Lucky Penny

Katherine Bitner

ISBN: 979-8-9870948-3-9

Book Cover by @rumaisa.artstudio (on Instagram)

Editing by Andrea Halland

1st edition 2025

Contents

Hello, my lovely readers! If you're new to me, I'm honored you picked up my book. While *Lucky Penny* is a standalone in an interconnected world, it's book #2 for a reason: if you read it before *Unravel Me*, the ending of *Unravel Me* will be spoiled—just a heads-up!

Also note that this book is a work of fiction, so while it takes place in a very real setting, many specific places are fictitious.

That being said, *Lucky Penny* was one of my favorite books to write. The characters are gritty and real, and for better or worse, there's a lot of myself in Penny.

And while every reader has their own meter for "spice," this book is open-door and intended for mature audiences.

Although the story ends with a happily ever after, it wouldn't be a true Katherine Bitner book without some heavier topics sprinkled in. If you'd like to know the content warnings, please check the next page (they may include mild spoilers). If you'd rather go in blind, feel free to skip them. Please take care of yourself!

Content Warnings:
- Lots of swearing – they love the F-word.

- Consensual sexual content

- Incarceration (past and present)

- Illegal drug use in minors (on page)

- Underage drinking, overconsumption, drinking as coping mechanism

- Family estrangement/parental abandonment

- Physical and verbal child abuse (mentioned briefly, no graphic depiction)

- Pregnancy + pregnancy related hospitalization (side character)

- Death of grandparent (past) grief over loss (on page)

To all the women whose strength has been mislabeled
as anger, I see you.
This is for you.

Lucky Penny Playlist

drivers license – Olivia Rodrigo
Fresh Out The slammer – Taylor Swift
Iris – The Goo Goo Dolls
Who Knew – P!nk
It's Been Awhile – Staind
Picture You – Chappell Roan
Stay – Rihanna, Mikky Ekko
Last Kiss – Taylor Swift
Photograph – Ed Sheeran
dont let me go – mgk
The Night We Met – Lord Huron
In the End – Linkin Park

1

Penny

NOW

"Wait—what did you say?" I sputter, the steaming water gently sloshing around me as I grip the sides of the bathtub. Hoping desperately that I had misheard my sister, I take the phone off speaker and hold it to my ear.

"I'm pregnant, Penny," Fia repeats herself.

A few beats of dead silence stretch between us as I close my eyes, leaning my head against the lip of the tub. My heart was already hammering in my chest from breaking one of my rules—no devices in the bathroom. This was supposed to be my time to relax and indulge. My twenty-dollar bath bomb is still fizzing around my legs, and a glass of chilled white wine is balanced on my bath caddy. I even lit a damn candle, the expensive soy jasmine one I bought at the farmer's market last week.

This was *my* time, and I've been looking forward to it all year.

Yes, *year*.

Because I'm a self-inflicted workaholic who rarely gets to rest.

But my little sister was never great at timing.

"Okay..." I finally find my voice, swiping a wet hand over my blonde, messy bun to make sure it's still in place. It is. "And you're, like, totally sure?"

"Yes, I'm sure," Fia chirps, annoyed with me.

I blink hard at the ceiling.

Being the older sister—older by seven years—means two things: hold it together when your little sister clearly isn't, and do not judge. Because the world already does enough of that.

"Alright, start from the beginning."

Fia exhales a trembling breath into the phone. "Brett's the father, obviously, but I haven't heard from him in weeks."

I jerk upright, no longer submerged peacefully in the rose-scented water, and grip the phone like it's Brett's neck. I never liked him. Never, *ever*.

The crisp white subway tiles on the surrounding walls blur together.

"First, I want you to know, I'm going to keep it," says Fia in a little voice.

I press my lips together, still stuck on the whole Brett ordeal, but exhale deeply through my nose, my jaw tense. "That's 100% your choice, you know I'll support you either way, but why didn't you tell me earlier? If I knew what you were going through, I wouldn't have nagged you so much over finals and Christmas details."

The sharp pain of a migraine hits me behind the eyes, and I pinch the bridge of my nose. I've been hounding her about nonsense, and the whole time, she was dealing with an unexpected pregnancy.

"It's okay... I knew you were busy with work. I've been busy trying to wrap my head around everything and didn't want to tell you until I got things in order." Her voice fades at the end of that sentence, which leads me to believe she *has not* been getting things in order.

It's no secret I've been consumed by my wedding photography business and filling my free time with social outings, but I would've dropped everything for this.

Us Hanson girls are stubborn and fiercely independent—we've had to be without the guidance of parents, raised by our single Nan since Fia was in diapers. However, that's where our similarities end.

Where I'm sunshine and fire, Fia is a gentle breeze. She doesn't plan; she trusts everyone immediately, and she is a kind, flowery soul. But that's all going to change for her now. A baby changes everything—I don't know if she's grasped that.

There's only one way to help her.

"I'm coming home early." I step out of the tub, wistfully looking at the still steamy water, and grab my white robe. Even if I wanted to, there will be no more relaxing tonight; my nervous system can't come back from this news bomb.

I tighten the robe around myself, still damp from what was a promising bath, and walk into my bedroom. The bed is perfectly made, all my white velvet throw pillows in line, the chunky beige knit blanket strewn across the comforter—just inviting me to sink into it, close my eyes, and forget the last five minutes.

"No, no, please, you don't need to rush here," Fia replies hastily.

I tune her out, crouching down to drag out my set of colossal suitcases from under my bed. I may not be spending my winter break in Raleigh, but that doesn't mean I have to schlep around Wilmington in sweatpants either.

I'm bringing clothes for any occasion, just in case: cozy neutral-tone lounge sets with the tags still on them, a cashmere turtleneck and leather miniskirt combo I've been dying to wear, and all the boots I can fit in a second suitcase.

"Listen," I say, speaking with as much patience as I can muster, "as you know, I took off the next two weeks, so I'm going to leave first thing in the morning, and I'm going to help you figure this out," I reassure her, even as my blood pressure and pitch rise with each word.

Fia remains mute on the other end, but I don't stop moving.

I storm into the kitchen, grabbing a pad of paper to make a list of everything I need to do and bring. Working in the wedding industry means I've gotten really good at being able to pivot.

Though, my plan up until five minutes ago involved mostly relaxing and catching up with friends over the next two weeks. Perhaps a fancy dinner downtown with my best friend Audrey, and maybe even letting the bartender who's been messaging me take me out for drinks. Then, eight days from now, I was supposed to drive to Wilmington, spoil my twenty-one-year old sister to a bougie Christmas celebration, and be back in Raleigh for a night out with friends before my next wedding shoot.

I had invited Fia to spend Christmas break with me, but she's been picking up extra shifts at her barista job, and now it's all making sense.

Fia sighs, her voice thinning. "You're making a big deal out of it, Pen. Really, I just wanted to tell you, I'm already working things out."

She's said she's *working things out* twice now, which doesn't give me any peace of mind, because I know my sister. "Working things out" means she probably picked out the baby's name.

I bob my head vigorously, even though she can't see me. "I'm sure you are, babe. But you shouldn't have to process this news by yourself. We need to talk about the house and everything else when I get there. Love you, see you tomorrow."

"Um...love you, too." She sniffles, sounding more hesitant than ever.

I end the call and toss my phone onto the marble kitchen counter, then yell out into my empty condo "Everything is going to be fine!"

Of course, no one can hear me but myself.

What I need is an hour-long meditation and to take a walk around the park, but there's no time, so I do the next best thing. I dart into my bathroom and snatch the lonely glass of white wine from the bath caddy, downing it in two gulps.

Not the best coping mechanism, I know.

But everything will be fine. I will remind Fia that having a baby isn't like rescuing a kitten, help her figure out finishing college and finances...and convince her to sell the family house, *and* we will have a jolly little Christmas together. I've accomplished more in two weeks.

Easy peasy lemon squeezy.

2

Penny

NOW

Cooler bags line my countertop, stuffed to the brim with groceries from my own kitchen, because one thing I can be certain of is that my little sister lives like a true college student. The last thing I want is to do a grocery haul in my hometown and risk running into someone from high school—honestly, I'd rather light my wardrobe on fire.

Once I triple-check my list, making sure I have everything—including the already wrapped Christmas gifts for Fia—I go room by room through my condo, shutting off the lights. A deep sigh rattles my lungs when I pull the plug on the little Christmas tree next to my TV, all decked out with pink ornaments and ribbons. I'd be lying if I said I wasn't disappointed to be spending my winter break away from here. It's my sanctuary.

I worked so hard, literally busted my ass all year, so I could take this time off just for *me*.

No editing bridal photos, no boarding destination wedding flights, no hotels, and absolutely no mothers-in-law shouting random instructions at me. Just me, the plush bubblegum-pink velvet sofa I splurged on when I bought this place, and an endless stream of holiday Hallmark movies.

But the fact of the matter is I'm the only reliable family member Fia has left, so what choice do I have? My twin brother, Danny, is in prison, and she might not be asking for my help, but I practically helped our Nan raise her. I can't let her down now.

After the final light is off, and my bags line the wall outside my front door, I exhale a bittersweet sigh and lock the door.

Every inch of my baby-blue Mini-Cooper convertible is stuffed, including the trunk, seats, and floorboard. Most days, I have nothing but adoration for this car I worked so hard to buy; it's a true extension of me—petite, stylish, and with just the right amount of sass. But as I turn onto the freeway, barely able to see out of the rearview mirror, I suddenly wish I had something bigger.

"Adios," I whisper, taking a sip of my green smoothie as the Raleigh skyline fades behind me.

Only two hours separate me from my coastal hometown of Wilmington, North Carolina. I begin the drive by playing my favorite true crime podcast, but end up pausing and rewinding it no less than thirty times, eventually giving up halfway into the episode. It was a futile attempt to distract myself from the continuous chatter running rampant in my head.

I touch the silver angel dangling from my rearview mirror. It hung in Nan's car my whole life, and now it accompanies me. Keeping me safe, I like to think.

"Nan, why did you have to let Fia read all those romance books?" I half laugh, half groan, talking to my late grandma out loud.

My sister is a hopeless romantic. Her bookshelves in high school were full of love stories, and she would much rather spend her days with her head between the pages than out with her peers. Nan thought that was a good sign, and so did I—until Brett came into the picture.

I still have no idea why Fia stuck with him for four years. Sure, on paper he's a catch. Brett comes from a good family and goes to UNCW with my sister. Plus, he has the whole classically handsome jock thing going for him. But I know how he treats Fia—like she's meant to be a trophy on a shelf and not much else. Pretty to look at, but to be seen and not heard.

Another hour passes, and I'm so worked up thinking about her loser ex that I almost miss my exit. I swerve, crossing two lanes, and fly down the ramp, immediately getting that same old tightness in my throat.

It doesn't matter that I haven't called this place home since I left for college ten years ago. And it doesn't matter that the people who hurt me no longer reside here, either. Their ghosts still haunt every corner.

I squirm uncomfortably in my seat and smooth my long blonde ponytail over my shoulder. Nausea continues to bite at my anxious stomach, and I wish more than ever I was arriving at a warm house where Nan greets me, where my sister isn't drowning, and where I can let down my walls. But that place doesn't exist, not anymore. The walls are crumbling—quite literally—and I have a sinking feeling that I'm the only one who can do anything about it.

As I turn onto my old street, warmth spreads in my chest, and I loosen my grip on the wheel ever so slightly. The houses on the street are a mix of grand Colonials and storybook Victorians, all strung with twinkling Christmas lights, and fresh green garland wraps the porches and pillars. It's beautiful.

But then I arrive at my family home, and the warm twinkly cheer in my body dims.

Our house is a faded-blue, century-old, Victorian-style home with clapboard siding, hurricane shutters that sit askew, and a front porch that was once stately but now sags slightly at the steps. The rose bushes Nan once lovingly tended to are now more thorn than bloom, no longer weaving through the scroll-iron fence in the front yard.

I roll up the bumpy driveway, my gaze locking on the front door with its dull sheen, and my heart sinks further.

A lonely wreath hangs crookedly over the brass knocker, but that's it. There are no swagging lights, no red velvet ribbon on the bannisters. It would be crazy to expect a twenty-one-year-old college student to handle the upkeep and decor of this house on her own. But nonetheless, it still hurts to see.

This will be the last Christmas she spends alone in this house, if I have anything to say about it. If she stays here, she too will decay. I have to get her out.

Drawing in a steadying breath, I step out of the car onto the cracked driveway. Tall weeds push up through the cement, brushing against the sides of my leather boots. The air is thicker here—warm and a little humid.

I have to shuffle the bags around the trunk just to get one out, grunting as I do. The largest one is stuck, so I leverage it with my boot against my bumper, and it flies out with a thud, right against Fia's car. My stomach drops at the sound of scraping, but then I remember Fia's car is made of scratches and dings. It was Nan's car, and she left it to Fia. Though it mostly sits there, because after driving for thirty miles, it begins to smoke. Fia said it's fine, *she enjoys walking* and owns one of those weird electric scooters.

I need to remind her you can't strap a car seat to an electric scooter.

The walk to the front door is difficult. I'm dragging half my wardrobe behind me. And I don't know what the hell to say to my sister when I see her.

Guiding her through college applications? Easy. Soothing her after her *first* breakup with Brett? I got it. Teaching her how to pace herself when she discovered alcohol? That's what sisters are for. I even showed her how to do her makeup to highlight her freckles, how to shave her legs without cutting herself, and how to tame her impossibly beautiful red hair.

But pregnancy and motherhood? I know nothing about that, literally zilch. Our mother left us two weeks before my eighth birthday.

However, I don't have time to consider the best way to phrase things, because as I gingerly step on the rotting porch steps, praying I don't fall through, shadows of movement pass by the front windows.

A chilly breeze rustles the last clinging leaves on the giant oak tree in the front yard, ushering me closer to the house, and I catch my breath on the porch, glancing up at the ceiling.

Haint blue.

It's Southern folklore that you're supposed to paint your porch ceiling this color to keep bad spirits away. That's what Nan used to tell us, anyway. But as I stand underneath it, I wonder who thought of that stupid idea, because this house is full of bad spirits. Or at least bad memories.

The door swings open, and my eyes fall on my sister's reluctant smile. Then my gaze drops again to the curve of her belly, gently cradled in her hand. I jerk my head back. I didn't expect it to be *cradle-worthy* yet.

"Hey, sis." She glances at me sheepishly, braided hair falling over one side of her UNCW sweatshirt.

I blink rapidly. Bewildered doesn't cover it.

"Hi... I..." I stutter as Fia's porcelain face flushes. "Can I come in?"

I cross over the threshold as she steps aside, dragging my belongings behind me into the foyer.

Fia shuts the door behind me as I spin to get a better look at her. From the side.

"I didn't expect you to have a belly," I say, followed by a tiny nervous laugh. Probably not the right thing to say.

Fia ducks her head, avoiding my eyes as she rubs the back of her neck. "Yeah, I know—"

"When you said Brett broke up with you *weeks* ago, I assumed you meant you *just* found out..." My sentence trails off because I can't wrap my head around this timeline, or peel my eyes off her mid-section.

"I told you Brett broke up with me weeks ago, but that's because that's when I found out."

"I don't understand..." I reply, folding my arms over my tan wool coat. The insulation in this house is non-existent, and there's a constant cool draft.

"I'm twenty-six weeks."

My eyes nearly pop out of my head, and I grip the oak banister beside me, rubbing my forehead. Holy shit. I quickly do the math...that means only three months left until there's a baby in this house.

"I swear I didn't know until a few weeks ago, okay? It's been a really stressful semester, and I thought I was just missing my period from all the stress and gaining weight. I had none of the classic pregnancy symptoms they teach you about."

I nod, unable to look at her.

My foot hits my suitcase as I take a step back, and the pale-yellow walls of the foyer suddenly seem to be closing in on me like a fun house. Even though Fia's the one who should be freaking out, she's standing there calm as a fucking cucumber. Which only makes my own spiral worse.

I've been here for approximately five minutes, and I'm already breaking my big sister rules.

"Okay. Okay. Okay," I repeat, and Fia furrows her brow, tracking my erratic movement with her eyes.

"I need a moment," I say, smiling way too brightly as I jut my thumb over my shoulder. "I'm just gonna grab the rest of my stuff, okay?" I don't wait for her to answer. I turn and clumsily step over my suitcase, speed-walking to my car.

Did I become an absent sister? Is this my fault? I'm supposed to keep an eye on Fia—Nan literally asked me to do so on her deathbed.

A wave of dizziness hits me as I pull more bags from my car.

My insides twist as I imagine my baby sister here, all alone in this big house, pregnant and heartbroken over a guy who's MIA. I was so busy working, doing lord knows what, barely having time to call her back all fall semester.

Truthfully, I want to rush inside and hug her. Pull her into my arms like I used to when we were kids and promise everything will be okay. But instead, I stomp into the kitchen and unload the grocery bags on the counter while she watches me from across the room, a wounded look flickering behind her eyes.

"This isn't exactly the Christmas greeting I was hoping for," she mumbles, playing with the hair tie on her wrist.

"I'm sorry, Fi. I'm just...trying to wrap my head around this too. You kind of dropped a bomb on me."

She shrugs, turning to grab a mug like we're discussing the weather. "There's not much to say. I'm having a baby. It wasn't planned, but it's going to be okay. I have a job, I only have one semester left—"

I wave my hand in the air. "You work at a coffee shop that barely pays above minimum wage. That might've worked while you were a student, but babies are expensive. Your car is on its last leg, and this house is falling apart. Not to mention there's *still* one more semester between you and your degree." The words spill out before I can stop them. No filter, no softness, just sharp-edge truth she needs to hear.

I wish I could hit rewind, take my words back, because the second they are out, Fia's pale face goes still. She stares at me like I just kicked her.

"Penny, I'm not a child, I *know* what I'm dealing with." She lifts her chin. "Can we just enjoy our holiday break? I don't want to do *this* with you."

"Do *what*?" My stomach grows hot, the unease crawling up my throat. I hate the way coming back to this place puts me on edge.

"Try to fix everything." She sighs heavily, like a mom exhausted with their repetitive child. "I love you, Penny. But believe it or not, I can handle this. So please—for now—can we drop the house stuff and job pressure?"

My fingers curl against the green-tiled kitchen counter. She has no idea what she's saying. Fia has never had to worry about finances or a living situation. This house is paid off, and Fia's been living on her part-time coffee shop salary, plus the money in the trust from Nan. But that's going to burn up quickly the moment she brings a child into the world.

I hate to do it, but I pull the Nan card.

"She wouldn't have wanted you to live like this, and you know it. She didn't leave the house to *trap* us. I'd settle for renting it out, and you can live somewhere that makes more sense. You can even move to Raleigh and be near me."

Her lips press into a hard line, fists clenched at her sides. I open my mouth, ready to say *something* to smooth it over. I should've taken care of this house issue a long time ago, but I thought giving her time to grieve Nan was the right thing to do. Now it's been two years, and I have to be the bad cop.

"I know you hate it here, Penny. But this is my home. And actually, I've figured out a way to pay for the repairs."

"Okay, so what's the plan?" I'm skeptical, to say the least.

"I have a roommate," she says, her voice careful.

"Who?" I glance toward the connected living room, noticing a large dog bed on the floor in front of the fireplace. *Great.* "Did they already move in?"

Spending the holidays with a stranger sounds less than pleasant.

Fia plays with the tip of her braid. "Yeah...they moved in, but this isn't how I wanted you to find out."

"Find out what?"

Fia steps forward, arms resting over her belly, green eyes searching mine. "I wanted you to be proud of me. I was going to tell you about the pregnancy once I secured a pay raise at the café, once finals were done, once I had a whole plan in place. But time is moving so fast." She grimaces, and uneasiness washes over me.

Did she rent a room to some drifter?

"Who is it, Fia?" I ask again, this time slow and clear. My hands settle on my hips like armor.

Seconds go by, and my sister just gnaws on her bottom lip.

"Is it Danny?" I ask but catch myself, because that's impossible. Danny is still in prison. I *know* the exact date he gets out—five months from now.

"No, it's Jesse," she finally whispers, and for a moment, everything goes numb. I couldn't have heard that right. There has to be another Jesse.

But her face doesn't waver.

My stomach flips, and I shake my head. "Fia...you didn't."

She nervously covers her mouth with her hand as she nods.

A wave of heat rises to my face. "How could you?"

I have to pause, remembering she doesn't know the truth about our falling out.

Fia scoffs, her brows furrowed. "Penny, come on... It's Jesse, not a stranger! He was your best friend and practically family! I don't understand why you are acting like this is bad news?"

The room tilts a little, but I plant my feet.

"I know you two fell out of contact, but everything will be fine." She offers me a cheerful smile. The same smile she gets when she's patching holes in her thrifted jeans, like she can fix anything if she just tries hard enough.

But some things can't be mended.

My mouth goes dry as the familiar squeak of the back door opens into the kitchen. Cold air rushes in, and I turn to look right into the green eyes of the man I never thought I'd have to see again.

He's the reason I never came back.

The reason I don't do relationships.

The reason I haven't visited my twin in ten years.

He's the only guy I've ever said I love you to.

The one who ripped my heart out of my chest and left me bleeding.

The one who became like a big brother to Fia.

Jesse Rivers.

And he's looking at me like I'm a color he forgot existed.

3

Jesse

NOW

It takes maybe two seconds to register that the amber eyes staring back at me belong to Penny Hanson. And then it takes roughly one more second to notice the stunned disbelief carved into her face.

I freeze.

The cold trailing in behind me snakes its way under my leather jacket, but that's not what's got me locked in place. It's the *way* she's looking at me—like I'm a ghost the wind dragged in with it.

Over Penny's shoulder, Fia's wide, doe-eyed stare darts between us, and all I can do is let out a gravelly chuckle, thin and dry, because it feels like someone just punched the air clean out of my lungs.

The last time all three of us stood in this kitchen together, Fia was eleven years old and I was a tall, gawky eighteen-year-old with no goddamn clue where I belonged in the world. I was just a lost kid who got taken in by a kind family.

"Hey," I say to Penny, nodding once. What do you even say to someone you haven't laid eyes on for ten years? What can I say without immediately opening every floodgate?

My gaze drops to her mouth, stuck on her lips that are still too full, too soft, too much, but I catch myself. This isn't my best friend I used to steal kisses from in this very kitchen.

That version of us is long gone.

She spins her body around so fast her blonde ponytail whips through the air—no doubt shooting daggers at her sister, who appears more ghostly than normal.

Fia clears her throat. "I've been trying to reach you for twenty-four hours, Jesse. Where the heck have you been?" There's a playful lilt to her voice, but her face reads *panic*.

It's still strange seeing her like this—grown. I've been here for two weeks now, but it still reminds me of how long I've been gone. I mean, *fuck*, just seeing her pregnant has me messed up too. She's like my little sister for all intents and purposes.

I've spent the better half of the last decade not being needed by anyone, not having to answer to a soul. No one's checking in on me. So it's a bit jarring to suddenly have someone needing to know my whereabouts. It's going to take some getting used to.

I click the door shut behind me, fully stepping into the kitchen, and shift around Penny's rigid body, not missing the way her breath catches as I do.

"Sorry," I mutter, scratching my jaw. "I stayed out late last night and left early this morning. My phone died sometime yesterday."

"Well, it's too late anyway." Fia exhales. "I was just trying to give you a heads up that Penny was coming." The corners of her mouth twitch, and she hesitates. "You know...*before* the happy reunion."

Penny lets out a frustrated grunt. The same one she used to make before slamming her bedroom door in Danny's face when we were all sixteen, under one roof.

"Does someone want to explain what the hell is going on?" Her voice cuts through the chill air, and Fia and I both stumble over our explanations, but mine's louder.

"I'm crashing here for a while. Thought you were made aware." It comes out clipped, unintentionally harsh. I can only imagine what thoughts are spiraling in Penny's head right now. Her stiff body and tense face say she wants to throttle my throat.

Penny was always a firecracker, someone who is unapologetically themselves. It's why I fucking loved her in the first place.

A lifetime ago.

Her attention snaps to her sister. "You couldn't find a nice girl your age to be your roommate? You had to choose *him*?"

Fia flinches but doesn't push back. This isn't the *happy* reunion she'd pictured. And I don't want to be the reason for a fight.

"Listen, I'll leave," I say, raising both hands in surrender. "I just need to grab Tank's food."

"No!" Fia crosses her arms, her voice sharp with emotion. "Please stay, Jesse. This is your home, too." She turns to Penny, frustrated. "Isn't this what you wanted? Me not living here alone? Look, I solved it."

Penny draws a breath sharp enough to cut, and I feel like I've stepped into an interrogation room with no exit.

"He used to live here, Penny!" Fia's voice cracks, full of disbelief. "I thought you'd be *happy* I didn't invite some random axe murderer to crash in the guest room!"

Penny jams her glossy pink fingernails into her temples. "You should've talked to me before you did this." Her voice comes out tight.

Fia blinks, thrown.

They're both talking like I'm not six feet away, so I inch toward the pantry, grabbing my dog's water bowl and food bin.

Fia moves quickly, reaching for the bin. "You're not leaving."

"And you're not grabbing forty pounds of kibble when you're pregnant." I hoist it over my shoulder, out of reach.

What the hell was I thinking, moving back in?

Oh, right. I wasn't thinking. Not with my head, anyway. My damn heart led me here—straight into what might've been a terrible idea.

Two weeks ago, I ran into Fia at the grocery store unexpectedly. I was grabbing another frozen meal to heat up in the motel mini-kitchen, and Fia was staring at cereal boxes blankly. I stared at her for way too long, unsure if I was really seeing the girl who used to tape coloring book pages to my bedroom door. When our eyes locked, something passed between us. Maybe a mutual relief?

"*Jesse?*" she asked, and without even thinking, I pulled her into a hug.

I hadn't told her I was back in town. Truthfully, I didn't know how to yet. It didn't feel like I deserved to just show up at her house, so I'd been holed up in a motel off the highway for six weeks, trying and failing to find an apartment. No one wants to rent to a tattooed guy with a record and a pit bull. I was used to that kind of judgment, but still, it had started to wear on me. Started to make me doubt why I came back here.

Fia and I had kept in touch over the last ten years. Just a text here and there, holiday wishes, Instagram likes, but seeing her in our hometown shifted something in me. Like a fragment of my heart was mending.

When I mentioned where I was staying, her face fell, then instantly lit up. She told me she was searching for a roommate and nearly begged me to move in. I wasn't comfortable with the idea at first, because coming back to Wilmington was one thing, but moving back into the house I lived in as a teenager was something else. She wouldn't take no for an answer, though. Fia may be the gentler of the Hanson sisters, but both she and Penny are like their Nan. When they have an idea in their head, no one can change it.

I found myself moving in a few days later, and it's been pretty smooth up until today.

I knew Penny was coming for Christmas, but I was supposed to have another week to prepare myself to see her. I didn't expect to walk in the back door and see her just standing there.

Penny taps her nails on the counter angrily. "Was I the last to find out everything? That my baby sister is pregnant, that Jesse is back from god knows where, and that y'all are playing happy family again like nothing ever happened?" Penny's sharp voice ricochets off the yellow-painted walls of this old house.

"I have a lot going on, okay? I'm sorry," Fia says, voice cracking. "I needed time to figure out how to tell you everything. I knew you'd try to control it all." Her hands are raised, helpless, and Penny shakes her head like she's building a wall brick by brick.

I've had women fight over me, but not like this.

I should've warned Fia that this wasn't going to be a sweet little homecoming. She doesn't know the whole truth about our relationship.

Past relationship.

The only people who do are Penny and I. And judging by the way she's clenching her jaw, she was planning on taking that information to the grave.

"I need a minute," she says, biting her lip before stepping around me and straight to the back door I just came through.

"Hold up!" I shout, but I'm too late. Tank, my dog who forgets he's not tiny, greets Penny the only way he knows how—uncontained helicopter tail, tongue ready to kiss, and head straight to the knees of his victim.

At least we got all the greetings out of the way.

4

Penny

THEN

Age 11, First Week of School

Nan will be so mad if she finds out we hung out at the park instead of going straight home, especially because the park isn't even on the way home from school.

We're in sixth grade now, which means no more after-school babysitters for us. I was excited about it—a chance to show Nan how responsible and grown I am. But Danny sees it as an opportunity to mess around. It's not like I hate when we goof off; my brother *is* the funniest kid at school, but I like to have fun at the appropriate times. And we're supposed to be going home right now.

But there's a new kid in Danny's class this year, and my brother must be trying to impress him or something, because he told him he'd show him the park after school today. Magnolia Street Park—where all the *cool* older middle schoolers hang out.

As we pass the street we're supposed to turn down to go home, I grab the handle of my brother's backpack and yank him back, interrupting their *riveting* conversation about skateboards.

I remind him that the instructions were pretty clear: During the week when Nan works day shifts, we go home, do homework, and no later than 4:15 p.m., go three houses down to collect our sister from the babysitter's house. Then we watch Fia until Nan gets home at six.

"Relax, Penny, she won't even know. We'll get Fia by four."

"What about homework?" I utter, burning under the hot September sun as I walk beside them on the sidewalk. My jean shorts with embroidered daisies were a good choice, but the yellow cardigan I paired with them is starting to stick to my back.

"Homework is for losers." He snickers and nudges his new friend, Jesse, but he glances back at me.

He's really tall for a sixth grader. His hair is almost black, and his eyes are super green. He smiles at me, and I peel my eyes away. Staring isn't kind.

We pass a house with a noisy lawnmower, and Jesse's mouth moves, but I don't hear him.

"What did you say?" I ask, brushing annoying grass clippings off my ankles.

"What homework do you have?" Jesse repeats himself, kinda shyly. "It's the first week of school."

I pull on my backpack straps and shrug. "I have a report to write on one of the books I read over the summer."

Danny flips his long blond hair—Nan's been threatening to buzz it off if he doesn't stop twitching his head to the side. She said his neck will get stuck like that.

"My sister is in the *advanced* classes," he taunts, rolling his eyes. "She read, like, all of the books on the summer reading list."

"Shut up, Danny." I shove him out of the way so I can walk between him and Jesse on the sidewalk. "I did it for the gift card prize, which I used for my new backpack. So who's the loser now?" I stick out my tongue at Danny.

"I actually read them all, too," Jesse chimes in, and I gape at him. "Well, all the ones the library had."

Danny starts to laugh, but I elbow him.

I glance up at Jesse. He's *got* to be a foot taller than me.

"Really?" I narrow my eyes at him. He's probably messing with me like Danny does.

He nods, shoving his hands in his pockets, looking down at the sidewalk.

"Do you have siblings, like a sister?" I ask, hoping maybe he has a twin. Danny would have a friend, and so would I.

Wishful thinking, but my best friend Julia moved to Pennsylvania over the summer, and I'm desperately searching for a new BFF.

"Nope, only child." He shifts his backpack from one shoulder to the other. It's duct taped together on the top.

When we get to the park, it's full of kids in the grade above us—at least twenty of them—and even some high schoolers. They're obnoxious, swinging from the monkey bars and yelling stupid things to each other.

I roll my eyes, groaning. I knew this would happen, but my brother never listens to me.

"Let's just go back to our house. We can make snow cones," I offer, crossing my fingers that my brother takes the bait.

Someone screams near the swings, and a car of way older kids pulls up. Yeah, Nan would kill us if she knew we were here.

Luckily, after a second of looking around, seeing there's really nowhere for us to hang out, Danny gives in to my idea.

Jesse murmurs a goodbye before he waves and turns in the opposite direction, but I skip toward him, grabbing his arm.

"Wait!" I yell, and he looks down at me, his cheeks growing pink. "You could come over, too," I offer.

Danny gives me a weird look. "Oh, so you're okay with breaking the rules *now*?"

I kick the mulch and shrug coolly. "I mean, technically, *I'm* not breaking the rules. I'll be doing my homework."

Jesse lets out a breath. "You sure your grandma would be okay with it?

"Totally, she won't mind," I lie straight through my teeth, which isn't easy. Lying makes my stomach tight, but I like Jesse. Not *like* like, I just think he's nice. Nicer than most of my brother's friends.

And he's new in town. Nan would be proud of me for making him feel welcome.

Danny smiles at me. "Well, gee, sis, thanks for finally being cool." He flicks my shoulder, and I roll my eyes.

"Whatever, let's just get out of here." I pause and spin to look them both directly in the eye. "But *I* am getting the first snow cone. This report isn't going to write itself."

Danny and Jesse play video games in the living room with a bag of chips open between them while I do my homework on my bed. Though I can hear their conversation all the way up here. Why do boys talk about such stupid stuff?

When four o'clock rolls around, my watch beeps, and I know Danny's not going to notice, so I slip on my sandals and trudge downstairs, making lots of noise with every step so he can't ignore me.

There are snack wrappers all over the coffee table, and Jesse's sitting back on the tan sofa, but Danny's up near the TV on his knees. He gets sucked into the screen, as Nan says.

"Danny, we have to get Fia now." I wave my arms from the other side of the living room.

He nods like he hears me, but doesn't take his eyes off the TV. Jesse quickly sets down his controller, though.

"I should get going anyway. My dad will be home soon." He puts his snow cone cup in the sink and thanks us for the snacks. At least he has manners.

Nan would like him, I think to myself.

"See you at school tomorrow!" He waves to my brother while I stand in the kitchen, arms crossed.

"Nice to meet you, Penny."

I smile politely. "You, too." My stomach feels weird, like there are butterflies in it or something.

"Danny!" I hiss at him, and he drops his controller and stands in a zombie-like state.

As Jesse's walking to the foyer, I whisper to my brother, "You should invite him to the beach on Saturday."

He looks at me with a blank stare.

"It's the nice thing to do. He's the new kid."

Danny races to the front door, and I stay put, straining my ear to hear their conversation.

"Hey, on Saturday we're going to Wrightsville Beach, want to come with us? I'll check with our Nan, but I don't think she'd care."

Jesse doesn't reply right away. Maybe he thinks we're weird. But then his voice cracks like Danny's does sometimes.

"Yeah, totally. I just have to check with my stepmom."

The front door opens and shuts moments later, and Danny comes back into the kitchen with his shoes slipped on.

"Julia's been gone like a month, and you're already trying to steal my new friend?"

I exhale dramatically and shuffle past Danny, grabbing his arm to pull him toward the door. "We can share friends, idiot. Jesse's cool."

He doesn't object, because he knows I'm right.

We walk to the neighbors' house to get our little sister, whose face is pressed against the front window. Her red pigtails look very messy. Maybe she'll let me practice my braiding on her if I bribe her with a snow cone.

We don't talk about Jesse on the walk there or back.

And I definitely don't mention that he is kinda cute...

When we get home, Fia lets me braid her hair, then she plays with her dollhouse in my bedroom while I sit on my bed and make three friendship bracelets. One for me, one for Danny, and one for Jesse.

I hope he likes blue and green.

5

Penny

NOW

These boots were not made for walking, not at this pace, but I can't slow down now. I can't put distance between me and that house fast enough.

Is this a nightmare?

I pinch my forearm then slap a finger to my neck, checking my pulse.

Nope. I'm wide awake. So it's a *living* nightmare.

My Pilates instructor's voice pops into my head: *Inhale through the nose, exhale through the mouth.* It's supposed to help.

It doesn't.

He moved in with his dog...like they are playing house. Does Fia think he is here to save the day? What the hell is he even doing back?

Last I heard, he was in Southern California, probably pretending his past didn't exist.

I brush the dirt streaks off my black leather leggings from his dog's paws—Tank—and stop to check myself out in a parked car's window. The window distorts my heart-shaped face, and even though I just got my thick eyebrows tamed, they look crazy. So I look as crazy as I feel right now.

I pull my vibrating phone from my pocket, seeing a missed call from Audrey. Straightening myself, I step to the side so a couple can pass me on the sidewalk and call her back.

"Hey, sorry," she says over the clang of metal mixing bowls and blenders. "Quick question for you."

Audrey is my best friend in the entire world. We've been inseparable since freshman orientation at UNC. Which also means she'll be able to hear distress in my voice—even a hundred miles away.

However, there's a lot Audrey doesn't know about my life *before* college. No one does, and I prefer it that way. When I left this town, I got to be someone new. I didn't have to be the girl whose best friend and brother were in prison, whose parents left her—none of that.

"Yeah, what's up?" I chew my lip, glancing back to make sure Fia and Jesse aren't following me down the sidewalk. They aren't. It's just me, speed-walking down an oak-tree lined street like a madwoman.

"Do you want to grab dinner Friday before we check into the spa? There's a new Mediterranean place opening north of downtown, and I can make a reservation."

My stomach drops. *Damn it.* The spa day we planned months ago is at the end of this week, on the opposite end of the state in the Blue Ridge Mountains. It was supposed to be a pre-Christmas getaway, an indulgent treat for both of us after a year of really hard work.

I stomp my heeled boot into the concrete sidewalk and toss my head back toward the gray sky. "You're going to hate me," I groan into the phone.

The whisking noise stops. "Uh-oh...what's going on, Pen?"

I exhale sharply and squeeze my eyelids shut. "I can't go this weekend." I brace for her disappointment. I hate letting people down.

"What? Is everything okay?" I picture her adjusting her perfect chocolate-brown hair.

"I've been in Wilmington for an hour, and everything's already fucked." I laugh—sharp and humorless—and stop at a crosswalk, debating which way to walk. Back isn't an option. I'll walk all the way to the ocean if I have to.

"Is Fia okay?" Her voice is gentle now, full of concern. I wish I could teleport to her front porch, where she'd hand me coffee, hug me, and let me rant.

"Other than the fact that she is six months pregnant...yeah, she seems great and totally aloof to her reality."

"Oh, shit."

"Yep."

I'm silent for a moment, running a hand through my frazzled ponytail, finally knowing which way I'm heading.

"What else is going on?" she asks carefully.

"Just...ghosts from my past." I'm not sure how much to divulge. I've kept that door sealed for years, but Audrey waits. She knows me—I always crack eventually, and she's the only person I trust right now.

"Okay, so Fia has a new roommate."

"Oh?"

"And it's my high school ex. Jesse."

"You're kidding me."

I shake my head, still in disbelief that those words left my mouth.

Audrey knows about Jesse in the generic high school ex-boyfriend kind of way. I kept it light, like it was just teenage drama, because that's all I could handle. She doesn't know Jesse is stitched into the fabric of my past in a way no one else understands.

It's a secret I was ready to take to the grave.

But him walking through that back door changes everything.

"Oh no, Jesse's not the father, is he?" she whispers.

I gag, lurching forward. "Oh god no! No. No. He's like a big brother to Fia. She trusts him for some stupid reason, and he needed a place to live. It's karma, huh?"

"Okay... So, how did it feel when you saw him?"

My eyebrows knit together, and I scoff, watching cars fly past.

"I wanted to choke his tattooed neck," I respond bluntly.

"Wait, I'm confused. I thought you were into that?"

I laugh, despite myself. "Audrey, what the hell! He's my ex...whatever... It was so long ago. I don't trust his intentions. I don't know why he's back."

After all this time. Why did it take him ten years?

"And he doesn't even look like himself anymore," I add for good measure.

"So, he's ugly now? Because I know you, and you're not exactly...*not* shallow when it comes to who you date," Audrey snaps back.

I roll my eyes. She's not wrong; I don't do relationships. I casually date, and if it's going to be casual, they need to be tens.

"No, he isn't ugly." If she saw the fullness of his lips or him standing at his full 6'4" height, she wouldn't even joke. He's painfully good looking. "But you're getting off topic."

"Well, I've never seen a picture of him. Give me his last name so I can stalk him on social media."

I puff out a laugh because the Jesse *I knew* would never have social media. He was a punk kid who didn't conform, and the idea would probably repulse him. Though I can't be totally sure. I've never searched for him, even when I was drunk. I knew it would be too painful.

It's one Pandora's box no amount of tequila could get me to pry open.

"No last name will be given." I sigh, my breath puffing in the cold. "He's tall. Dark hair, green eyes. Tattoos from his knuckles to his jawline...I'm assuming. Still wears all black. Probably spends too much time lifting. He's a douche, okay?"

"Mmhmm," she replies smugly.

"I'm serious. Nothing about this is fun for me."

"Okay, okay. But...he sounds hot? I mean, you don't *date*, so what's the harm in warming up to him?"

The idea has me clenching my phone, and I look back over my shoulder, even though I know he's not following me.

"I think you're forgetting that my delusional little sister is having a baby in a few months, the house needs probably fifty grand in repairs, and my ex-boyfriend just moved into the spare room. It's *complicated*. And you know I don't do *complicated*."

The bell chimes in her bakeshop, but she keeps talking to me.

"I know, I know. I'm just trying to ease the tension. This isn't like you."

I nod, expelling a shaky breath into the cold air. "I'm never myself when I'm in Wilmington."

I know Audrey, of all people, will understand the pain of going back to the place you grew up in, the way it surrounds you like a suffocating cloak.

Returning here reminds me of all the beautiful things I miss most, like my Nan, the ocean, and my sister. But it also strips me of all the stability I've worked for.

She is right, I'm not being me.

I'm a positive person, annoyingly so. Always searching for silver linings, always ready with a pep talk. I schedule my fun so I never miss it. Always in control, that's how I stay safe.

That's how I've built a successful life.

I stepped onto that campus ten years ago with a shattered heart, but I made a choice to let it build me rather than bury me.

So I decided to become sunshine.

Even when it was hard. Even when I wanted to crawl back home and disappear.

I stayed in control.

Another bell chimes over the door of Audrey's bakery. "I'm so sorry, babe—someone just came to pick up their cake," Audrey says. "Text me, okay? You're going to be fine. You're *Penelope Hanson.* Literal boss bitch."

"I love you. Thanks, Aud."

"Love you, too. And seriously—send me a pic of your tattooed ex."

"Never," I say, and we hang up.

The last thing on my mind, the last thing I would ever do, is let Jesse back into my life.

Fia may think she knows what's best, but I've got two weeks to convince her otherwise and fix this mess.

Audrey is right, I'm Penny Hanson. Literal boss bitch.

Five minutes later, and roughly a half mile from the house, I stop at the edge of Magnolia Street Park. The swings are no longer the jagged sun-faded rubber I remember, and the mulch is replaced with an expensive looking rubber flooring.

I gaze across the park toward the magnolia trees lining the back fence. My chest eases just a fraction when I spot it.

The bench.

It's still there, worn and weathered.

A mom pushes her toddler on a swing nearby, but she doesn't look up as I cross the brittle, winter-dead grass. I keep my eyes on the bench like it might disappear if I blink.

When I reach it, I sit slowly, cautiously, not wanting to draw attention to myself.

The moment I settle, a weight presses into my chest and floods down my legs, anchoring me to the old wood slats like the bench *knows* me.

I drag my fingertip along the board beneath me, tracing until I find it.

J + P

Jesse and Penny...it's etched deep.

Deep enough to outlast ten years.
Deep enough to outlast *us*.

6

Penny

THEN

Age 15, September Sophomore Year

Jesse strides toward me, his long arms ending in the pocket of his favorite black hoodie—the one I secretly wish was mine. His dark hair swoops across his forehead, and the gold flecks in his green eyes catch the fading light. He pushes his hair back and smirks at me, his dimples doing that thing to my heart again.

God, I hope he can't tell how nervous he makes me.

"Hey!" I wave to him from across the grassy park. The streetlights flicker as the sun dips down, casting an artificial glow over the city park.

Magnolia Street Park has a beautiful name, but it's nothing special. Just a small park directly between the historic neighborhood with mostly nice homes, including mine, and the other side of town. The side Nan tells me not to hang out in. The side Jesse lives on with his dad and stepmom. Over the last four years, it's become our spot. Danny, Jesse, and I.

"You got my note." I smile, and he nods. I slipped it into his locker after geometry with very detailed instructions. Jesse's phone broke last week, and he can't afford a new one, so we've returned to hand-scratched notes passed between classes. Something I find romantic, but I doubt he finds anything but bothersome.

I told him to meet me here, at our bench, at 9 p.m.—an hour after Nan leaves for the night shift at the hospital, late enough that

Fia will be fast asleep and Danny too stoned in front of his TV to know what day it is, let alone notice I'm gone.

I wanted to see Jesse alone.

The bench bends a little as he sits next to me. He smells like body spray and stale cigarette smoke that's not his.

I stare at the holes in his ripped black jeans, steadying myself for what I need to say.

"I brought you your favorite." He slides a crinkled pack of Starbursts from his hoodie, and I smile. "Don't worry, only the pink ones." He uncurls his fingers and places six into my hand. My pulse kicks up as his fingers brush mine.

"Thanks." I glance up quickly at him before popping the sweet taffy-like candy into my mouth to buy myself a few seconds.

What I have to say is good news...but it's uncomfortable. And really, it should be coming from Danny, too, except lately, he's been totally checked out. I do everything for this family, even though my brother is technically ten minutes older.

Rubbing my palms on my legs, I shift my gaze to Jesse's face. "So, obviously, I didn't want to bring this up at school today, but we talked to Nan last night."

What I don't say is that I couldn't wait another day to tell him. Not after he showed up to school with a black eye last week. Not with things getting worse at home for him.

Jesse's hair falls over his eyebrows, but he doesn't fix it. He peers down at the ground, and his knee begins to bounce lightly.

"Oh yeah?" he asks, wariness in his voice.

"She said you can stay with us," I blurt out, a smile tugging at the corners of my mouth before I can stop it. "As long as you want, of course."

His head lifts, and a crooked grin spreads across his face.

"Shit, really, Penny?" Jesse exhales, barely. His shoulders ease just a little, and I can tell this means more than he'll ever say. He always plays it cool—so annoyingly calm and composed, which makes it even more baffling that he's best friends with my hothead brother, who once punched a wall over losing at Mario Kart.

"Nan said you just have to check with your parents."

"They won't care," he says, holding back a smile, eyes still on the night sky. "They probably won't even notice I'm gone. My stepmom will be fucking thrilled."

He laughs, but I don't.

I'd notice if he was gone.

I don't understand how anyone could hurt him. Jesse is made of pure goodness. He's thoughtful—like really thoughtful. He brought my Nan her favorite flowers on her birthday last year. And he's super patient with my little sister. He's always willing to help me whenever I need it, no questions asked. I don't think Jesse has a mean bone in his body, which is ironic, considering his dad is the meanest man alive.

"Well..." I search for the right words to say. "It's settled, you'll move in this weekend? Nan says you can sleep in the guest room across from mine. It's kinda tiny and the bed isn't awesome but—"

His jaw ticks. "Trust me, it's an upgrade from where I've been sleeping."

I don't ask; I'm not sure I can handle knowing. Danny and I have never seen the inside of Jesse's house. He's never invited us in, and we've never pushed.

"Sweet." I slip another Starburst into my mouth. "So, see you in Spanish tomorrow?"

He stands and stretches. I follow suit, but standing next to him, I barely reach his shoulder.

"Yeah." He cracks his knuckles and watches me with a new look on his face. One I've never seen before—it gives me butterflies for some reason.

"Hey Penny?"

My breath catches.

"Thank you."

I wave him off. "It's not a big deal. It's like an extended sleep-over."

"Maybe not to you." His voice drops, quieter now. "But you kinda saved my life."

"Oh," I whisper, my lips pursing.

He gently bumps my shoulder with his knuckles. "Told you. You're my lucky Penny."

In every book I've ever read, every romance movie I've watched, there's a moment—something small but pivotal—when a character crosses a line they can't come back from. Something shifts, and they're never the same again.

As I walk away from the park that night, Jesse heading in the opposite direction, I feel it in my heart.

I crossed that line.

Everything will be different now. There's no turning back. I've entered a new territory, and my heart aches with both fear and love.

7

Jesse

NOW

"Don't worry, she'll be back." Fia flashes me an apologetic look. "It's freezing out, and Penny hates being cold."

I trail my fingers over Tank's smooth back as he sinks onto the braided rug at my feet next to the sofa. The kitchen opens into the living room, so no walls to separate Fia and me as we sit in the quiet wake of Penny's storm. Fia hasn't moved, still leaning against the kitchen island, as if anchored there. It's only been minutes since Penny walked out, but the aftershocks of her earthquake are still very present.

"The last thing I want is to cause trouble here." I pause, trying to find words that won't unravel whatever trust I've managed to rebuild with Fia. "Me and your sister have our history. But I'm not trying to pull you into the middle of it."

"I know." Fia's nails hover at her mouth—an old nervous habit. Nan used to give her hell for it. "This isn't how I had it planned."

Her plan was shaky at best, but I didn't have time to get to the bottom of that.

My stomach rumbles, interrupting my thoughts. It's almost lunch time, but the alarm on my phone reminds me that there's no time for that.

"Shit, I gotta go." I silence my phone, stand, and grab my keys from the hook near the back door. I pause to look at Fia. "You sure you don't want to come with me?"

She shakes her head. "I'll stay here and wait for her to come back. Next week, though?"

Danny's going to be bummed, but I bite my tongue. "Yeah, of course. You cool with me leaving Tank?"

Fia crouches to his level, letting him slobber all over her cheek. She turns, laughing, and throws me a thumbs-up.

I'm still second-guessing being back here—not just in this house, but Wilmington. It was time to come back, settle up some things I left undone, but nothing about that is easy. There's no roadmap to follow.

But seeing Fia on the floor with my dog makes me think that at least Tank's happy and Fia's not alone. That's gotta be worth something, right?

"I'll be back late. He gets one scoop of kibble for dinner. Thanks, Fi. I owe you."

I tap her shoulder and head out through the back door, the cold slapping me the second it opens.

The sky is gray, and the wind whips against my car as asphalt stretches endlessly in front of me. Seventy-two miles left until I reach the state prison.

The plastic table between us bends, my elbows weighing it down. My knee bounces a bit under the table—this is not a place I ever wanted to return.

I've been on Danny's call list for seven years—ever since I got out. It's taken most of that time to untangle our messy friendship. Ten years inside gave him plenty of time to screw up, but also to grow. Still, being back here is a mindfuck. I don't really know what I'm doing—I'm just trying.

Trying to fix things.

Trying to show up.

Last Monday was the first time I'd seen him face to face in years, and the first time I'd stepped back inside this prison since my own release. And now I have to explain why I showed up alone.

Danny asked me to bring Fia when he called last week, which didn't surprise me since she's the one person he brings up every time we talk. I found out she's been visiting when she can, maybe twice a year, three if she's lucky. But her life's been rough lately. Her car barely makes it across town, and with her classes, her job, and now the pregnancy... It's a lot.

And today, she's at home waiting for Penny to storm back through the front door.

"Hey, man, how you've been? You look like shit," Danny starts, and I laugh, looking down at my faded black jeans and dark-green shirt under my old leather jacket, wishing I could shove him like we used to when we were dumb kids. But there's a whole room full of inmates and guards with eyes like lasers.

I glance at the signs on the wall: *No touching*. And I try to ignore the metal mesh on the windows. Seeing them makes me feel like I'm back in this fucking sardine can.

But I'm here for *him*.

Despite everything.

I forgave Danny because I made a promise to myself to stop living with grudges. They'll rot you from the inside out if you let them.

I crack a grin. "Nice to see you, too, asshat. It's been a day."

"It's 2 p.m., what the hell could've happened so far?" He throws up his hands. "You get a speeding ticket on the way up or something?"

I chuckle and lean back, black leather tugging at my shoulders. Danny's always been a smartass, but ironically, prison might've saved him. He's sober now, learning to weld, and talks about life after release—five months to go. Not the usual stuff, like fast food or chasing girls. He wants to visit Nan's grave, volunteer at the shelter with me, and more than anything, show up for his little sister.

"Not that," I say, tilting my head back. "But I did get accosted. By your sister."

"Fia?"

My mouth opens, hesitating for a moment. "Your other sister."

He lets out a low whistle and leans toward me. Amber eyes—the same as hers—watch me too closely. "How...how is she?"

There's that ache that never healed laced in his tone. What happened with Danny and I fractured his family, the same one that welcomed me with open arms when I was barely sixteen. The same one I ran from, the same one I'm trying to make amends with.

"She's..." I pause.

She's Penny. A wildfire. Beautiful in ways she never understood. The girl who considers me public enemy number one. But that's not what Danny needs to hear.

"She's good." It's a white lie, for Danny's sake. No need to tell him she was about to decapitate me. "She showed up today, to be with Fia for the holidays, I guess." I shrug, ready to chat about anything else.

But Danny traces a circle on the table, a mischievous grin on his face. "I'm glad she's still there for Fia." He hesitates, hunched over the table. "She seem happy?"

"I only saw her for maybe ten minutes." I rub my stubbled jaw. "She's processing a lot. Seeing me. Finding out about the baby..."

The clock on the grimy white wall ticks, and Danny nods slowly.

"Yeah, Fia called me yesterday to tell me about the baby. Still shocked. But that's a lot for Penny, too."

"But hey," I say, straightening my spine, "at least Penny got out of this town and she's doing what she always said she'd do."

Just saying that makes my heart twinge, an old scar pulsing inside my chest.

"That's what Fia says." Danny leans back, his smile returning. "Ever think back to those summers, all of us raising hell? We were wild, but Penny always kept us in line. Well, she tried."

I laugh. "How could I forget?"

The memory of us flying down back roads in high school with Penny screaming in the passenger seat hits out of nowhere. I haven't thought about that in ages. The true miracle isn't that Danny's alive, it's that all three of us are.

He tilts his head, studying me. "Hey, man...you think she'd come with you next time? To visit me? It's almost Christmas. Maybe she's feeling generous."

Danny doesn't know Penny anymore, not that I really do either. But nothing about what I do know or saw today makes me believe I'd be able to get her here to see her brother. If I did succeed, she'd probably be the next Hanson sibling to land themselves behind bars.

"I'll try, but no promises man." I crack my knuckles. "She's stubborn, you know that. And I'm not sure how long she's sticking around."

Danny shrugs, masking disappointment, and I feel for him. "Nah, I figured. Just wishful thinking. I haven't heard from her in a decade...what would change now?"

A jolt of stubbornness hits me, because why did I come here, why did I move back if I wasn't here to fix things? I don't really owe Danny anything, but I'm trying to make things right.

Maybe this is my good karma deed to get the ball rolling.

"I'll see what I can do, okay? Penny used to like me, maybe it can happen again," I joke, but Danny takes it to heart.

"I appreciate it!" He slams a palm on the table and points to me. "I believe in you. Do your magic."

I don't mention the way she looked at me today—like I was something broken she never wanted to touch again.

Instead, I nod as the guards give us the signal.

As I walk out, I turn back to see Danny shuffle toward the locked doors. He raises a hand before disappearing through them.

I don't know what it will take to get through to Penny, but I do know I've got my work cut out for me.

What Danny doesn't know is that today might've been the first time I laid eyes on Penny in ten years, but not a day has gone by that I haven't shut my eyes and seen hers.

Or thought about that final kiss I planted on her sleeping face, knowing I was about to break her heart.

This wasn't going to be easy.

Everything is quiet and dark by the time I get back to the house.

I ate dinner at a roadside diner, alone, and ended up driving around Wilmington aimlessly for a while. Driving eases me. When I first moved to California, I would drive Highway 1 up and down the coast for hours when I couldn't sleep. And tonight, I knew I wouldn't be able to sleep, but I didn't want to be the reason Fia and Penny didn't.

The glow from the living room catches my eye, and I peer in on my way to the staircase. Fia's fast asleep on the sofa, the TV still flickering, Tank squished beside her like he's always been her dog. A thick fleece blanket is draped over both of them.

Tank's block head is wedged between the back of the tan sofa and Fia's growing bump. He cracks his eyes to look at me, lets out a small sigh as he nestles in closer to her, and shuts his eyes again.

Traitor.

Three years ago, I rescued him from the LA shelter I was working at. It took ten minutes of playing with the dirty four-month-old puppy to decide I needed him as much as he needed me. He's been my ride or die ever since. Well, up until I moved here; now he's attached to Fia's side. But I'm not mad about it. Dogs know when someone needs them.

I head upstairs and hear faint sounds—sudden music, an electronic-sounding voice, another sudden song, like someone is scrolling a social media app. The moment my boots hit the upstairs hallway floor, it creaks, and the bedroom across from mine falls silent.

I guess Penny returned...and she's awake.

I shake my head, step into my room, and switch on the light. Not much has changed in here since I was a teenager. Forest-green walls with a wallpaper border of mallard ducks. The same pine bed frame that still groans in protest when I lie on it. But everything I own fits in here, considering I left anything that didn't fit in my Camaro back in California.

I toss my leather jacket on the back of the chair in the corner and strip down to my boxers. The promise I made to Danny plays again in my head as I lie down, staring up at the same ceiling I memorized over a decade ago.

Nothing lights a fire in my chest like the odds being stacked against me. But the stubborn blonde across the hall is a challenge I'm pretty sure might kill me.

8

Penny

NOW

When I finally came back to the house, I apologized to my sister. She doesn't see that I'm trying to protect her, but I didn't want to harp on it all evening. Things stayed awkward, and I bit my tongue as 7 p.m. came and went with no sign of Jesse.

Of course, he left his dog here for us to take care of. Fia seemed totally chill about watching Tank, adding to my growing frustration. She spent her entire childhood obsessing over dogs, reading every dog book, begging Nan to take her to the shelter to adopt one. So in any other circumstance, I'd be thrilled for her to have a companion.

Instead, I sat in the chair next to the fireplace, seething in silence as my sister peacefully dozed off to sleep, Tank curled up next to her. By 8 p.m., the house was silent, aside from Tank's snoring and the heater working for its life in this house, so I got up and called it a night.

I grabbed the large fleece blanket from the back of the chair and draped it around Fia before heading upstairs, turning up the thermostat as I went. Not that it would make a difference—the ancient radiator system in this house is beyond my understanding, and I wouldn't even know where to start fixing it. Still, it desperately needs repair.

After anxiously watching every passing car from my bedroom window, bracing for his return, exhaustion eventually overtakes me. I force myself to unpack, shoving my clothes into the tiny closet.

Perched on the bed, I scroll through my phone like a sulky teenager desperate for distraction—until a floorboard groans in the hallway. I jolt upright, slamming my phone onto the covers.

My pulse spikes as the shadow stretches beneath the door, because my body can't tell the difference between a lurking ex-boyfriend and a serial killer who's broken in. However, as quickly as it happens, he's gone. I didn't even know Jesse was home.

Collapsing against the headboard, I squeeze my eyes shut, listening until the door across the hall clicks closed. I feel like a prisoner in a house I technically own.

The moment my head hits the pillow, I'm wide awake again, and I toss back and forth relentlessly.

I hope I wake up to find out that none of this was real.

My hair feels like a rat's nest piled on my head—wavy and hanging around my cheeks, the rest of it twisted into a messy bun—as I meander down the stairs.

Something's burning.

Something cheesy, maybe. Or eggs.

I pull my sweatshirt sleeves down around my fingers, and brace myself for whatever mess I'm walking into. Probably Jesse burning shit.

Rounding the corner, I collide directly into Tank, knees knocking against his solid gray body. He doesn't so much as glance my direction as drool beads on his mouth.

"I'm sorry!" I apologize to him. It's not his fault that he is owned by Jesse.

I follow his intense gaze to my sister.

Fia curses under her breath, and tears stream down her face as two black discs sit in front of her on a plate.

"Good morning," she greets me meekly, wiping her nose on the sleeve of her terry cloth robe.

I circle the island to get a look at whatever is on her plate.

Two hockey pucks, it appears.

"I just wanted a bagel." She inhales, staring longingly at the sad, burnt food in front of her. "It's all I've been craving, and this is the last one, and I had to pee so bad, and it stayed in the toaster oven too long, and it's burnt now and—"

"It's okay, Fi." I wrap my arms around her narrow shoulders and pull her into a hug. Clearly, she's got the fragility of an eggshell right now.

I grab the plate and toss the bagel in the trash—much to Tank's dismay. I snag a paper towel and hand it to her. Fia blows her nose, peering at me pathetically.

This is what I do best. Clean up messes.

"Forget about the bagel. There's a new café by the beach, they serve brunch, and it looks really good. Plus, I need to get out."

She perks up, fiery red hair falling from behind her ears. "Okay." She sniffles. "That sounds good."

"Great." I try to muster some semblance that I have my shit together today. "Let's leave in thirty."

I stand at the sink, blow-drying my hair in the only upstairs bathroom this house has, when my phone dings. After a quick shower, I admittedly feel a bit better. Jesse was nowhere to be found this morning, and maybe today, Fia and I can have a nice, normal afternoon doing stuff we're used to.

Audrey: How's it going today? Robert was asking about you at pilates. He invited us to his and Dave's xmas party, but I told him you're out of town :(

I set down the dryer, typing out a response.

Penny: Damn, I really need to sweat out this rage inside me. Instead I'm dealing with the aftermath of my sister crying over a burnt bagel.

Audrey: I hear those pregnancy hormones are no joke. How's the ex situation?

Penny: He's made himself scarce. I'm hoping he gets the hint and just leaves. I need Fia to focus on her life, not be distracted by her estranged "brother" showing back up.

Audrey: It's really messing with my brain when you refer to your ex-boyfriend as a brother. Do you really think he'll leave?

Penny: Sorry, it's just she acts like he's family but he is NOT. He doesn't belong here, not in this house, not in this town. Nowhere near me. I don't care if he paid rent. I'm making him leave.

Audrey: Well it sounds like you have quite the day ahead of you.

Penny: HA. Thanks for the moral support.

I swipe on some matte-pink lipstick and fluff my hair in the small medicine cabinet mirror, the light yellow and harsh. Another text lights up my screen.

Audrey: Just play nice...maybe he's changed. Also, still waiting for that pic of Jesse. How can I hate him with you if I don't even know what he looks like?

Penny: Seeing him won't help. Trust me.

Heat rises in my cheeks. Do I really think that? I mean *fine*, he is attractive. But my best friend having that knowledge won't help my case.

I need to keep my eyes on the prize, not have Audrey reminding me that the guy renting a room in my family home was the center of my universe once upon a time.

"Want to walk on the beach?" Fia asks after taking the last bite of her asiago bagel. The color has returned to her face, and her green eyes are no longer filled with tears now that she's eaten.

I agree to the beach, because even if it's cold, the beach has always been our happy place. Maybe that'll make what I need to discuss with her easier.

Sinewy clouds linger in the blue sky. We walk over to the public beach access, and the moment I hear the waves, the tension in my shoulders slowly melts. Fia pulls her hood up; the baby bump is barely noticeable under all her layers.

The ocean is dark today, with only a few seagulls scattered along the stretch of sand. The wind whips my hair across my face, and I brush it back, eager to enjoy this walk, eager to hold on to the peace it brings me.

Fia turns to face me as we walk along the cold sand, a shy smile playing on her lips. "I can't wait to bring my baby here one day. Hopefully they'll love the water just as much as we did as kids."

"Of course they will, it's part of our DNA," I say, still fighting the surreal feeling around Fia being pregnant. "Hey, have you talked to your school to figure out how to finish your last semester?"

Fia nods. "I'm going to finish school online next semester and probably take some classes over the summer. Then, when the baby is old enough for daycare, I can work full-time."

"Isn't daycare pretty expensive?"

"I'll figure it out. I have some time." She shrugs, and my shoulders tense.

I can't figure out why she isn't taking this more seriously.

"Nan raised three of us on a nurse's salary." She smiles, walking wistfully beside me.

This feels impossible. I know Fia's resourceful, and she's wicked smart, but she's not thinking clearly. She can't raise a baby with no family around, in an old house, on minimum wage, *and* finish college. Something has got to give.

We come across a patch of sand filled with shells, and I bite my lip, my lungs tightening. Two fishermen with long poles walk by, nodding at us, and I muster up a smile before turning to see Fia squatting down, sifting through the shells. She picks up a large one with orange striping. "A treasure," we would've thought as kids.

"For the baby's room." She shoves the shell in her pocket. "I'm going to do a bohemian beach theme."

I nod, my list of worries growing longer in my head. "Which room are you going to turn into a nursery?"

"I was thinking about your room." We both stop, and her lashes blink rapidly. "If that's okay with you? It's next to mine and has good lighting."

"I have a proposition for you, actually," I say, even as nausea rolls through me.

"What?" Fia asks, studying the seashells near her shoes.

I steel myself. I came here without a real plan, just knowing I had to clean up this mess and help Fia, but now it's become evident that there's only one plan that makes sense.

"I think you should move to Raleigh. Like move in with me."

Fia's eyes snap up.

"I have a large spare room with its own bathroom," I say, hurrying through my words. "You wouldn't have to pay rent, you wouldn't need a car, and my condo building is new and safe. I could help you find a good job in the city, so you can afford daycare and—"

"Wow..." She cuts me off, twirling the toe of her white sneaker in the sand, avoiding eye contact. "That's extremely generous of you, Penny...but I can't just leave."

"Why not?"

It's the ideal solution. No one is going to come to save her, and I'm offering an olive branch.

The wind blows a lock of red hair into Fia's eyes, and she tucks it behind her ear, shrugging. "Jesse paid me rent in advance, I can't kick him out now."

My heart rate mimics the white-capped waves pounding the shore, but I ball my fists and try to reason with her.

"So give him it back," I snap, shoving my fists into the deep pockets of my wool coat. "He can find a new place, he's a grown man."

"I'd never do that to him!" Fia gapes at me. She's too kind, too delicate.

I bite my tongue so I don't say everything else I think about him. Like that she can toss him out on the damn street for all I care.

"Plus, I don't want Danny living in a halfway house when he gets out. I want him to move into the family home."

Inhale through the nose, exhale through the mouth.

Sure, invite the brother who literally ignored you and ruined this family back in. Where is my sister's logic?

"This isn't *Full House*," I stutter, feeling like I'm losing my grip more and more with my sister. "You have a baby on the way, you need to stop thinking about Danny and Jesse and think about what's best for you. Be selfish for a moment!" I pull back, realizing I'm nearly yelling.

Fia pauses to study me, her green eyes far away. "Being selfish doesn't come easily to everyone."

"What does that mean?" I know exactly what it means, but I *want* her to say it.

Fia looks out over the white-capped waves, her eyes glassy. "I just mean…you left when you were eighteen and never looked back. You forgot all about us. It was easy for you. But some of us can't let go like that." She flaps her arms at her sides and turns, walking away before I can reply.

I stare at the water, unblinking, numb.

Being selfish was the only way I was going to survive. Nothing about leaving was easy, but she'll never understand that.

Christmas music plays on the radio, but there's a serious lack of cheer between Fia and me as we drive back toward town. I brushed her comment under the metaphorical rug, because I'm not getting anywhere with her with this approach of *big sister knows best*. So I bribe her with something I know she can't resist.

I glance over at my sister with her pink cheeks and hair falling out of her braid. She sits stiffly in her seat.

"Hey, we need to get sweaters."

"I'm not really up for that this year," Fia responds glumly.

"Come on, it's tradition, Fi. You look forward to it every year." We stop at the light, and I swivel toward her, but she keeps her eyes focused on anything but me. "Don't you want to have a photo to show the baby one day of their pregnant mom in an ugly sweater?"

I'm trying.

Her green eyes brighten, lips struggling to fight back a smile.

"Fine," she replies and points up ahead. "Pull over there—there's a new thrift store called Cause for Paws. All the proceeds go to the animal shelter."

The thrift store is in an old hardware store downtown, with a narrow sidewalk out front. Asphalt grits under the tires of my convertible as I turn the wheel, pulling into the last spot.

"Why the hell is it so busy?" I mumble, but Fia flashes me a smile and leaves the car.

This is what I asked for, but of course any flicker of satisfaction is fleeting—because when I look up, reality smacks me in the face in the form of one tall, tattooed guy donning a Santa hat.

Jesse's standing next to a table with the Humane Society's banner taped crookedly across the front. Stacks of brochures and colorful papers line the table, held down with stones to keep them from blowing away in the salt air. And he is ringing a bell.

I have to be dreaming.

"Jesse? What the heck are you doing here!" Fia laughs, almost giddy, stepping up to the table he's standing beside.

I remain a few feet back.

For his own protection, of course.

He doesn't seem phased by me, which irks me. I want him to feel uncomfortable.

"I'm volunteering for the shelter today," he informs Fia casually. "Trying to raise awareness of the new program I'm running—the rehab and rehome one I mentioned to you."

Fia carefully takes a pamphlet off the table. "I'll put this up at Good Grinds." She slides it into her pocket.

I roll my eyes.

When I glance back, he's staring right at me. Green eyes piercing mine, his jean jacket over his signature black hoodie.

"What're you two up to today?" He's looking directly at me.

It takes me too long to find my voice, and when I do, it comes out squeaky. "We're shopping."

Fia glares at me.

"Come on, Fi, I'm cold." I pretend to shiver, rubbing my arms.

I'm actually burning up, I simply don't feel like standing on the sidewalk as my ex rings a bell, looking like rockstar Santa while people walk by, slipping money into his pail.

This is the opposite of a sweet Hallmark movie. It's hell.

"We're getting ugly sweaters for our annual Christmas photo," Fia tells him as she takes slow steps toward the shop's door. "Actually, Jesse, you need one, too!"

That's it.

I reach out and grab my sister's arm, yanking her toward the store. "Nope, Jesse does not need to participate. This is just between us!" I smile tightly at him as he watches, confusion in his eyes but amusement on his lips.

Inside, the store is warm and has that distinct thrift store smell—like everyone's different laundry detergents, or lack of, mixed together. There are too many people in here doing god knows what, and I'm ready to leave the moment we step inside.

But there's tradition to uphold.

Fia rips her arm from my grasp, pacing behind me down the tight aisle of sweaters. "What the hell, Penny? That was so rude!" she whisper-yells as other people stare at us.

I grab a red sweater, barely looking at it but needing to keep my body moving, and face my sister. "Listen, I know you're just trying to be nice to him, but I want you to be careful, okay?" I sigh, shoving the sweater back onto the rack. It's not ugly enough. "Jesse breaks promises, and you trust too easily."

That's an understatement, but I'm not trying to make her feel like shit about herself. I simply want her to be cautious. If he broke Fia's heart, I'd have no choice but to hunt him down and seek big sister revenge.

"What's that supposed to mean?" Fia blocks the aisle, arms crossed over her chest. "Jesse is a good guy."

"You don't know him that well, Fia. Just don't get too attached, okay?"

We lock eyes, and I hold it here until she nods.

She grabs a sweater and holds it up to herself. It's hideous. Which is perfect.

"I know you're being protective, but remember what Nan used to say?" she muses, and I shake my head. My Nan had a lot of southern sayings she'd throw around. "When someone shows you who they are, believe them."

I stifle a chuckle. "So, what's Jesse shown you, then?"

Fia throws her hands up. "That he's grown up, that he cares!" She stops shifting through the rack and looks right at me with that little sister shit-eating grin. "But don't take my word for it, the two of you can catch up tonight."

"What's tonight?" I stutter, my mouth going dry.

"Family dinner. It's Tuesday." She winks, and I shake my head. "If you can bring back the ugly sweater tradition that Nan started, I can bring back family dinner while you're home."

First, this isn't my home. Not anymore.

But also, she's got me. I don't know if I can maneuver my way out of this one. The great thing about me is that I can be silent all dinner long. Jesse can talk, and I will just disassociate and pretend I'm at the spa, soaking in a mud bath.

"Fine, *one* family dinner. But I'm not in the mood to cook." I'm about to pull out my phone and order takeout when Fia puts her hand on my arm, stopping me.

"Correct. I'm cooking."

Great. *Bon appétit.*

9

Penny

NOW

Fia sighs deeply from her napping position on the sofa. I plop down into the overstuffed chair next to the fireplace and tuck my legs under me, getting comfy. This was Nan's favorite chair—thick rolled arms, plaid fabric softened from years of wear, and ornate walnut feet. I'm not a sentimental person, not like the other women in my family. Both Fia and Nan had a tendency to hold on to things. Every corner of this house has knick-knacks and mementos, a living time capsule of Nan's life and all the grandchildren she raised.

But not me. When something is done, I cut the cord and move on.

This chair is the one thing I'd hold on to, though. Maybe I'll take it back to my condo with me if...no, *when* I get Fia to move out.

I glance over at my sleeping sister and sigh. She opened up a bit more to me this afternoon after I convinced her to browse a few more stores down by the Riverwalk. We chatted about the baby and school, but she didn't want to talk about Brett. Neither did I.

By the time we got home, we were both exhausted. Fia crashed, and I considered closing my eyes as well, but I had too much jittery energy running through me from the week's events—and it was only Tuesday.

So I open my laptop and pull up a browser. There are no emails to send or brides to collect invoices from, and I don't have a wedding

"

to shoot until the weekend after Christmas. But there is one thing I need to figure out—something I've been putting off.

I need to know what it would take to sell this house. Fast.

To sell it, we *all* need to agree.

Danny has to sign, too, which means I have to talk to him. I can't just send a lawyer to show up unannounced. I doubt my quick-tempered brother would take that well.

I glance at Fia with my fingers hovering above the keyboard. This is the only home she's ever known. But if we don't sell, she's going to drown here—with the baby, school, and the endless repairs this place needs. We need to do this while the house is still worth something.

Convincing her won't be easy...but that's Tomorrow Penny's problem.

Quickly, I type up an email to the attorney who handled the house deed and Nan's will. I'll have a much better grip on things once I understand how I can properly execute this whole ordeal.

I hit send just as Tank stirs at the base of the chair. I didn't invite him to lie there, but he curled up anyway, like we're besties.

I glance down at his gray and white face and his paws twitching in his sleep. He's pretty damn cute, not that I ever plan to admit that out loud. I'll just admire him from here. And take a picture of him to send to Audrey—she's got a thing for misfit dogs.

In the silence, it dawns on me that I could google Jesse.

Just type in his name and see what comes up. Find out if what he's told Fia about his business and life in California is actually true. That's reasonable, right?

I start typing his name, my fingers stiff, my throat going tight like I've swallowed something too big. I don't even know what I'm afraid of finding.

No, that's a lie.

I know exactly what I don't want to find. The same reason I never looked him up for ten years, because knowing he existed somewhere without me—that he kept going, living, becoming someone I didn't know anymore—was unbearable.

I type his name in the search bar, but my finger hovers, hesitating.

What if he has a girlfriend?

The breath leaves my lungs like I've been punched. I slap my laptop lid shut so fast it makes Tank jump and bark. This is ridiculous...I am not doing this. I don't care if he has a girlfriend. I have no right to care.

Fia stirs from the sofa, opening her eyes and reaching for her phone.

I study my nails, pretending to be relaxed, even though my heart's racing way too fast for someone merely lounging in a chair.

"Shoot, I need to start dinner," she says, stretching before shuffling into the kitchen.

"Cool, cool." I swallow. "Need any help?"

She shakes her head, totally oblivious to how *not chill* I am right now. Fia pulls her hair back and grabs an apron—a habit she picked up from Nan.

"Nope, I got it," she replies, propping her phone up with the recipe open.

I watch from the sofa, useless, while she waddles around the kitchen. I really wish Nan hadn't torn down the wall between the kitchen and living room twenty years ago, turning this old Victorian into an open-concept space—because right now, all I want is to hide and be alone with my thoughts.

"I'm just happy to have someone to cook for besides myself," Fia yaps mindlessly, as she pulls a bundle of vegetables from the fridge.

The pantry surprisingly isn't empty, and there's actual produce in the house. Bringing my own food only crowded the kitchen.

I don't know when my sister suddenly became a real adult.

I stand, and Tank licks my hand as I set my laptop on the coffee table.

"Isn't he the sweetest?" Fia asks.

"He seems very well trained," I say, patting his head. His fur is silky smooth, eyes like little honey-colored marbles.

"Well, he should be—considering that's what Jesse does."

I freeze. "What...does he do exactly?"

Fia chuckles, already slicing an eggplant. "Wow, sis. You literally know *nothing* about him, do you?" She laughs again, like it's so damn funny. "He's a dog trainer."

You have no idea how much I know about him.

How he kisses softly and slowly. How he runs his large hands up and down my back until it's safe enough to sneak back to his own room. How he used to call me princess to piss me off, until it became his pet name for me. How he made me a playlist with songs that reminded him of me, of us, and how, for ten years, anytime one of those songs comes on, I have a knee-jerk reaction to turn it off as quickly as possible, like my sanity depends on it.

"I guess I don't." I play along. "So, that's where he goes all day?"

"Yeah. He had a pretty successful business in Los Angeles, I guess." She shrugs, reading the recipe. "He works with dogs that've basically run out of chances," Fia says, her tone light, like this isn't about to knock the wind out of me. "The ones people think are too far gone. His specialty is rehabbing them and getting them adoptable again." She drops that in so casually, like she's reciting a fun fact. "I guess he was on some huge podcasts and had this crazy two-year waitlist. But now he works with rescues. Just look him up, he's kind of a big deal." She chuckles. "He was even on the cover of that tattoo magazine last year. So crazy, right?"

My throat constricts, and I peel my eyes away, even though she's not even looking at me. She's too focused on preparing the meal, but I feel exposed regardless.

Because that's exactly who the Jesse I knew would've grown up to be.

Helping the voiceless, helping those who are forgotten.

Even when he had nothing left to give, when he was the one who should've been angry at the world, he wasn't.

I blink away the emotions clouding me and open my mouth to ask more, desperately hungry for a bit more detail about why he's here, then, why not stay in LA?

Fia seems to be a well of random Jesse trivia, but she squeezes her legs together and whispers, "Shoot I gotta pee!" before scurrying off to the bathroom.

As the bathroom door clicks shut down the hallway, the back door swings open, and Tank jumps up, alert. His whole body starts to wiggle back and forth so hard that his defined gray spots become a blur.

The doorway fills with dark jeans, scuffed black motorcycle boots, and broad shoulders that block out the last of the light. Jesse's green eyes cut through the room until they land on me.

"Hey," is all he says.

Before I can even whisper my breathless, raspy *hi*, he's already crouched to pet Tank with one hand, the other arm wrapped around a twined bundle of firewood.

"Thought I'd build a fire," he says without looking up. "It's supposed to get cold tonight."

"Sorry. Fireplace doesn't work," I retort.

He looks up at me now.

I scrunch my nose, feeling not-so-bad about bursting his bubble. I turn my back to him, planting myself in the chair next to the fireplace again.

He doesn't just get to swoop in and play *hero*.

10

Jesse

NOW

Miss *I Know Everything* is about to learn a lesson.

I push past Tank and drop the firewood bundle next to the fireplace while Penny watches me, wide-eyed. I squat in front of the brick hearth and pull open the mesh screen.

"Let's just test it." I wink at her—much to her horror—and push the sleeves of my Henley up. I carefully begin to stack the wood inside the redbrick fireplace.

"If you light that up, you're going to burn down the whole house." She inches forward in the chair, long blonde hair flopping over her shoulder, like she isn't above physically trying to stop me.

I would love to see her try.

Fighting back a grin, I continue to slowly stack the logs, relishing in how torturous this is for her. I take an exaggerated inhale of the fresh pine I cut early this morning.

Her eyes drill into the side of my face. "Are you daft?" Penny kicks her feet free from the fleece blanket on her lap, the slap of her soles on the hardwood loud enough to echo. "I told you, *Jesse*, the fireplace doesn't work."

With the final log in place, I slip my lighter into my palm, baiting her. My thumb strums the lever, and I flick my gaze at her over the blue flame, a cocky smirk on my lips.

Her eyes narrow, then drop to my lips—parted just enough.

The moment stretches, tight and electric, like she's about to leap at me, stop me.

But I smile.

"Relax, princess."

Shit.

The nickname spilled out like fucking word vomit, but I play it off. Maybe she forgot about it.

"I got the fireplace serviced last week," I add, lighting the kindling. I stoke the fire and glance over at her.

She *did not* forget about the nickname.

It's written all over her shell-shocked expression. The same look she wore when I walked through the door yesterday.

I'm not a betting man, but I'd wager that no one calls her princess. Probably because she'd never let them.

Fia strolls into the living room, and the tension evaporates like smoke.

"Oh my god, thank you. My toes are frozen! I totally forgot to tell you, Pen—Jesse paid for someone to fix the fireplace. Wasn't that nice?" She beams at her sister and hurries back to the stove, oblivious to Penny's stone expression.

"Aren't you just a fucking hero," Penny mutters as she pushes herself out of the chair and waltzes into the kitchen.

I've never felt like a hero.

Penny doesn't leave her sister's side until dinner is ready, and I take Tank for a quick stroll in an attempt to clear my head. He loves walks here—there's a lot more trees and grass to pee on than in LA.

The neighborhood I once called home has changed a bit in the last decade. More houses being are being renovated, and wealthy investors are moving in. Wilmington suddenly seems like the place to be, which is funny, because all Penny and I wanted to do was get out of here one day.

I guess the grass is always greener when you're young. Which makes for an easy cover story as to why I moved back here.

Why'd you return here when you lived in Southern California?

Ah, I missed the small town feel. There's no place like the Carolina coast. Cost of living is too high in LA. Sick of the crime.

They were all things people would buy at face value, and none of them were flat-out lies.

But they weren't the full truth either.

Nan—the only woman I ever considered a mother—died two years ago, and I found out too late to come back for the funeral. I was surrounded by people in LA who acted like they knew me, and maybe they did to some degree. They knew Jesse, the dog trainer, Jesse the former tattoo artist, Jesse the guy who won't date you but will take you for a ride on his motorcycle and let you warm his bed for a night.

One morning, I woke up and something in me had shifted. Not in my bones—nothing that obvious. It was deeper, somewhere in my chest, like a weight I'd been carrying finally pressed too hard to ignore. Maybe it had been there for years, festering quietly beneath the surface. But one day, it got loud.

Loud enough to pull me back here—to this port city that once felt like home, even as it carved me up in places I'm still learning to patch. I didn't just leave this city. I left it wrecked in my wake. This whole state is littered with people I hurt, hearts I broke, lives I walked out of without looking back.

Three months ago, I knew I couldn't keep running. Maybe I really am just a masochist—stupid enough to believe in second chances. But either way, something in me said *enough*. So I started the slow work of turning around.

Because as much as I wanted to move forward, I knew I couldn't—not without facing the ghosts I left behind.

At least, the ones still alive to talk to.

Running into Fia at the grocery store was serendipity, if you believe in that sort of shit. I'm beginning to not have a choice if I believe in it or not, because the universe keeps throwing things my way that are impossible to ignore.

The angry blonde who slept across the hall from me last night is one of the ghosts I came back for.

And I can't believe I just called her *princess*.

11

Penny

THEN

Age 15, December Sophomore Year

The mall is packed with moms and their daughters shopping for dresses. Sophomore year winter formal is a big deal. It's a dance hosted at an outside venue, and some of my friends have their driver's license, meaning we don't have to get dropped off by parents anymore.

But I won't be sixteen for another month.

Nan, Fia, and I quickly pass every store I *want* to go in, full of dresses I've seen in the magazines. The ones my friends will be wearing.

I gaze at the colorful window displays, sighing.

We head to the back of the department store, straight past the mannequins with the gorgeous sequined gowns that would probably fit me like a glove, and to the dimly lit, forgotten corner where the discounted dresses are thrown on broken racks.

The fact that Nan agreed to buy me a brand new dress is a big deal, though—even if it's off the sale rack.

"Oh, this is pretty." Fia grabs a purple dress and twirls around in front of the mirror.

I sift through dresses that look very *three seasons ago,* but try to smile. "I want a pink dress."

"We'll find you something," Nan reassures me, looking through dresses in my size. "And remember, even if it's ripped or too big, I can fix it."

My enthusiasm wavers because everything on the rack looks frumpy, last season, or full of big flower patterns that appear like they belong on a tablecloth.

However, ten minutes later, I'm in the fitting room, trying on dresses that Nan insisted would look beautiful on me. She can be very convincing.

A pale-pink one with beads on the straps and ruching on the sides catches my eye. It's the only one that doesn't look like it belongs on a mother-of-the-bride, so I slip it on and come out into the dressing room corridor, doing a little spin in my socks.

From the floor she's sitting on, Fia gives me two thumbs-up, and Nan drops her jaw dramatically.

"Are you sure you didn't get asked to the dance? Because you are a beauty queen, missy." She comes over, rubbing the pink satin fabric between her fingers. "I find it hard to believe that not a single boy asked you."

My cheeks grow hot, and I look away.

I hate lying to Nan—it's the worst feeling.

"No one did, but it's okay, Nan! Really." I twirl, checking out my backside. The dress is tight enough to show off my ass, but not too tight that Nan says no. "I'm excited to go with Grace and Evie."

Nan grabs the tag hanging out the back, putting on her tortoise-shell readers. I already looked—it's 60% off, so I think she'll say yes.

"Plus, Danny and Jesse will be there," I add, shrugging.

"Yeah, because no girls would ever say yes to them, they are so gross." Fia rolls her eyes.

"Seriously," I add, pretending to agree. Well, actually, my brother is pretty grungy.

Nan flashes us a stern look.

"Yeah, well, lucky for them, Grace and Evie agreed they could go with us as a group," I add, and Nan's gaze meets mine in the mirror.

"Oh good, you can keep an eye on them. Make sure they don't get into trouble." She winks at me, and I nod, keeping my face as serious as I can.

"I'll try my best, they are wild animals," I joke and quickly slip into the fitting room to change out of this dress.

"Let's stop at the shoe store, they have a buy-one-get-one sale," Nan says, reaching a hand over the door to grab my dress.

"Thanks, Nan, I appreciate it. I love the dress," I say when I come out and meet them at the register. She kisses my cheek, and I get a whiff of her signature jasmine perfume.

"Sure thing, honey."

I always pictured my first dance differently. I thought my boyfriend would pick me up at my house, bring me one of those fancy flowers for my wrist, and Nan would take pictures of us on our steps.

Instead, my boyfriend lives in the room across the hall from me, and no one in the world even knows we're dating.

They can't know.

Jesse passed me a note under my door three nights ago after everyone else went to bed, and I've reread it so many times, the paper's getting soft.

P,

You know there's no one else in the world I'd rather go to home-coming with than you, right? It's killing me that we can't go together like normal couples at school. I know we'll all be together as a friend group, but I need you to know, in my heart, it's just you Pen. Always just you.

It's going to be torture not being able to dance with you, especially if they play our song. But if another guy tries to grind up on you, I can't promise you I won't knock them out. Not even sorry for that.

I can't wait to see you in your pink dress. I'm not sure how I'll hide my reaction from everyone, because you're going to look so damn stunning, as always.

xo,

J

I always had a crush on Jesse, but I never meant to fall for him like that... It just happened. One day, he was my best friend—the one who always knew when something was wrong without me saying a word, and then suddenly, he was everywhere. In my yard, laughing with my brother. On the couch, eating cereal like he'd always lived here. And he did belong, which is what made this so impossible.

I couldn't say anything. If Nan found out, Jesse would have to leave and go back to his awful family, or foster care. Somewhere away from me. Where I couldn't make sure he was safe.

So I kept quiet as long as I could. I pretended I didn't get butterflies when he brushed up against me in the hallway, didn't feel a pang of jealousy when he was partnered with other girls in biology.

But then came the beach day.

Maybe it was the hazy pink sky, or how it had been the best day ever with him and all our friends. Everyone else wandered off at one point, and it was just Jesse and me. We sat in the sand under the pier at Kure Beach, overlooking the waves, but I couldn't take my eyes off his sun-kissed face.

"Jesse... I like you." It slipped out small and shaky, and I instantly wished I could suck it back in.

Jesse froze for a second, and I thought I'd ruined everything. But then he turned an adorable shade of red and glanced over at me. And without a word, he scooted closer in the sand and wrapped his arms around me like he'd been holding back all day.

"I like you, too, Pen...a lot."

Now I turned bright red and hid my face behind my beach-tousled hair.

My heart was pounding so loud I almost didn't hear him say, "You have no idea how long I've wanted to kiss you, Penny Hanson."

I looked up, and he leaned closer.

"Can I?" he asked.

I nodded with my heart in my throat, and Jesse pulled me closer, kissing me right there as the sun was setting. It was magic, pure fucking magic.

I still replay it in my head every night as I drift to sleep.

He's better than the movies, he's my real-life prince charming.

But no one knows about the kiss, or him being my boyfriend—which we established about three minutes after that kiss.

Even my best friends, Grace and Evie, don't know because they can't keep their mouths shut, and it would get back to Danny. I don't think he'd tell Nan, but it would make things pretty awkward. And if Fia found out, we'd be totally screwed. Good thing my sister's always in la-la land.

So for now, I keep my mouth shut and hope one day Nan forgives me for lying.

12

Jesse

NOW

Six hundred bucks. That's what it costs to get the fireplace up and running again and ensure we don't freeze our asses off. By the time I get back from walking Tank around the neighborhood, it's already done its job, making the house warm. A vast improvement from two weeks ago, when Fia was stuffing ratty old towels under the doors to keep the draft out.

It pissed me off beyond belief that there was a guy roaming this town who knocked her up and hadn't checked on her once this winter, knowing damn well she was here alone. Probably for the best now that I'm here, though, because if he did decide to show his pretty little face, I can't guarantee her I won't be taken away in handcuffs.

I settle into the house, noticing Penny has ditched the pink hoodie she had on before, so she can glare all she wants, but she's not shivering. In fact, she's moving around the dining table in nothing but a skin-tight workout top and barely-there yoga pants.

The way the thin fabric clings to her curves should be illegal, and when she catches me staring at her, she smiles knowingly—and then proceeds to flip me off.

Ah, that's my girl.

"Dinner's ready!" Fia calls out, slightly out of breath as she brings the glass casserole dish to the big oak table.

I drop down into my usual seat—same one I sat in all those years ago. It's an old habit I don't think much of.

It didn't feel weird until Penny walked in and halted.

Her eyes flicker to the empty seat beside me—her seat. She hesitates, and I try not to overthink it. Does she really hate me so much that she can't sit next to me?

She puffs her cheeks and quickly drops into the dining chair across from me.

Danny's spot.

"Damn, chef, you didn't have to do this." I grin at Fia, who exhales, proudly scanning the meal she's prepared. Wafts of hearty roasted vegetables and warm tomato sauce fill the air between the three of us.

"This is fun for me. Plus, when else is my family all going to be under one roof?" She glances at the empty chair. "Well, *almost* all."

I don't miss the shadow that passes over Penny's face.

"Yes, thank you. It was very thoughtful," Penny chimes in, sounding robotic. "Is this Nan's recipe?"

Fia nods, scooping a large square of lasagna onto her blue ceramic plate. "Yes! It's my first attempt, so I doubt it's as good as hers, though."

Fia continues talking, something about a friend, maybe school or work. To be honest, I'm not really listening.

I'm watching Penny, sitting rigidly upright in her seat, eyes trained down.

She's barely touched her food, she just drags her fork in slow circles around her plate. She nods at all the right moments, even mumbles a few polite responses, but she's somewhere else entirely.

And I know that look. I've seen it before—when she's lost in her head, trying to sort through something she doesn't want anyone else to notice.

But I notice, and when I have a chance to pull her back in, I do.

"So photography, huh?"

"What?" Penny's eyes flick to mine, her brow creased.

"You're a traveling wedding photographer, no?" I take a large bite.

"You're phrasing it like it's a question." Her voice is cool and controlled. "But it's clear you already know the answer."

"You're right," I bite out, sharp, as she stares at me, daring me to continue. "I found your social media account. You have quite the following."

From the corner of my eye, I catch Fia pressing her lips together, barely holding back a smirk.

"She's huge," she jumps in, throwing an arm around Penny's shoulders. "She got hired to shoot a pro hockey player's wedding in Tulum a few months ago."

Penny closes her eyes with a groan, peeling Fia off her, and mutters, "Let's not go there, *Fia*," before stuffing an oversized bite of lasagna in her mouth.

"Tulum, huh?" I lean back in my chair, arms crossed over my chest. "Never been."

"Oh my gosh, Penny, you have to tell him about the grooms-men!"

Penny shakes her head furiously, a blush crawling up her cheeks.

"It's a wild story." Fia wiggles her brows at me.

"Jesse, why don't you tell me about your job." Penny tries to shift the conversation, but Fia continues as if she didn't hear her sister's interjection.

"So the groomsmen were NHL players, too. Naturally, they got completely wasted and ended up in Penny's hotel room! They drank the minibar dry and trashed the place. Then they fell asleep...in *Penny's* bed. Three of them! She couldn't get them to wake up and leave."

I glance at Penny. Her jaw looks like it might crack from how hard she's clenching, and she throws her head back, guzzling her red wine.

"So," Fia continues, scooping more food onto her plate, "Penny went through their pockets while they were passed out, stole their room key, and slept in *their* penthouse instead. When they knocked on the door in the morning, Penny pretended she didn't know what the problem was." Fia giggles, and I glance at Penny, who's swirling her wine glass, mouth in a hard line. "The bride was so mortified that she paid double for the photography. And one of the players is still obsessed with Penny. He keeps calling, and I told her she should just go on a date. I mean, the guy's got *hella* money."

Penny turns, pinching Fia hard.

"Ouch! What the hell!" Fia yells, and Penny buries her face in her palm.

I push down the sharp, hot pang in my ribs. Jealousy isn't something I need to feel right now.

Penny can do whatever the hell she wants, with pro athletes or anyone else. They'd be idiots not to want her. Hell, it's probably a bonus if they're into pain, since she seems hellbent on making every interaction as uncomfortable as possible.

"So, you work for the shelter?" Penny shouts across the table, her voice echoing off the wallpapered dining room, startling everyone.

I cock an eyebrow at her.

I don't know if I've ever witnessed someone in such distress at a dining table. She's like a damn feral animal that needs to be put out of their misery.

Fia, jaw still tight, rolls her eyes and stabs her fork aggressively into the lasagna.

I'll need a miracle to survive these two women.

"Penny, what is *wrong* with you?" Fia snaps, exasperated.

"I'm enjoying dinner," Penny says sweetly, finishing off her wine. My eyes linger on her plush lips. "And I'd like to know what Jesse does. Like you said earlier, Fi, I have a *lot* to learn about him." Her voice is dripping in sarcasm, but I don't take the bait.

"You were talking about me?" I smirk as I lick my lips, a cocky habit I know she hates.

Penny grins sarcastically. "Yep. Nothing good."

"You're both acting like children," Fia groans, tossing her hands up. "It's the holiday break, and I'm determined to make you two civil." She brings her hands together in front of her, exhaling loudly. "Can you *at least* stop being so awkward when you're in the same room?"

Penny and I stare at each other, unblinking.

"Please? For me? Think of it as a Christmas gift." Fia bats her lashes dramatically at her sister.

"Fi, let it go," Penny warns. "Jesse and I are *fine*, aren't we?" She crosses her arms and tilts her head, daring me to disagree.

"Yeah," I reply, dry as hell. "We're grand."

We are absolutely *not* fine.

But the moment to hash it out isn't over lasagna and Fia's naively twisted dream of a perfectly blended family dinner.

"Well, I have to work tomorrow evening," Fia adds casually. "So you two will have a chance to catch up."

I swear Fia throws a wink my way.

"Right," I say at the exact moment Penny blurts, "Absolutely not," and lets out a sharp, almost panicked laugh.

So that's how it's gonna be, huh?

13

Penny

NOW

"What are you and Jesse going to do tonight?" Fia's way too chipper as she grabs her puffy winter jacket off the hook.

She got called into work at the coffee shop a few hours earlier than expected, which means the house will be empty, giving me alone time before Jesse returns from work. And I intend to use that time exactly how I want.

I shrug, feeling my heart rate rise again. "I don't know. Why are you so obsessed with us being best friends anyway?"

I was hoping Fia forgot about the conversation over dinner last night—the one that keeps replaying in my head. You know, pregnancy brain and all that. But apparently that's not how it works.

She pulls a hat with a fluffy pom-pom over her bright-red hair and exhales like *I'm* the difficult one here. "Because I know you're jaded when it comes to men. But Jesse's going to be here for the next six months, maybe longer. Every time you come to visit me and the baby, he'll be here."

Not if I can help it. He'll be gone.

She pauses, then softens her tone. "For my sake, and for yours, it'd be nice if you two could at least get along."

I shift, leaning against the staircase banister in the foyer. "I'm not *jaded* by men. I just don't do relationships. And how can you be so sure he'll be here in six months?"

Fia zips up her coat. "I never said you had to be in a *relationship* with him." Her eyes lock on mine, and I pretend to gag.

"And he paid me six months' rent up front, that's how I know. People don't do that unless they are committed."

Six months? I choke on my saliva.

"I just don't want you to be disappointed or anything, Fi. That's all."

She stops fidgeting with the zipper and pauses by the front door. "You're beginning to sound like a broken record, you know that?" she says flatly.

My defenses simmer as she wraps a scarf that looks home-made around her neck.

I want to be mad at her, but when I watch her bundle up for her walk to work, sadness pulls at my core. I've missed a lot since leaving Wilmington, and I didn't worry about Fia much because she had Nan and friends and a busy life with college, but now she just has me. The last thing I want is for Jesse's sudden arrival to drive a wedge between us.

"Okay." I shut my eyes, knowing I'm going to regret this. "Fine. I will try with Jesse."

"Oh, thank you!" she exclaims a bit dramatically. "You two used to be so close, I honestly don't understand how you could still be mad at him. Whatever happened, let it go and just show him the fun version of Penny *I* know."

It's completely innocent, *I think*, but I quickly pull her into a hug so she doesn't see my reddened cheeks.

"Well, I sure hope he likes sushi and true crime docuseries, because that's on my agenda tonight."

My sister rolls her eyes, hand already on the front door. "Okay, love you, I'll be done around nine."

"You sure you don't want me to drive you?" I ask again, but Fia shakes her head.

"It's a fifteen-minute walk, and I read that walking is good when you're expecting."

Huh.

"Okay, well text me, I'll pick you up at nine." I smile and lock the front door behind her.

What the hell did I just agree to?

The stack of firewood falls over again. Apparently, there's a right way to build a fire, but I was never a Girl Scout. This was Danny's job growing up. I also can't get anything to catch on fire, and I'm not trying to burn this place down, so I step back and shut the screen, pulling my cardigan closer around me.

I miss my condo and the little light switch next to the fireplace that turns on the modern blue flame. I'm not built for a pioneering lifestyle, and this hundred-year-old house was not built for me.

Back when I was in high school, Nan used to grumble to the neighbors that one day she'd have to bite the bullet and replace all the windows in this house. I'm not sure how that job somehow ended up falling to me, but...here we are.

Out of morbid curiosity, I pull out my phone and look up what that might cost for a house like this.

The moment I see the estimated price range, a startled squawk escapes my lips.

Yeah. No. Absolutely not.

I slip my feet into pink fur-lined slippers, fall back onto the sofa, and find the local sushi restaurant's menu on my phone. At least good food is still an option tonight.

I'll take my wins where I can.

The menu looks promising, but as I'm adding my picks to the cart, it dawns on me that Jesse will probably be hungry when he gets home. In the following moment of weakness, or kindness, or whatever you want to call my soft spot for Fia, I add a few different dishes to the cart for him and hope he likes something I selected. I add a noodle dish for Fia and her inevitable late-night cravings, too.

It's a peace offering. A fresh start.

With a few hours to kill before I have to pick up dinner, I decide to check my emails.

I skim the reply from my attorney, and my stomach flips.

It's confirmation of what I've been dreading—I need Danny to sign off on the sale.

In eleven days, I have to be in Raleigh to shoot a wedding, and my calendar is fully booked through January, giving me no time to come back to see Danny. But Fia only has three months before the baby arrives, meaning time is of the essence—I don't have the luxury of debating this for another day.

I type a response back to the attorney without hesitation: *Please draft the letter.*

If I were home in the city, I'd have an endless supply of things to do, but here, I feel like I'm twiddling my thumbs, waiting for my enemy to return, so I attempt to do something productive.

I take stock of what's in the house.

Within minutes, I'm engulfed in *stuff*, because it's no exaggeration when I say every nook and cranny of this century-old house is full. I open the cabinet under the steps and am met with clear plastic bins labeled *Easter decor,* and behind them is a bin labeled *art projects, third grade. My* third-grade art projects. A lump forms in my throat as I stare at the accumulation. It's too much. I shut the door, having to lean my body into it to get it to click shut.

Partially, this feels like my fault.

When Nan died two years ago, I didn't want to throw everything out or sell it right away. Fia was commuting from the house to college, and she insisted on staying here. I thought moving out would be more change than she could handle, and I didn't want to push her. I was just happy she was keeping up with school and work. But as months passed, life got back to normal for me—busy. I was booking more destination weddings than ever, and it was easy to push the idea of cleaning out Nan's house from my mind.

But now I can see that this isn't something we can put off forever. I also can't do this without my siblings' support.

"Fuck this," I mutter, walking away, and flick on the TV, killing the next hour.

When it's finally time to put my coat on and walk out the door, the picture of Nan near the back door gives me pause. I bring my fingers to her face, touching the glass.

"I really hope I'm doing right by you, Nan."

I take the long route to the restaurant, through neighborhood streets. I drive past Magnolia Street Park, my old high school, and without even realizing it, Jesse's old house. My chest squeezes as I halt at the stop sign and glance at the small white house with a sagging front porch. It looks like it should be condemned by the city, but to be fair, it didn't look that different when we were kids.

I don't know if Jesse ever contacted his family again, after everything. A knot forms in my stomach when I remember how he'd come to school with bruises. But then headlights approach behind me, and I hit the gas, moving along, willing the memories away.

Hoping my pump-up playlist can drown out my impending thoughts about Jesse, I crank the music in my car. Because how am I supposed to spend three hours alone with an ex-boyfriend-turned-roommate? Where's the manual for that, because I'd love to know.

What should I ask him first, "How was prison?" or "Do you remember when I went down on you in the back of the car after prom?"

Like I said, it's complicated.

But not for Fia.

It's black and white for her—she was only eleven when he and Danny were sentenced. Nan protected her from a lot of the gritty truth. She was heartbroken the only way an eleven-year-old could be, she missed her annoying older "brothers." Then I left, too. Now she's got me and Jesse back for a bit.

I can't entirely blame the kid for being hopeful.

Jesse's black car sits in the driveway when I return from the restaurant, and a loud groan rips through me. But I catch myself.

Nope. I promised Fia I'd try.

I can be sunshine.

When I walk in the house, bracing myself for his presence, it's eerily quiet. I wait for Tank to barrel into me, but there are no signs of that slobbery gremlin either. I drop the takeout containers on the kitchen counter and turn on a light, wondering if he took his dog and bailed on us, on foot? Then my phone starts ringing.

Audrey's calling to FaceTime me.

Maybe Jesse and Tank just went for a walk, but I'm not going to risk my conversation being heard, so I pop in my earbuds and answer the call.

"Hey, babe!"

Audrey's face fills the screen, half-covered in flour. "Where are you?"

"Sorry, I just got back to the house. Went to pick up some sushi for tonight."

Audrey's mouth falls open. "You do know that pregnant women shouldn't eat raw fish, right?"

I roll my eyes. "Duh—it's not for Fia. She's at work. It's just me and Jesse tonight."

Audrey raises her brows, saying nothing. Which says it all.

I dig around in my purse for lip gloss, feeling extra fidgety. "She pretty much begged us to act like functional adults because she's in a blissful state of mind where we are all a happy family."

"That's kind of sweet, though, right?" Audrey replies.

"Sweet, naive...same difference." I unclip my hair, letting it fall around my shoulders as I lean on the counter. "But I want her to be happy, so if being nice to Jesse makes her feel all warm and fuzzy inside, then fine, I'll *try*."

The words burn like vinegar on my tongue.

"Wouldn't it be easier to simply tell her the truth? That you two had a romantic falling out?"

I laugh, short and bitter. "That chapter is closed. Fully and completely."

I put on the pink lip gloss I find in the bottom of my purse, a mindless habit.

"I feel like she'd understand, right? And considering you're going to be there until Christmas, that's a long time to pretend nothing happened," Audrey chimes in, always with logic.

"I'm not pretending. Nothing is currently happening because it's ancient history. And telling her would only make things harder. She'd feel guilty for inviting him to live here if she knew the truth, then she'd feel like she had to take my side in this, and she doesn't need that stress right now."

Audrey tilts her head. "You don't want her to do that...because you care about his feelings being hurt?"

I nearly knock my phone to the floor. "I *did not* say that. I'm avoiding drama, that's all! I ordered him dinner, and I'll hang out with him *for one hour*. We'll play nice and move on with our lives. Happy holidays."

"Right," Audrey replies slowly, observing me with narrowed eyes. "You know best."

I head for the stairs, nearly tripping over Tank, passed out in a melted puddle at the bottom step. His limbs are all bent, tongue half out, snoring. World's worst guard dog.

The stairs creak as I make my way up to the dark second floor, and I half expect one of them to just give out. I wouldn't mind being swallowed whole right now.

"Hey, I wanted to talk to you about throwing a baby shower for Fia," Audrey says, and I can't believe that didn't pop into my head.

"You know that's actually not a bad idea, she's going to need everything. It will have to be in February, though, January is already full for me," I reply.

"Perfect! I'm happy to handle the food for her, I was just thinking that would be nice."

"Seriously? That's so thoughtful, Aud, I owe you. While I have you, let me show you the sweater I picked up at a boutique yesterday. I love it, but I feel like the burnt-orange color might look better on you."

I adjust the phone to switch on the hallway light.

"Hold on, let me flip the camera—" I press the button, then freeze.

A yellow glow spills from the narrow slit under the bathroom door, and before I can register what's happening, it swings open, steam billowing out.

Jesse steps into the hallway, shirtless, ruffling his wet hair with one hand, the other pulling the door shut behind him. Water clings to his skin, drops trailing over tattoos and a six-pack of muscle that I have *absolutely no business* noticing. But I do.

God, do I.

What happened to the Jesse I knew? The tall skinny emo kid?

And his towel sits criminally low on his hips...like pornographically low.

Like barely an inch above his fucking dick.

He sees me, pauses, eyebrows lifting just a little like he knows *exactly* what he's doing.

"Everything okay?" he asks, voice gravelly, and my mouth opens, but no sound comes out.

"Holy shit." Audrey's voice brings me out of my chokehold.

I spin, nearly body-slamming my bedroom door, and hurl myself into the room, kicking the door shut behind me like a middle school girl who just saw her first R-rated movie.

I pinch the bridge of my nose, eyes squeezed shut like I can erase what I just saw, even though I know, without a doubt, that image is going to be seared into my brain for a very long time. I turn the video call back toward me.

My face is beet red.

"Well," I mutter, breath still shallow, "that's Jesse. No photo needed. You just saw more of him than anyone ever asked for."

Audrey's eyebrows are still halfway up her forehead when she smiles devilishly. "That's Jesse?" She lets out a whistle. "You are so screwed."

I nod, unable to make eye contact.

I'm well aware of just how screwed I am.

14

Jesse

NOW

The timing of my life is just...classic.

I glance at myself in the mirror, almost laughing. *Is the universe playing a joke on me?*

Penny's reaction keeps looping in my head while I move around my room, attempting to get dressed. She gawked at me like she'd never seen a half-naked guy before.

Nope. Don't like that thought.

Imagining her seeing *anyone* else like that makes my neck pulse. I'm not a jealous guy, but when it comes to Penny, I'm like the territorial alpha male dogs I train. Absolutely feral.

Either way, it can't be true.

Penny's laugh is contagious, her smile is borderline criminal, and her body...

Not that I've been witness to any of those things since she got here.

She's serving me up fire only.

I have promises to uphold to both Danny and Fia regardless, and thinking with anything but my head won't get me far.

Several minutes have ticked by since Penny nearly slammed into my freshly showered body, but it's still dead quiet across the hall. I'm beginning to question if she'll ever come out of there.

I glance at my phone—it's barely 6 p.m.—and I'm not about to sit here in my room and rot. I dig through the dresser until I find a plain black t-shirt and throw it on, then step into gray sweats.

Right before I step out of the room, my phone buzzes on my nightstand. I kneel on the bed, leaning over to grab it, but accidentally knock the phone clean off the surface. It lands between the nightstand and the wall with a thud.

"Shit," I mumble, lying flat on the bed so I can push the nightstand back and reach around behind it.

My fingertips graze something small and round. I grab it along with my phone.

"You've got to be kidding me." I blow the dust off the silver ring in my palm and rub my thumb across the green stone. Sea glass, to be exact.

I haven't seen this ring in ten years.

Right before our high school graduation, I took Penny and Fia to the mall one Saturday. Fia wanted to buy a pretzel with her chore money, and Penny needed a dress for all the graduation parties we were invited to. I didn't know why she couldn't wear any in her closet, but there was a very specific one she had in mind.

We were walking around when she saw a ring in a display cabinet at a fancy boutique and came to a dead stop, eyes glued to it. She dragged us into the store, drumming her fingers across the racks of expensive clothing and smiling wistfully, announcing that one day she'd be able to buy anything she wanted from that store. I didn't doubt her for a minute; Penny worked harder than anyone I knew. She's the only one out of the three of us who was able to save up and buy a car senior year, for fuck's sake.

But she kept coming back to admire that ring. I pretended not to notice, but when she and Fia walked out, I quickly stole a peek, committing it to memory.

The next week, I came back to the mall and used all the money I'd made that month to buy it for her.

I slipped it on her finger, telling her it was the first step to her getting everything she ever wanted.

What a stupid thing to promise, but what did I know back then?

The sea glass ring is still stunning, and a piece of my heart warms knowing she didn't toss it in the trash. If I had to guess, she probably threw it across this room in a blind rage that summer.

After I was gone.

Movement sounds in the hallway, and light footsteps tap down the stairs.

That's my cue. Maybe the night *is* still on. Maybe I can get her in a good enough mood to bring up Danny and entice her to visit her estranged brother.

I place the ring in the nightstand drawer and wish myself luck.

"Need help with something?" I clear my throat as I walk into the kitchen.

Penny jumps, cracking her head against the cabinet. "Fuck," she mutters, rubbing her forehead before turning to grace me with a scornful glare.

"You're freakishly quiet for someone your size. I didn't even know you were down here." She turns back around, standing on her tiptoes, reaching for a bottle atop the refrigerator.

Before I can think twice, I step behind her and easily wrap my fingers around the glass neck, my chest brushing her back in the process.

She snatches it from my grip like I burned her.

"Thanks," she says quickly, ducking under my arm.

I watch silently as she unscrews the top with one hand while moving around the kitchen like she's on a very important mission. A smirk pulls on my lips, and I lean back against the counter.

Penny grabs a lime, seltzer, and a glass. She approaches me, waving her hand. "Can you please move, you're blocking the utensil drawer."

Hey, at least I got a *please* out of her.

"What do you think will happen if you touch me?" I ask, tilting my head.

Her amber eyes snap to mine. "Excuse me?"

I lean down. "You heard me, Penny." Her lips part, but I don't allow her time to think up a wise-ass comeback. "With the way you've skirted around me the last forty-eight hours, you'd think I'm a dangerous man. You afraid of what will happen if you accidentally touch me?"

Penny's poker face has gotten better, I'll give her that. But I notice the subtle things; the way her chest rises rapidly, her eyes searching mine.

I oblige anyway, moving so she can grab a spoon from the drawer. She hip checks it shut.

"I'm not avoiding you," she mutters. "Maybe I just don't *want* to touch you."

She doesn't make eye contact with me as she stirs her drink—hard enough to chip the glass.

"See, I think you're worried that it will bring up something. You won't even look at me," I add, my tone bordering on cocky.

I know I'm goading her.

It's a risk, but if I'm going to keep my promise to Fia and Danny, I need her to talk to me again, and unless she's willing to bring up the past, I don't know if we'll have any type of future.

And until I saw her again, I didn't know how badly I wanted a future, of any kind, with her.

I'd settle for being civil.

She takes a long sip, so long I wince. That much vodka could strip paint. But she drinks like it's water.

"Don't flatter yourself, *Mr. Rivers*. Maybe I just don't like what I see."

I push back my hair and can't help but smile. "So you didn't like what you saw in the hallway?"

She glares at me like she wants to throw the glass at my face, but I don't flinch.

"You're insufferable," Penny spits out.

"I think staying in the same house and avoiding the elephant in the room is insufferable," I reply sharply.

If I learned anything over the last ten years, it's to say what you really feel. I'm not going to lay it all out at once and overwhelm her, but shit, I have a lot to say.

"I'm not here for *this*." She points between us. "I'm here for my sister. You're just a leech who wandered in."

Well shit, tell me how you really feel.

"Okay," I say, pushing off the counter, hands raised. "You win. I'll back off."

She grabs a takeout container from the counter and shoves it toward me.

"What's this?"

"Dinner," she says flatly.

"I didn't think we were on *dinner* terms." I'm not complaining, just confused as hell.

"I'm not a complete bitch, believe it or not." Penny snatches the other container. "Actually, I'm a pretty fun and upbeat person. But your presence has turned me into someone I hardly recognize."

There's exasperation in her voice, but underneath it is hurt she disguises with a lashing tongue. For a second, I feel like a complete asshole. I never meant to make this harder for her.

I just want to talk, to get it out. Because pretending we didn't blow each other's lives apart is slowly driving me insane. But I've learned how to wait.

Prison teaches you that.

So I'll weather Penny's storm...because sooner or later, she's going to have to look our history in the face.

If she doesn't murder me first.

"I appreciate it." I hold up dinner. "Really." I smile at her.

Kill her with kindness, right?

Penny silently exits the kitchen and heads upstairs, presumably to eat her food in peace, away from me. Sushi and vodka soda seem like a horrible mix, but I'm not about to give her any advice.

I slide onto the barstool, open the container, and laugh. Despite her bratty behavior, which isn't totally unwarranted, she actually ordered my favorite meal. Sesame chicken with heaps of rice and broccoli.

As I dig in, I know that my chances of talking her into visiting Danny are off the table today. I'll try again another day.

The food is good, better than the lunchmeat sandwiches I've been making for dinner every night. Tank seems to think so, too, because he's watching me from his dog bed in front of the fireplace, drooling. He knows better than to beg, but he'll certainly stare like he's never eaten a day in his life.

"Do those eyes work on Fia?" I ask like he'll respond, and his gray ears perk up at her name. His big brown eyes settle on the back door in anticipation of her return.

I've been replaced by a girl who wraps my dog in fleece blankets and kisses him goodnight. I'm pretty sure if I ever move out, she's going to steal him with little resistance from Tank.

My phone buzzes on the counter.

"Speak of the devil," I mutter.

Fia: How's it going?? Penny promised me she'd chill out, so I hope y'all are having fun!

I look around the kitchen, the silence thick. The aftermath of being alone with Penny.

Jesse: She got me dinner...a peace offering I think? Penny can be...
Fia: ruthless?

She has her reasons. But I'm not giving up

Jesse: Nothing I can't handle
Fia: I'm so sorry, I feel like this is my fault. Fingers crossed for you!

My chest cracks a little. I flip my phone face down, scrubbing my palm across my jaw.

Could it be possible that I'm *not* the reason Penny's pissed?

Maybe she has a boyfriend and they're going through a rough patch, and I'm just the easiest target to take it out on. Maybe someone else hurt her—though that thought doesn't sit any better with me.

It would be insane if she's gone ten years without a serious boyfriend, though, right?

Ten minutes pass with those thoughts swirling in my head, and I take the last bite of dinner and look over at my dog.

"Wish me luck, boy."

His eyebrows shift, but he doesn't follow as I shove off the stool and take the stairs two at a time, adrenaline lighting up my veins.

This time, I'm not leaving without a real conversation.

Penny can hold grudges and push me away all she wants, but Fia and Danny are the closest things to family I still have. Fia deserves someone she can depend on, and I want to be able to look her in the eye tomorrow and say I gave it my best shot to smooth shit over with her sister.

When I came back here, I didn't know what would happen with Penny and me. Truthfully, I thought it would take months to even figure out how to navigate talking to her again, given how things ended between us. Mending the fence, so to speak.

But I didn't expect this. I didn't expect that seeing her would ignite something in me the way it has. Something uncontrollable.

I knock—three sharp raps on the oak door between us.

It's silent for a few seconds before I hear shuffling.

The door cracks open, and Penny's standing there in a baby-blue cropped hoodie, sleep shorts that really should be considered panties, and white fluffy socks up to her knees. I school my face, trying not to check her out. Trying harder not to physically react.

"I made a promise to Fia, and I intend to keep it," I say, point-blank.

Her gaze flickers at *promise*, something all I do is break in her mind, but I keep my composure. I know I have to gain back her trust, but I can't do that if she doesn't even let me try.

I lean against the doorframe, blocking her in. She crosses her arms, pink lips twisting, and for a split second, I wonder if they taste the same as they did back then.

"*Listen*, your perseverance is admirable, but I'm not feeling it." She attempts to shut the door on me, but I don't move. It bounces right back at her.

"I don't remember you having such a smart mouth," I reply, and her jaw clenches.

"You want to play the *big brother* so bad? Fine. I'll treat you like one." Penny slams her palms against my chest, but unluckily for her, I'm pretty quick on my feet. All those years of boxing paid off.

In one clean motion, I squat, grab behind her knees, and haul her over my shoulder. I duck out of the doorway so she doesn't hit her head.

I might be rowdy, but I'm a gentleman.

"JESSE! Put me down!" she yells, pounding on my back.

"Nope." I grip her thighs tighter. "You owe me fifteen minutes. That's all. Just long enough so I don't have to lie to your sister's face."

Penny kicks and wiggles, but it just takes one arm wrapped around her ass to keep her pinned to my shoulder. I'll give it to her—she packs a punch for being such a tiny thing.

"Keep squirming like that," I mutter, "and I'll start to think you're enjoying this." I trudge down the steps and deposit her into the oversized chair next to the fireplace.

Her bun's half-falling out, cheeks flushed, eyes blazing. If she were a cartoon, steam would be coming out of her ears.

"You can't just manhandle people to get what you want!" she snaps, jumping out of the chair and jabbing a sharp finger into my chest.

"Fifteen minutes won't kill you."

Penny crosses her arms over her chest and looks away from me.

"You've been pissed since the second I walked through that door." I nod toward the back door, the memory still vivid in my mind. "How long do you want to keep pretending like nothing ever happened between us?"

Penny doesn't look at me. "We were eighteen," she mutters. "It was a long time ago."

"Then why do you look at me like I set the whole damn place on fire?" My voice sharpens, but I can't help it. "You talk like it's ancient history, like it was *nothing*, but you treat me like I'm the fucking devil."

Her body goes rigid, and she squares off with me. "You want to talk?" she asks, and I nod. "Fine, Jesse, let's *chat*, shall we?" A wicked grin spreads across her face, and Penny starts pacing back and forth in front of the fireplace.

Tank watches her, tail wagging, like this is a fun game.

It's not.

"First of all," she starts, hands flying, "I busted my ass this year so I could take time off. Spa days, holiday parties, binge-watching trash TV, some actual peace for once. Christmas with my sister."

Her voice fills the room, heat pouring off her.

"Then she tells me she's pregnant, the baby daddy's MIA, and to top it off, you walk in, like some movie hero who never left."

I keep quiet, letting her get it out. She deserves that much.

Penny stops pacing, eyes locked on mine.

"You don't just get to show up and decide you're back in our lives," she spits out. "You left us, Jesse. You left *me*. Like it was nothing, like we didn't have a future planned."

"So, that's where we're going?" I take a slow step forward. "You think I *chose* prison? I thought I was doing the right thing."

She laughs, sharp and shrill, and I throw my head back. "Everyone has a choice, Jesse. You just made a bad one."

My jaw tightens. "You want to talk about that night—or the three years that followed. How you never contacted me, never once set foot in that prison?"

She freezes, and the room goes still with her.

"No," she says, her voice low and bitter. "I don't want to talk about any of that. You broke my trust. Why the hell would I give you my time *then* or *now*?"

I pause, my tongue brushing over my bottom lip, and I crack my knuckles.

I lean down so we're eye to eye.

"Sorry to break it to you, *princess*, but you're forgetting the part where *you* disappeared, too." Her mouth opens, but I don't stop. "You keep acting like I abandoned you, but the second they cuffed me and Danny, you vanished. We were ghosts to you before the door of that prison cell even slammed shut."

Penny's eyes catch the light of the fire, and for a second, it's like time folds in on itself. I didn't realize how long I've been holding those words in, waiting to say them to her face.

She thinks she was the only one shattered that night. But she never saw what it did to me. How it battered me down.

"You don't know what you're talking about," Penny replies, her voice small. "And don't call me princess."

"You want to know why I came back to North Carolina?" I ask, and for the first time, she doesn't fire back, she just listens.

Ten years of unsaid words settle thick between us.

"I was eighteen when I got locked up with your brother," I begin. "That might've been ten years ago, but it still feels raw. And no matter what you think, I never wanted to leave you. That was never the *plan*." My voice is pained, sharp.

She begins to protest, but I grab her waist, touching the exposed skin under her hoodie, steadying her. I do it without thinking.

"After everything you were to me, you honestly think I went a whole decade without thinking about you?" I demand, my voice gravely. "Look me in the eye and tell me you really believe that."

She doesn't speak. Doesn't move. She just watches me like she's trying to memorize every word out of my mouth.

I release her from my grip. I've said what I needed to say to her.

My heart rages behind my ribs, and Penny doesn't blink.

"Penny, I'm—" I start, but she puts a finger to my lips, silencing me.

Our eyes hold steady until hers drop to her finger, time stretching between us.

Before I can move, she pulls the finger away and replaces it with her mouth.

Soft. Certain. She kisses me like she means it, and suddenly, nothing else exists. She's so close that I see every gold fleck in her eyes before she closes them.

My heart slams against my ribs, wild and unrelenting, and as fast as it starts, it ends. Her fingertips feathering across her lips, like she can still feel me there.

"Fuck, I shouldn't have done that," she hisses, shaking her head.

But I reach for the curve of her throat, pulling her back in, because I'm not sorry.

This time, I kiss her the way I've been dreaming about since the day I lost her.

Slowly, my tongue sweeps across hers, and she lets out a little moan that unlocks a part of me I've been smothering for ten damn years.

She melts under me, my fingers gripping her tiny waist, like it was molded for my hands, and for a breathless moment, everything fades away.

The hurt, the past, it's just us.

And then—the heat kicks on.

Tank barks. Penny startles, heart pounding against mine as she pulls back, breathing unsteadily.

We stare at each other, stunned in silence. I want to grab her, pull her back in, touch her until she remembers everything, but she steps further back, out of reach.

"I can't do this with you, Jesse," she whispers, voice cracking, arms wrapping tight around herself.

And then she's gone, running away from me. Just like that.

Watching Penny walk away brings back the ache like it never left.

But underneath it, there's something else. That kiss gave me something fragile I haven't felt in a long time—a glimmer of hope.

15

Penny

NOW

There are moments in life that leave a lasting mark on your memory, some good and others bad. Things I'll never forget, even if I want to. They are part of me, like a scar.

The day Fia was born, and I held her for the first time at the hospital. *Good.*

Nan taking all of us to the beach as kids, chasing us down the sand, wearing her ridiculously large sunhat. *Good.*

Getting paired with Audrey as roommates freshman year. *Good.*

Burying Nan unexpectedly. *Bad.*

Waking up to find out Jesse and Danny had been arrested a week before I left for college. *Bad.*

Driving to the university without him. *Bad.*

And now, as I lean back in the worn clawfoot tub, hair plastered to my skin, the water growing tepid, my fingers brush my lips as a strange, looping sensation plays in my brain.

Kissing Jesse tonight... I can't decide which category it fits in. *Good* or *bad*.

Everything about Jesse in the last two days has been neither black nor white. It's somehow in the messy middle, the gray, where my heart struggles most.

Tears slip down my cheeks because this was not supposed to happen. I've spent years pushing the image of his green eyes from my memory, trying to forget how it felt to be held in his arms. He's right, he's not the same guy he was at eighteen. But that one kiss somehow brought me right back to that heartbroken girl who had everything planned.

16

Penny

THEN

Age 17, Summer After Junior Year

The June sun is scorching, but I find a cool spot under my favorite magnolia tree, sitting on the weathered wooden bench. I joked with Jesse that when we leave this town, we need to do a secret night ops and steal this bench. It has our initials carved in it, for fuck's sake.

It's kinda crazy that it's almost been two years since Jesse moved in. He fits into our family like he was meant to be here all along. This week at day camp, Fia even made a sign for Jesse's bedroom door that says *#1 Brother* with a bunch of seashells glued to it. On one level, it's weird because he is my boyfriend, but also, it's not like Fia has a role model big brother, so I'm also grateful Jesse fills those shoes.

I think the whole sign thing pissed Danny off, but he'll never show it, plus he's always in a mood anyway. It's his own fault—he's a dick to Fia, always ignoring her or acting like she's a baby. Jesse and her bonded quickly, probably because he didn't grow up with a sibling, and I think he likes having an adopted little sister. But that's also just Jesse. He's kind to everyone, even my asshole brother, who is a piss-poor "best friend."

Sweat dribbles down the back of my neck as I fan myself, unable to roll my jean shorts up any higher without my entire ass cheeks hanging out. All I can think about is the slushie we're supposed to be getting right now. That's the whole reason I let the boys talk me into walking ten blocks in the blazing afternoon heat, but Danny, of course, surprised us with a *quick pit stop along the way*. Quick, my ass.

Even glaring at him right now feels like an energy waste, but I can't help it. The heat makes me grumpier than usual. And Danny's been really pushing my buttons lately.

"C'mon, Danny, hurry up," I croak as a tall shadow blocks the sun momentarily. I glance up at my hero, and instant relief floods me, along with a few butterflies in my belly.

"He says he'll be five more minutes, then we can go." Jesse plops down next to me, pulling his baseball cap over his eyes to block the sun. His T-shirt hangs over his shoulders like a rag, and I try not to stare at his bare chest, but it's hard. His muscles are long and lean, and he's starting to fill out a bit more. Other girls in my grade are definitely noticing, but Jesse only has eyes for me.

"Five minutes is like thirty in his world," I remind him.

Jesse lolls his head toward me, smirking.

"What?" I ask, and if I wasn't so hot already, I'd probably be blushing.

"I'm making him buy us the largest blue slushies they have." He squeezes my knee, and I laugh.

The jarring sound of car doors slamming shut startles me, and my eyes snap toward Danny, who's standing across the park. He sways awkwardly, hands shoved in his hoodie pockets even though it's 90 degrees out. He paces in front of the car, and I shake my head, glad Jesse isn't over there with him, getting wrapped up in that shit.

"Who even are those guys?" A pit forms in my stomach. My brother was always a troublemaker, but he's not a bad kid. He's got manners and is kind to everyone at school. I hate that he's being this dumb.

"Who knows... His hookup, I guess? He's using all his money to buy weed."

"He's an idiot. I love my brother, but fuck, I don't know what happened to all his brain cells."

"I'm trying to get through to him, Pen, but he won't listen to me." The strain in Jesse's voice makes me sad. Danny's his best friend, and the distance growing between them lately couldn't be more obvious. Jesse's making plans; he's leaving behind his deadbeat parents, but I'm not sure what's going to happen to Danny. He needs an intervention, but he's the most stubborn person I've ever met.

I peel my eyes away from my brother's shady dealings and smile at Jesse. "You know what I'm thinking about right now?" I close my eyes and picture it. "We just landed in Aruba and got dropped off at our resort."

Jesse plays along. "Alright, should we hit up the pool or ocean first?" He muses, and my smile grows.

"The pool, of course. Unlimited nachos and iced drinks with straws."

He laughs. I love that sound. "They serve nachos poolside in Aruba?"

I shove his leg playfully. "I don't know, but it's *my* daydream! I get nachos. Extra jalapeños."

It's our favorite game. It started when he moved in last fall. When he was having a bad day, and we'd be walking home from school, we'd play "where would you want to be right now?" and we'd envision all the places in the world we want to go. We'd make up stories like we were rich and planning our vacation.

I always had a wanderlust soul, as Nan called it. Jesse told me he never thought he'd leave Wilmington, but now this game is our favorite pastime.

But it's not just a game for me—I intend to make it all real one day.

"Fine, whatever you want, princess."

As Danny approaches, I turn on the park bench, my heart pounding. Jesse and I have to get out our words when we can. Sure, we can text, but nothing beats the feeling I have when it's only us, just our secret dreams alive between us.

"I'm not traveling the world alone. Remember our pact?"

"Hey." He locks eyes with me. "Where you go, I go." He winks just before Danny saunters into earshot. We'd probably need to be more careful if my brother weren't always high. He barely notices anything these days.

I wish Jesse could hold my hand and kiss me, and we could have a normal relationship like other people our age. I wish I could tell everyone I love him, but we can't.

We only have to make it one more year and some change. At the end of next summer, I'll be packing to leave and hopefully be a student at the University of North Carolina in Chapel Hill, and Jesse will go to trade school nearby, and we can be open about our status. It's what I've worked so hard for, and if I stay on track, I'll get a pretty good scholarship.

The mere thought of it makes me so happy I nearly jump off the bench.

"Let's go!" I yell at my brother, whose face is still scrunched in paranoia, but Jesse wears a small smile on his perfect lips.

And only I know why.

17

Penny

NOW

"How'd last night go? You haven't said anything about it." Fia leans forward in the passenger seat, pulling down the mirror to swipe on mascara as I drum my fingers on the steering wheel.

I stare at the red light, willing it to turn green, because Fia's question is burning a hole in me, and I need to move. There's a Santa on the corner ringing a bell. I'm just glad it's not Jesse.

"It was fine," I reply quickly. "We ate dinner and chatted." I accidentally slam on the gas too hard as we head toward Fia's doctor's office.

"Damn, Penny!" she yells.

The seat belt jerks against my ribcage, and I wince, glancing at Fia.

"Sorry," I mumble.

Fia reaches for the grab handle, like I'm about to drag race through town. "Just slow down," she replies, and I roll my eyes. "But seriously, you two used to be so close... What happened?"

"Nothing, we drifted apart. It happens," I say with as much control in my voice as I can. "Do *you* still keep in touch with your high school friends?" I raise my brows at her, knowing damn well she doesn't.

Fia lets out a slow sigh, then smirks. "Well, anyway, when I came downstairs, Jesse was whistling."

"What do you mean he was *whistling*?" I scoff.

Fia shrugs, but she's eyeing me closely now. "I don't know, he seemed like he was in a good mood. So whatever you did to smooth things over, it must've worked," she adds cheerfully.

I kissed him. That's what I did. And I shouldn't have.

It was reckless and stupid. But I couldn't stop myself. Because standing in front of the fireplace with him brought me right back to that love-sick teenager who would've lassoed the moon for him.

I'm terrified by how easy it was to slip back into that version of Penny.

I can't let it happen again. That's a dangerous, slippery slope.

I force a smile and wave dismissively. "Well, now that everyone's happy, maybe we can stop obsessing over Jesse and talk about something else. Please."

"Fine," Fia says slowly, but there's a twinkle in her eye. "We'll move on. For now."

There's no way Fia could know about Jesse and me. She was an oblivious child, but she's an adult *now* and not as naive as I had originally believed, unfortunately. The tension between Jesse and me is thick, and Fia can read me like a book.

Sister intuition, or whatever.

But I can't afford to even begin to let her guess.

I whip the car into a parking spot in front of an old brown brick building with a sign on the front of a mother and baby. Fia has her twenty-six-week checkup today.

"Alright, let's get this over with." I muster up some cheer, because I'm not thrilled about being here, but I wasn't going to let her go alone. Nothing about pregnancy entices me—in fact, it freaks me out entirely. But I'm trying for my sister.

It's not until I reach the double glass doors that I realize Fia hasn't followed me. I turn to see her still sitting in the passenger side of my car, unblinking, staring straight ahead at the row of hedges.

What the hell?

She lowers the window when I knock on it.

"You coming in or what?" My patience wearing thin has nothing to do with her, and everything to do with my nerves around last night. So I try again, nicely, when she doesn't answer. "Fi, talk to me, what's going on?"

Her bottom lip trembles, and for a moment, she looks so young. She *is* young, but suddenly she doesn't look like the twenty-one-year-old who has a lot of big decisions ahead of her—instead, I see the little girl who used to sit on my bed, clutching her Barbies, watching me do my makeup.

She doesn't answer at first, just blinks hard, shaking her head, green eyes misty.

"I don't think I can do this." She sniffles, rubbing her nose with the sleeve of her oversized green sweater.

"They're just going to measure the baby and check vitals," I repeat what I read on Google this morning, because I know absolutely nothing about what happens at these appointments. I don't mention that they will probably do bloodwork, or that I gagged reading about the cervical checks.

My sister bites her lip, and I grip the edge of the door, looking around, because right now, I'm not sure how to handle this.

My famous "Penny Pep Talks" have apparently decided to leave the station today.

"You were right," she says suddenly, so quietly I almost miss it.

I glance back down at her. "About what?"

"I'm not ready for this. I have *nothing* ready. This isn't how it's supposed to be." Her hand lands on her stomach, and she breaks, a sob rolling through her.

This is way worse than bagel-gate.

"Fia..." I crouch down beside my car, guilt stirring in my gut. "If this is about what I said, I didn't mean to sound so harsh. I have a lot going on...and I was just trying to drive home how serious this all is."

She swipes a tear, shaking her head. "I texted him two days ago."

"Texted *who*?"

She gazes at me, her tear-stained face growing red and blotchy. "Brett. I thought maybe…I don't know…that after a few weeks, maybe he'd had time to think. Maybe he came to terms with it. I told him where I'd be today and that I'd like him to come," she explains breathily.

I already know what's next before she says it.

"He read it. And didn't reply."

My knuckles whiten, a fist clenched at my side. I avert my gaze, a silent scream held in until I can release my breath.

"Listen to me." Like word vomit, my pep talk comes rushing out. Too loud and too much, but Fia's eyes snap to mine, and I know she's hearing me—truly hearing me. "He is an idiot! Him not being here has no reflection on you, or indicates how your future is going to be. Do you understand?"

She nods and wipes a stray tear.

"I have let so many people walk out of my life, Fia," I say, surprising even myself. "And yeah, it hurt like hell. But if someone wants to leave, you *have* to let them. You can't build your future around people who don't have the decency to stay. I wasted years waiting for apologies that never came.

"You're going to go in there"—I point at the sad looking brown building—"and they're going to show you your baby on the monitor or whatever the hell they do." This gets a laugh out of both of us. "And we are going to hang the picture of your damn uterus on the fridge. You're going to be the best freaking mom ever. So screw Brett, it's his loss. And your baby will have me and a million other people who will love the hell out of it."

"Like Jesse and Danny," she adds wistfully, and I unwillingly nod.

Sure, maybe.

"I couldn't do this without you." Fia smiles at me.

She offers her hand like she used to when she scraped her knee or got scared of thunder, and I pull her petite frame out of her seat.

"I know," I say, smiling as I nudge her shoulder. "Come on. Let's go see what kind of weird shit they do in there."

I open the door, hit with the smell of musty plants, and Fia steps through. She pushes the little elevator button, and I smirk, reassuring her.

"Hey, after this, let's get mani-pedis."

"And a bagel?" Fia asks, and I laugh.

"If you eat so many bagels, your baby is going to come out addicted to gluten," I say as we walk into the suite.

An hour later, I'm trailing out behind my sister—only slightly traumatized.

But she's grinning ear to ear.

"An early Christmas gift," she says, holding up the little scroll of photos they printed off for her—she's having a girl.

Looks like we're adding another stubborn Hanson girl to the clan.

I stare down and wiggle my glossy cotton candy toes. I don't care that it's winter and no one will see them—I didn't fly all over the world this year to not treat myself to small luxuries like deluxe pedicures.

"God, I *needed* this." Fia moans as her shoulders are rubbed while her toes are painted a cherry red—for the holidays, of course. She's a traditionalist.

"You deserve it," I say, leaning my head back against the heated spa chair.

I open my phone and see an ad for a new rooftop bar down-town. The kind with heat lamps and modern firepits and drinks that look like science experiments.

"Oh my god, I just realized something—I never got to take you out for your twenty-first birthday."

Fia snorts. "Penny, that was months ago." It was only three months ago. "You sent me money and told me to 'raise hell responsibly.'"

"It's not the same. I wanted to take you somewhere," I say, frowning.

"It's fine. Honestly, I don't even really enjoy drinking, you know that. And obviously..." She rubs her small belly. "That's a hard pass right now."

"Well, we could still go out," I offer. "Somewhere low-key. You could get a mocktail, maybe live music or something chill. We can't just sit at home every night."

Her eyes brighten slightly. "Nothing crazy, though..." she trails off, then perks up like she's just had a brilliant idea. "What about Rebel Tavern?"

My spine stiffens against the leather massage chair, and I sit up quickly. She *has* to know, why else would she suggest that place?

"Rebel Tavern?" My mouth goes dry. "That little dive bar down in Carolina Beach?"

Fia nods, pulling her phone out, half listening to me. "Yeah, that one. It seems chill, they have live music on Wednesday nights, and Jesse mentioned it before."

My fingers dig into the armrests of the spa chair, and I rack my brain for a response.

The last time I was in Rebel Tavern was just weeks before everything went to hell.

Danny was out doing something sketchy, and Jesse and I snuck into the bar, crawling through the bathroom window from the alleyway, and danced in the corner of the wood-paneled, smoke-filled dive bar.

We felt free, his hands on my hips, his lips on my neck, his whispers in my ear telling me he loved me. The taste of cheap beer, the way the lights blurred, and when they closed, we ran down to the beach, buzzed and alive, the moon the only light around us.

The way he kissed me—wild yet sincere. I remember everything.

That was the first and last time I ever set foot in that place.

"Hey, you sure you don't want to go somewhere uptown? There's a new rooftop bar that looks fun. They have tapas." I grin, knowing I can entice my sister with food, but she shakes her head, eyes glued to her phone screen.

"Tempting. But no. I don't want to risk running into anyone..." Her smile falters.

Right. Brett.

I let out a breath and nod. "Okay. Rebel Tavern it is."

I'm not sure there's enough liquor in all of Rebel Tavern to erase the memories of that night.

Fia and I walk over to a coffee shop after the nail salon. It's peaceful now that the morning rush is gone and just calm enough, with the indie playlist and aroma of espresso beans.

I begin to feel my nervous system relax after the whole Rebel Tavern memory relapse. This week is truly going to be the test of my emotional stability, I already know it.

Fia crumbles the paper bag in her hand and rubs her belly.

"I feel so much better." She smiles after demolishing her second breakfast. "Do we still have time before we need to go home?"

I crinkle my brow. "Time for what exactly?"

She swivels in her seat, staring up at the chalkboard menu on the wall. "I wanted to bring Jesse a coffee."

Well, the peaceful feeling is now obliterated.

"Isn't he working?" I ask way too fast.

"Yeah, a few streets away at Long Leaf Park." She's squinting at the menu. "He's training there until two today, I think."

I roll my eyes, scoffing. "He's probably busy, Fia, let's not bother him."

"It's cold out today, I'm sure he'd appreciate hot coffee," she says, annoyingly thoughtful.

Damn it. Nan really did instill kindness into this girl.

"God, you're such a mom already," I tease, peeling the label off my coffee cup with my nervous energy.

"It will take like two minutes to swing by, and anyway, you said you two are cool, right?" She stares at me a beat too long, and I nod vigorously.

"Yeah, yeah, we're two civil beings." I clear my throat. "Go order his stuff."

I walk up with Fia as she places the order.

"A tall latte...oh, let's add vanilla," she cheerfully tells the barista.

"No!" I snap, and everyone near the counter turns to look at me, including Fia. Her eyebrow arches into surprise. "He only drinks his coffee black. Or with hazelnut flavor," I add, bringing down my voice a few decibels as heat crawls up my neck.

Fia raises her eyebrows at me. "Okay then..." She turns back and corrects the order.

I walk outside, needing cold air to breathe.

"So, you know his coffee order?" Fia questions me when she joins me on the sidewalk.

"We were best friends in high school, we drank a lot of coffee back then. It's ingrained in my memory..." I trail off, shrugging, because it doesn't matter. "I don't think his tastes have changed."

"I feel like I'm not getting the full truth."

Damn straight you're not.

I start walking toward the park so she can't see my face.

"It's normal to remember someone's coffee order," I say loudly.

Fia doesn't reply, and I don't look at her.

It *doesn't* mean anything.

Ten minutes later, I spot him in the distance on the other side of the grassy field. It looks like he's wrapping up a session with a dog, and they are heading to a bench, his back to us.

As we get closer, Jesse looks up, shielding his eyes from the sun, and smiles.

Why does his smile have to do that?

I adjust the collar of my jacket, ignoring the annoying little jab in my ribs.

Fia waves enthusiastically, and Jesse strolls toward us, a leashed dog at his side.

"Isn't he a cutie, Penny?" Fia starts, and I glance at her with a surge of confusion until I realize she's talking about the dog. Not Jesse.

Holy shit, I need to get out of this park. Maybe out of this state.

Is this what one kiss does to me?

Jesse stops in front of us, leash in hand, black hoodie sleeves pushed up so his arm tattoos are exposed. Something about that black hoodie makes my heart flutter. It's just a memory, that's all.

Surely it can't be the one he wore all those years ago—he's probably got seventy-five extra pounds of muscle on him now.

"This is Lulu." He gestures to the dog at his side. "She's a sweetheart."

"We were just around the corner at the coffee shop and thought you might want something," Fia says brightly, handing him the steaming cup. "I almost got you a vanilla latte, but Penny nearly bit my head off. She said you only drink it black."

His gaze drops to mine.

"Or with hazelnut," Fia adds.

"You didn't have to do this." His brows twitch, and my cheeks get hot, so I look away.

"It was Fia's idea."

Jesse nods, still looking at me, and it's like all the air has been squeezed from my lungs.

Fia kneels down toward the dog. "May I?"

"Knock yourself out, kid." Lulu wags her tail, accepting Fia's affection like she's known her forever.

"Aren't you a little lovebug?" she coos.

I watch, unable to move, unsure what to say, stuck in an unbearable standoff with Jesse.

The park isn't busy. There are no toddlers screaming on the play gym or college students jogging by. It's quite still, actually. Nothing to distract me.

"Oh, Jesse, do you have plans tonight?" My sister asks out of the blue.

His eyes flick between me and Fia for a moment.

"No, I was just going to hit the gym after work." *Of course, he was.* "Why what's up?"

I realize now what she's about to ask. It wouldn't be appropriate to wrap a hand around your pregnant sister's mouth, though, so I'm forced to watch in slow motion as Fia ruins my night.

"Penny's taking me out for my twenty-first birthday...something laidback, for an hour or two. Obviously, we aren't partying hard." She grins. "You should totally come."

Jesse hesitates, though his green eyes light up. And I feel bad for a moment, because I'm sure he doesn't have that many friends here in Wilmington anymore.

"If that's okay with you?" It takes a moment for me to realize he's talking directly to me.

My voice catches. "Uhm, sure, I mean, if you want?"

"Cool. I'll be there." He taps Fia's head. "Where we going?" he asks, sipping his coffee.

"Rebel Tavern," Fia answers mindlessly, now rubbing Lulu's tan belly.

Jesse's smile falters just slightly. He bites his lip, eyes on me again. "Oh...interesting choice," he says, and I don't say anything back.

I don't have to.

18

Jesse

NOW

The smell of musky cologne fills my small room as I dip my head down to take a look in the mirror above my dresser. All it took to get ready for the night out was swapping my faded gray work shirt for a clean black one, and I even added a small silver chain around my neck.

I can't say it was the same for Penny and Fia, but I know better than to rush two women doing their hair. Or whatever they've been doing in Fia's room for the past hour.

As I walk into the hall, they both glance up through the open bedroom door. There's a soft glow from the lamp and purple painted walls, and I pause.

Fia offers a small grin from her wicker vanity seat while Penny stands behind her, fixing her hair. From behind the safety of her sister, Penny runs her eyes shamelessly up my body, and every muscle from my calves to my throat tightens.

I haven't been able to stop thinking about those lips on mine, her tongue between my teeth. Fuck, I got so hard last night thinking about her, I had to relieve myself like I'm eighteen again.

And now she's looking at me like she knows.

Like she's proud of it.

She drops her sister's long hair and mists it with hairspray.

"All done." She sets the aerosol can down, fluffing Fia's red curls. "You look stunning."

I shouldn't linger, but I do. "You both look great," I say gruffly, but I mean it.

Fia shuffles around for something in her closet.

"Do you own anything other than black?" Penny asks but doesn't wait for an answer before leaning into the mirror and seductively tracing her lips with cherry-red lipstick.

Her eyes meet mine in the small oval mirror as her open mouth puts me in a trance.

I'm beginning to think her hot and cold attitude toward me is on purpose. A little torment for good measure.

My dick is certainly starting to think so.

Even if Penny wanted me the way I want her, she'd never admit it.

Fia emerges from her closet, brown boots in hand, and walks past me with raised eyebrows but remains quiet as she heads down the steps.

But Penny pauses in the doorway, scanning my outfit.

I glance down to see what she's scrutinizing. "The shirt has a pocket and no stains. I thought it was fine?"

What the hell do I know about fashion? Though no woman ever complained about my outfit choices.

"It's a dive bar," I remind her, and she tilts her head, eyes narrowing in on me. "Ever been to one, or has time made you forget that you used to dance on the tables in them, *princess*?" I wink at her.

Penny's face goes red, her eyes snapping to mine. "I was a different person back then," she rebuttals.

"Were you, though?" I ask and turn my back, skipping down the steps, not waiting for her.

Two people can play this little game.

The look on her face as she struts into the kitchen, all beauty and ice, says she remembers everything.

The last time I was at Rebel Tavern with her, she was wearing barely-there shorts, dancing on the bar—wild, young, and free. I remember the sound of her shallow moans, her nails digging into my shoulder as I held her against the wall of that tiny bathroom, doing unspeakable things.

There's no way she forgot about it.

"You ready?" Penny asks, and Fia nods, grabbing her phone and purse.

I lock the door behind us and meet them in the driveway.

Penny's digging in her tiny purse for her keys, and while I have a moment to stare, I do. Thigh-high black boots encase her legs, a red leather miniskirt that's dangerously short hugs her perky ass, and a tight black turtleneck sweater leaves nothing to the imagination. Her hair falls around her shoulders in bouncy curls, and red lipstick lines her pouty lips.

She catches me looking and cocks her head at me. I wish with every fiber in me that I was taking her out on a date right now.

Instead, I'm somehow playing chaperone to these two chaotic sisters.

"We're taking my car." Penny nods toward her baby-blue convertible, and I bark out a laugh, spinning my keys on my finger.

"I can't fit in that car."

Fia glances between us like we're bickering parents.

"We'll drive separately, then," Penny suggests, and I shake my head.

This is where I lay my foot down.

"Miss *has one vodka soda and is tipsy*? I'm DD, like it or leave it."

Penny looks pissed, but Fia pipes up before she can even respond. "Works for me!" She nearly skips to my black muscle car, and I unlock the doors, smirking at Penny in the dim evening light.

Checkmate.

Penny obliges, though she wears a scowl as she crawls into the seat next to me. I adjust the mirrors, making sure everyone is comfortable, before pulling out into the street.

I'd be lying if I said Penny's presence in my passenger seat isn't surreal as hell right now.

Ten years ago, this was all I dreamed about. *This* was my dream car, and I worked my ass off after prison to be able to save for a down payment. I took the first tattoo apprenticeship I could get in LA and trained dogs every spare minute. I was working eighty-hour weeks just to stay afloat. Just to keep my mind off everything I left behind.

I got the dream car, but I never had my dream girl.

So seeing Penny look like *this* in the front seat of my car fucks with my mind.

As I pull onto the dark street, the twinkle lights from nearby houses cast light on her face, and our eyes catch. She doesn't look away right away.

She just looks at me like I'm fire that will burn her life down.

Nostalgia hits me like a ton of bricks the second I step inside Rebel Tavern behind the girls. It's not even late yet—the band's still setting up, and the crowd's thin—but the air already smells like cheap beer and poor decisions. It's been a long time since I've stepped foot into a dive bar like this, but they are all mostly the same.

I kind of dig how nothing has changed. The neon signs still buzz over the pool tables. The old dartboards sit in the dark corner, where college bros have pitchers of beer sloshing around. My boots still stick to the floor.

And one other thing's still the same—every head turns when Penny walks in.

Only this time, I don't get to wrap an arm around her, pull her close, and stake my claim.

This time, she's not mine.

Penny and Fia follow me to the long wooden bar, and as I attempt to pull my credit card out, Penny beats me to it, sliding hers across to the bartender.

"First round is on me." She doesn't smile, but she's standing so close to me I can smell her vanilla-scented hair and feel the heat coming off her body.

"Glad you don't find me dangerous anymore," I whisper in her ear, her hair brushing my lips.

Her shoulders snap tight, and those amber eyes find mine. A flicker of something passes between us. Maybe a memory, maybe regret, but it's gone in a split second.

She hands Fia a pink fruity mocktail like nothing happened, and I grab my whiskey from the bartender.

"Cheers!" Fia lifts her glass, and we clink.

"Happy belated twenty-first Fia." I nod, and she scrunches her nose.

"I hope no one judges me for being here."

I lean down as the music gets louder. "Fuck 'em. You're not doing anything wrong. You're allowed to have a little fun drinking your Shirley Temple, kid."

She laughs as I hug her, and Penny watches us over her shoulder.

She smiles softly at me, but her eyes say something else. Something I can't decipher.

But before she can say anything, the doors swing open and a rush of cold air and voices pour in. A large group of women floods the area around us, loud and already tipsy. I recognize the tall brunette immediately.

Laura.

She spots me and cuts across the floor like I'm a magnet.

Penny and Fia step aside just in time for her to slam into me with a hug that's way too touchy.

"You little liar!" she shouts, slapping my chest like we've got history. "You said you didn't go out!" Her face is all smiles as she bats her eyes at me.

"I don't," I deadpan, gesturing toward the girls.

Fia smiles and sticks her hand out like the polite lady she was raised to be. "Hi, I'm Fia. We're out celebrating my birthday. I'm Jesse's sister."

Warmth spreads through me at the way she naturally claims me as her brother. It feels pretty damn good to be wanted like that.

Penny's face, on the other hand, is cold as ice, but then, like flipping a switch, she beams a smile so bright I know it's fake.

God, she's good.

"I'm Penny." She offers no other labels.

But Laura doesn't really care, turning all her attention back to me, still hanging on my arm, reeking like strawberry wine coolers. "Jesse's been working with my rescue," Laura says to Fia. "We've been trying to get him to come out for happy hour, but he's been playing hard to get."

I groan, but luckily the music drowns it out.

Laura's hand doesn't leave my chest, and Penny's eyes haven't left her hand. I never gave an inclination that I had any interest in this chick, and I have a very strict no mixing work and pleasure policy. She didn't get the memo.

"You smell so good," Laura adds, rubbing her nose into my chest, and Penny nearly chokes on her drink.

"Girls, look who I found!" Laura yells out, and the rest of the group swarms like bees.

Fia winks at me and grabs her sister's hand, motioning toward the little stage in the corner. "We're going to go check out the band."

Penny flips her hair as she walks off, not giving me another second of attention.

Tonight's going to be interesting.

19

Penny

NOW

My pulse thrums in my ears as Fia drags me through the growing crowd near the small stage. I don't look back—I don't have to. I can still feel Jesse's eyes on my back, even with that tall brunette wrapped around him like a snake.

Why wouldn't she be? He's magnetic and mysterious and beautiful, and that's always been his problem.

Or my problem.

Fuck. I really am little miss one-vodka-soda.

I glance at my phone, it's only eight thirty, the band comes on at nine, but it's already feeling late.

I'm getting old.

"Up for a game of darts?" I raise a brow, and my sister smiles. I lace my hand through hers, leading us toward the darts in the back corner. Jesse's leaning against a nearby wall, still cornered in conversation with Laura and her posse, but I can feel the weight of his stare tracking me. He doesn't hide it well. He never did.

Fine. If he wants to look, I'll give him something to watch.

Mr. Cool, calm, and collected.

Fia sighs beside me. "Shoot, none of them are open."

They are indeed all in use. But then I see an opportunity.

"Give it a minute." I slide her my credit card. "Go grab me another drink?"

She hesitates but listens as I smooth my skirt and take a step toward the pack of frat guys around the dart board. Their eyes rake across my body, and though I want to say something feisty, I force a slow, practiced smile.

"Excuse me boys," I purr. "Think my sister and I could take a turn?"

They all eye each other, faces caught in half smirks.

"Sure, you can have the board if you can hit the bullseye." One of the guys winks at me, and I force a giggle. Off to the side, I notice Jesse become alert, peeling his shoulders from the wall. He crosses his arms tight, watching me like he's paid to.

Perfect.

I shake the guy's hand, and he turns his baseball cap backward, showcasing blue eyes and a chiseled jaw. College Penny would've had his number in about three minutes, but right now, I have one mission.

Blue Eyes hands me a dart, fingers lingering just a second too long. He knows what he's doing, but so do I. I suck the corner of my bottom lip seductively between my teeth, not because I want to—but because I know Jesse is watching. And I know it will drive him nuts.

"I think I deserve a warm-up shot," I tease in the flirtiest vibrato I can manage.

He grins. "Sure. Show us what you got."

I turn toward the board, adjusting my stance deliberately, and tilt my ass out just enough to drive attention to my miniskirt.

The dart is sticky in between my fingers, but I turn to Blue Eyes. "Can you...show me?" I pout. "I've never done this before. My form's probably awful."

He closes the gap between us without hesitation. "May I?" he asks, reeking of cheap beer, and I nod. His arm wraps around the outside of mine, and he murmurs in my ear, "Just like this."

I let him guide my fingers and release the dart when he says to, his lips too close to my earlobe. The dart flies and hits the board—barely.

When I turn, he's close, *too* close. His smile is cocky, dimples deep. But I'm not looking at him.

I'm looking at the brooding guy ten feet away, who's now standing straight as a board, jaw tight, no sign he's trying to hide it. The bar is filling in, but it wouldn't matter if there were five hundred people in here. I know how it feels to have his eyes on me. Like my whole body is buzzing with electricity.

"I think I'm ready to try by myself," I say sweetly, brushing past Blue Eyes and his friends, yanking the dart from the board.

Fia returns with my drink and stops to take in the scene unfolding before her. She looks at me, wide-eyed, and I wink back at her.

Lining my feet up and turning my body, I wiggle my arms to loosen up, feigning nervousness. Then without missing a beat, I throw the little metal dart.

It flies right into the bullseye, just like I knew it would.

The group of guys all holler, gripping their heads, like I just scored a touchdown.

Fia's jaw is on the floor, and she laughs, walking cautiously toward me as I gather all the darts.

"Oopsie! Beginner's luck," I muse, shrugging.

"Fair is fair." The same guy hands me all the darts. "But hey, lemme get you a drink." He smiles, clearly thinking he's going to score. I barely have the heart to tell him to scram, but I don't have to.

Jesse's voice cuts through the crowd, low and solid. "She's already got a drink."

His arm snakes around my shoulders, his presence swallowing me whole. I glance down at his tattooed knuckles curled around his whiskey glass, veins flexing under his skin. The inked words catch my eye—HOPE. HURT. One on each hand. I noticed them when he was stacking wood into the fireplace the other day.

Blue Eyes pales and steps back. "My bad, man. Didn't realize..."

Jesse's arm stays there, heavy, like an anchor across my shoulders. I could move easily if I wanted to, but for some reason, I don't really want to.

Maybe for one split second I want to pretend I got everything I ever wanted, even if it's far from the truth.

"What the hell was that?" Fia whispers, and I'm pulled back into reality. I'm not sure if she is mortified or impressed by her big sister.

"Those guys had no good intentions," he says stiffly, and Fia's eyes drop to his arm still around me. He promptly drops it, coming to stand next to me instead. A pang of hurt reaches up and grips me.

Jesse snatches a dart, steps up, and throws it.

Bullseye.

"Damn, are you both professionals?" Fia laughs, and I grab Jesse's drink from his grip before he can object, throwing back the remaining whiskey.

Jesse looks me up and down, a punishing look on his face.

"Shit, I have to pee," Fia blurts out, leaving her drink on the high-top.

"I'll come—"

"I'll be fine, it's right there." She's gone before I can argue.

The second the door swings shut behind her, Jesse leans in toward me—elbows on the table, head tilting to meet my gaze.

"Didn't peg you as a cougar," Jesse says casually.

"And I didn't take you as the jealous type—"

"They were getting a bit handsy." He cuts me off as a quick flicker passes his green eyes. Then he's back to cool and collected.

"I can handle myself, thank you very much. I've been with plenty..." This time, I cut myself off.

Jesse smiles softly at me.

"Teaching your little sister how to swindle men out of dart boards, that's a new low."

I snort, throwing my head back. "That was hardly it. Fia needs to toughen up—I'm teaching her not to let the world screw her over. How to get what she wants. Fair and square."

Jesse's eyes drop to my mouth. His voice lowers when he asks, "You really don't trust people, do you?"

My stomach steels. *What is his problem?!* Intervening where he has no right and asking questions like he's my therapist.

"I trust people," I lie straight through my teeth.

"But you don't trust me, princess."

The nickname slices me open, and suddenly, I'm not here.

I'm eighteen, messy hair and cheap sandals, salt air licking my skin. Jesse's arms are not full of ink, and I can feel the worn cotton of his heavy metal band T-shirt.

Back when I trusted him with the world.

Maybe a tiny sliver of me still does, but I silence that part. It's not safe.

"You gave me a lot of reasons not to." I blink, looking away. The bar blurs and sharpens again. Then his hand is under the high-top, fingers brushing against mine.

I don't pull away when he touches my hand, so lightly, but it feels like fire on my skin.

"I want to fix that."

I can't look at him, I can't talk about this right now.

He gets closer, so close I can smell his cologne, our faces inches from each other as the music grows louder. "Pen, you here with me?"

"I don't know…I don't know where I am these days," I whisper back, too tipsy to filter my words.

Jesse's jaw tightens, and before I know it, his fingers thread tightly through mine like they remember how.

Like they never forgot.

"You're here, and you're safe," he says firmly, and for a moment, I believe it.

But then Fia returns, cheeks pink and smiles wide. "Well? Let's play. You earned it."

I let go of Jesse's hand before she can see it. I need to breathe.

"I'll grab our last round," I say quickly.

"Nothing for me, I'm driving home," Jesse adds.

I nod, turning toward the bar, choking back tears.

20

Jesse

NOW

"You got her?" Fia asks, yawning in the hallway with Tank on her heels. The overhead light casts a soft golden haze, catching in her tired eyes.

I shift Penny's limp weight in my arms. Her head rests on my shoulder.

"Yeah," I reply quietly. "She's gonna feel this in the morning."

Fia just shakes her head and disappears into her room without another word.

I nudge Penny's half-open door with my shoulder and step into her room.

It's spotless—too spotless. Nothing out of place. Like she could pack it all in five minutes and disappear without a trace.

She whimpers softly against my chest, the sound low and vulnerable. I lower her gently onto the bed, trying not to jar her. She smells like vanilla and lime, and I try not to notice how soft her hair is against my jaw. I flick on the lamp, the light washing the room in amber as I catch her reflection in the mirror above the dresser.

"Jesse?" she murmurs, voice thick with sleep, her head rolling to the side.

"I'm here." I drop into a squat next to the bed, and her eyes adjust to look at me.

"I can't sleep in my boots," she whispers, almost pouty. She lifts a leg an inch off the bed and lets it drop. "Help."

Of course, she can't. She didn't get the nickname *princess* for nothing.

I sigh, not bothering to answer, and reach for her foot.

"You have to unzip them first," she adds, watching me through heavy lashes, her brown eyes glassy but still sharp enough to sting.

She tries to sit up and fails, falling back with a laugh that rattles me, making me exhale deeply.

I told her not to take that fifth vodka soda. She didn't listen. She never does.

She's lucky I was there. Every eye in the Rebel Tavern was on her, and I fear she would've been eaten alive tonight.

The zipper starts at her thigh.

Fuck.

Careful as hell, I grab it, my fingers trailing the warm, smooth skin of her inner leg, and it's a kind of slow torture I wouldn't wish on anyone. I keep my jaw locked, eyes averted, pretending this isn't the closest I've been to her in a decade.

She watches me the whole time. Not speaking. Just...watching.

I get both boots off quickly and drop them at the foot of the bed like they burned me.

I straighten up, running a hand through my hair, trying to ground myself. "If you need anything, I'm just across the hall," I say, jerking my thumb toward the door.

Penny sits up slowly, her hair messy and falling in waves around her heart-shaped face. She looks like a fever dream in this light—drunk and heartbreakingly real.

"Wait."

I freeze mid-step.

She blinks heavily then whispers, "Stay. Please."

I close my eyes. Her voice—raspy, quiet, *needing* me—wrecks whatever composure I was hanging on to. I turn to face her, against my better judgment. The room has gone still, and I have to remember to breathe.

"Penny," I reply, almost a warning.

She shakes her head as she flops to one side and clumsily pats the empty space on the bed next to her. "I don't want to be alone tonight, Jesse," she says, softer now. "Please."

I haven't heard my name sound like this on her lips for a long time. Not bitter. Not sharp. Just bare.

I should say no. I *should*.

But how many times have I thought about crawling into bed next to her? So I stay, because I can't say no. Not to Penny.

"Okay." I move slowly to the bed where her arm stays outstretched in welcome. "I'll lie here."

Just for tonight.

And only because she asked nicely.

Even if it tears me apart.

I kick off my own black boots with a grunt, then strip down to my boxers—I am not getting on the bed in my full clothes. But I'm also not about to ask Penny if she needs to change. That's a boundary I will not cross tonight.

Penny shifts toward me as I lie down next to her on the pink floral quilt, her body curling on her side like it's the most natural thing in the world.

I reach over her for the lamp and pull the cord, and for a second, the room is swallowed in stillness. My heart starts to settle.

And then, in the dark, her voice slips out soft and sleepy. "Do you remember our bench, Jesse?"

Her words hit me like a sucker punch. My lungs forget how to function, and a lump lodges hard in my throat.

Of course, I remember. God, I remember *everything*.

But before I can force a single word out, she murmurs, drifting into sleep, "Our initials are still carved in it."

Silence again.

Except now it's louder than before, echoing with memories I haven't let myself feel in years.

I lie there frozen, staring at the ceiling in darkness, blinking back something I won't name. She's asleep within seconds, peaceful, completely unaware that she just cracked me wide open.

I stay awake for another hour, maybe more, wondering how the hell I got here.

Wondering what I'm supposed to do now that she remembers us, too.

21

Penny

NOW

The low hum of the heat through the vents stirs me, warm air brushing over my legs where the soft quilt slipped off. I reach toward the nightstand, hand fumbling for my water bottle or cup—anything to quench my dry throat. There's a dull and rhythmic pounding in my head, making it impossible to think. I drag my hand across my forehead, feeling grossly slick.

Shit. I slept in my makeup.

Something I haven't done since my drunken college days.

When I sit up, gently so the nausea doesn't worsen, I wince. The zipper of my red miniskirt digs into my ribs. I need to get this off ASAP.

Much to my surprise, the rest of the room looks orderly. Good to know I didn't rampage through here like a bulldozer last night. Everything is in place...except for the fact that I feel like I was dropped into bed by an airplane and splattered on impact.

With my feet dangling off the side of the bed, I roll out my sore ankles.

What the hell did I do last night?

The moment I sit up and see my raccoon eyes in the mirror, the memories come in quick flashes—the rock band, dancing on stage, the sting of too many vodka sodas.

I really wish it was a bad dream, but my body screams with movement, ensuring me it was real. A *really* bad decision.

My black turtleneck sweater is stretched oddly across my chest. Nothing is worse than sleeping in a push-up bra.

If it wasn't for *him*, Fia and I would've had an easy-going night out like she asked for. We would've been home by eleven. I can't even tell you what time I got home last night, or how. I don't remember anything after...

Oh my god, I think Jesse pulled me down from the table where I was attempting to dance like I was in *Coyote Ugly*.

It's his fault.

When he's around, I can't think straight. I am completely off the rails.

Jesse makes me act reckless.

My stomach protests as I down the lukewarm water next to me. I should probably make my way to the bathroom before I throw up in bed. That would be icing on the cake.

So much for being the big sister who takes care of things.

As I swing my legs slowly over the edge of the bed, the other side of the bed catches my attention in the mirror.

Is that...an imprint in the sheets?

Why does the pillow look like it's been slept on? A sharp twist that has nothing to do with this hangover hits me like a ton of bricks.

Did Jesse sleep in here? That would be crazy.

No, I probably just thrashed in my sleep like a wild animal.

Just then, the bedroom door creaks open.

"Help, I'm dying," I croak, hoping it's Fia with a bottle of Pedialyte, but it's not.

It's Jesse. No shirt, just gray sweatpants that shouldn't be as sexy as they are. And a steaming mug of what smells like coffee.

I don't know where to look—the coffee that's a godsend or the very large, very real, tattooed proof that something *might have* happened last night. He's smirking at me like he has a secret.

"What's that?" I ask stupidly, hoping the coffee is for me. I can stomach coffee.

"I made a pot. Fia and I have been downstairs watching Christmas movies for, like, two hours." He sets the mug down beside me. "You slept in."

"Oh." My voice comes out thin. I wasn't prepared for *this* version of the morning. "Thanks," I mutter.

"You talk in your sleep, you know that?" Jesse muses.

I groan in response. "I was so loud that you could hear me from your room?" I ask, bringing the coffee to my lips, needing something to do with my hands. I glance up at Jesse, who runs a hand through his messy dark hair. Bed head always looks good on guys. I look like I just rolled out of the back of a trash collection truck.

"You don't remember last night, do you?" he asks, almost seeming shy. Not something I've ever seen him be. "I slept right next to you."

I burn my tongue on the first sip of coffee.

That indent in my bed is real—and really not mine.

Three awkward silent beats pass by before I muster the courage to look up at him.

"Nothing..." I start, my voice cracking. "Did something happen...between us?"

He shakes his head, and I sigh in relief. "You just didn't want to be alone."

That's somehow worse.

"Right," I bite out.

The black mug burns my fingers as we remain in this loud silence, but Jesse mercifully breaks it.

"I'll let you get yourself together."

I nod, unable to hide my shame.

"I'll be downstairs, join us when you're ready?" he asks, and I nod, needing to be alone.

But my eyes catch the ink sprawled across his back as he turns to leave, and everything in me pulls tight.

"What's on your back?" I stutter, my heart pounding unsteadily against my ribs as he freezes mid-step. He drags a hand down the doorframe, shoulders tense, then reluctantly glances back at me.

I don't meet his eyes. I can't.

I'm too busy tracing the lines etched into his skin.

It's unmistakable.

"Move closer," I command, and he does.

Lucky Penny is scribed in black ink, settled deep into his skin, right beneath the bench. Our bench. A magnolia tree shelters both.

This whole time, it's been there, intertwined with all his other tattoos...our story, my *name*, on his skin for the whole world to see.

Jesse turns the rest of the way around, and I see the magnolia branch stretch over his shoulder, vining across his chest until it stops—right over his heart.

Though I'm barely moving, it feels like this bedroom is spinning around me.

"Why do you have that tattoo?" I ask, not sure I truly want to know the answer.

He's covered in ink—a whole life catalogued across his skin. But I don't have to clarify which one I mean.

His gaze finds me again, and it locks. Everything I've buried starts clawing its way up. Every unspoken thing. But it gets trapped right at the tip of my tongue.

"Some things I never wanted to forget," he says quietly. "Some stories are permanent."

The floor creaks behind him, but neither of us break our gaze. My lips part, breath half-caught, teetering on the edge of something more.

Then the door opens with a soft push, and Tank's black nose comes through first, with my sister close behind.

"Glad to see you're alive, Pen," she remarks, sassy and unaware.

A shower and two more cups of coffee bring me back to life—enough to throw on lounge clothes and join Jesse and Fia. But before I do, I pull out my phone, needing to discuss the life-shattering tattoo news I discovered an hour ago.

Penny: On a scale of 1 to 10 of "WTF" what would you rank discovering that your ex-boyfriend has your name tattooed on his body?

Mere seconds going by before three little dots appear.

Audrey: 100!? Your name? I feel like there's something you're not telling me. That is not normal high school boyfriend activity.
Penny: Oh nothing about this is normal. I have to go, but just needed to see if I was in the right for feeling like I'm losing my mind.
Audrey: Don't hate me, but I'm kind of living for this. Are there other lovers' names on his body? Because if not, and it's not covered up, he is 100% still in love with you.
Penny: Please don't call them lovers.

The sounds of crackling wood and Fia's laughter pull me into the cozy living room, and I slip my phone into my pocket. Fia keeps her eyes on the screen—*Elf* is playing, her favorite Christmas movie. She probably watched it a million times as a kid.

At the opposite end of the khaki-slipcovered sofa is Jesse, casually taking up so much space. He glances up as I enter the living room, and his green eyes settle on me. We haven't spoken about what happened at Rebel Tavern.

We didn't talk about the way he held my hand under the table, or how he slept next to me all night.

I don't mention the enormity of my name being inked on his body either, even if it's all that occupies my mind as I look at him.

Instead, he pats the empty space next to him, like he was expecting me.

"She lives," he says with a small smirk.

"Barely." I sit next to him, the few inches of space between his body and mine making my alarms go off.

"No work for you two today?" I ask, needing to draw the attention away from the fact that Jesse puts his arm up across the back of the sofa, and if I just lean a bit to the left, I'll fall into the curve of his chest.

"I work tomorrow and have to pick up a Saturday morning shift. But today is my day off," Fia replies.

Jesse's eyes wander out the window. "Work gets quiet for me closer to Christmas."

I nod, sucking in a deep breath, and look toward the kitchen.

"Is that a stack of waffles on the island?" I ask in disbelief, though I know I smelled cinnamon and vanilla.

Fia pulls the fleece blanket up to her chin, and that's when I realize Tank is curled up on the other side of her. He is as close as he can get to her without crawling into her sweatshirt.

"Yeah, I made breakfast. Not all of us did shots last night," Fia shoots back, brows raised.

I close my eyes temporarily, if only to block out my sister's expression. "I did shots?"

"You had fun," Jesse adds, and I turn my head to stare at him, wondering if he's teasing, but his eyes are gentle, his mouth relaxed.

We're too close with my head turned, so I scoot to the edge of the sofa and lightly clap my hands together. "How about a game?"

"A game? Has hell frozen over?" my sister asks, and I narrow my eyes at her.

I play with the knotted ties on my pale-pink hoodie and avoid eye contact. "I figured it's cold, and no one probably wants to do anything today." Wishful thinking, since neither of them are hungover like me. And if I was at my condo, I'd be binge-watching Netflix in bed and getting a smoothie delivered. Ultimate laziness and pure bliss.

Jesse leans forward on his elbows, brows pulled down, and turns to me. "What game?" His tone is serious.

"Let's see what there is." I hop off the sofa and wander to the pine wardrobe in the dining room, throwing it open only to see that nothing has moved. It's like a time capsule of my childhood. The day I perused this house—I didn't get far. I certainly didn't open this wardrobe that appears like it would lead to a magical land, because I was certain things would fall out. I wasn't wrong.

"Holy shit, did Nan seriously not get rid of *anything* in here?" I swipe a finger across a dirty board game as stacks of cards fall onto my slippered feet.

Fia slowly gets off the sofa and comes to stand next to me, hands on her hips. "Nope." She shakes her head absentmindedly. "She was so sentimental about our childhood stuff."

That's an understatement.

I also don't see how this doesn't bother Fia. Her baby could open this and an avalanche of board games would come down. *When do infants even start crawling?*

"No way! She kept my special edition Monopoly!" Fia squeals, reaching for the box. She precariously pulls it out. The game hasn't been played since we all lived under this roof to-gether, I'm sure of it.

"This was your and Danny's favorite game. Do you remem-ber how you two never let me play with you? It was *for adults only*," Fia teases, but I look away.

"Yep. I remember."

"I was thinking..." Fia twirls her hair, the board game tucked under one arm. "Maybe we can call him on Christmas, since we're all here. I know it would make him so happy." She smiles, and my stomach drops.

"Please...let's not go there right now." I offer a tiny smile.

Her face falls, and now I feel like a bitch.

Fia's always respected my distance with Danny; she never pushed it. I know I have to face our brother, sooner than later. But I need to figure that out on my terms, not with her.

Especially when I'm going there to convince him to sell this house.

"That's like a four hour game, are you sure you really want to play it right now?" I change the subject, trying to lighten the mood that I just ruined.

"Yes. I do."

"Fine," I resign.

Jesse's already clearing the coffee table, and Fia's kneeling to set up the old board game. I hope I don't regret this, but then again, everyone's in a good mood. Maybe I can finally get Fia to talk about the house.

"Who wants hot chocolate?" I ask, remembering that I brought a hot chocolate kit with me from my house. God only knows why I even had one to begin with, but Fia and Jesse both smile like little kids.

Tank follows me to the kitchen while I heat up the milk and fill the space with the scent of sugary marshmallow and chocolate. Sifting through the cabinet, I find three Christmas mugs. Nan was a mug collector. There must be fifty in here. It would be insane for two people to live here with fifty mugs.

I even fill a plate with Christmas Oreos, using a fancy tray, and walk to the living room. Jesse jumps up from the floor to help me.

"I got it, thanks," I say and set it down. I offer him the reindeer mug with a small smile.

I sit next to him but slyly call Tank over to sit between us on the floor. A buffer, if you will.

Fia's about done setting up the game, a chocolate cookie in her hand and a smile on her face, and I decide this is the best time.

Because I have to try.

"You know, we could do a big estate sale after the holidays with all this stuff. Did you know Nan has like fifty mugs, and that's *just* what's in the cabinet. If you sold even half the stuff, you'd have money for the baby. You could probably furnish a whole nursery." I smile, but Fia shrugs, like I suggested that she pick a different game piece or something trivial. Not like the well-being of her unborn child. "If you sold all the stuff in the attic, all those antiques, that might even be enough for a down payment on a car."

Jesse casts his face down but glances over at me, giving me a knowing look.

I know what he's thinking. He thinks I'm pushing my luck. But when the baby comes, and I'm back to a busy work schedule, it will be ten times harder to get anything done.

Something *has* to give.

Fia takes a sip of hot chocolate. "Wow, is there peppermint in here? This is so good."

Trying to butter me up with compliments. Of course, there's peppermint; I know how to make a drink.

"Honestly, Pen, money would be great, but that sounds like so much work right now. Plus, I can't even imagine living anywhere but here."

I stay silent, and Fia finally looks up at me, continuing. "This is my home." Her voice is clipped.

In Nan's will, she specifically stated that anything that happened with the house would have to be agreed on by a majority vote. The will was drafted after Danny was in prison and I hadn't spoken to him in years. It's like Nan had a plan all along, knowing this house is what would tie us together.

But maybe she forgot how stubborn her three grandchildren were.

We start the game without another word, and I push the frustrations out of my head the best I can. It's nearly Christmas, and I don't want to ruin every waking moment with my nagging reminders that reality is a bitch.

So we sat around the coffee table for the next hour, playing Monopoly.

And I decide to let today just be today. I won't talk about the house.

I do steal glances at Jesse, however, who I can't help but laugh at with the reindeer mug in his giant tattooed hand.

The gravity of this moment isn't lost on me, and my stomach is riddled with anxiety. We aren't kids anymore, Jesse isn't afraid of returning to an unsafe home, Nan isn't in the kitchen making dinner, Danny's not coming up with new ideas that will get us all in trouble.

For a moment, I let myself imagine it. A happy family.

But that's ridiculous.

Fia's having a baby, and Jesse is simply passing through. He'll leave, onto something bigger and better, and it will go back to being Fia and I.

"I can't believe next Christmas there will be another little girl here." Fia places a hand on her belly, smiling. She's glowing, really.

It's surreal to think about, and before I can catch myself, I'm pouring salt on the wound.

"You know, if you need my help, I'll be two hours from you." I frown, because the idea actually does make my heart twinge.

"You could look at it the other way around, too," Jesse adds coolly, even though I wasn't talking to *him*.

"What do you mean?" I ask.

"What if *you* need help, and *we* are both two hours away?" he asks, and my breath stills in my lungs.

We. Like he's part of this family.

"You talk like you're staying around." I laugh, but my heart is skipping beats, waiting for his response.

Jesse leans back, his hands behind his head, biceps flexing.

"Who said I'm leaving? Like Fia said, this is home."

This house? This city? Where? A million things I want to say rush to mind, but Fia smirks, her green eyes glinting at me. "You're outnumbered, sis. Sorry."

As I sit on the scratchy woven rug, in a house that's a time capsule of my childhood, and watch Jesse and Fia laugh over a game, Audrey's words come to mind.

What would happen if my sister knew the truth? What if she knew the complicated past of her sister and the guy she looks up to like a big brother?

I hate keeping things from her. I tell my sister everything, but *this* is different. She needs me now more than ever, and if I tell her, she might not trust me. I can't risk fracturing our relationship.

I consciously have to keep pulling my knees back to my chest, so my foot doesn't accidentally brush against his, and I know I'm reaching my limit. How many more times can I hear his laugh and not stare at his face like he was the sun and stars at one point in my life?

How much longer can I bite my tongue until I taste blood to keep the words from clawing their way out? Confusing and painful words that have every fiber of me begging to decipher them before I do something stupid.

Because everything about Jesse makes me feel like I'm walking a tightrope.

And I know that eventually Fia's going to see it. I can't keep this charade up forever.

"Earth to Penny, it's your turn." She waves at me, and I roll the dice quickly to save face.

"Sorry, still a bit out of it," I apologize, though the hangover has nothing to do with my dilemma.

Jesse's phone sits face up on the table and begins to vibrate during my turn. He quickly grabs it before I can read the name of the caller—not that it's any of my business.

"Sorry—gotta take this." He stands abruptly, staring at the screen with a bewildered look in his eyes.

"Okay..." I murmur as he walks to the foyer.

"I accept." He talks in a hushed tone, like he doesn't want anyone to hear. I strain my ear to listen, but the front door opens and closes behind him.

I can't ask Fia what that's all about without raising suspicion.

"I need another snack anyway, want anything?" She stands, and I do too, walking to the front of the fireplace to warm up. I step up on the brick hearth, not to get closer, but so I can see out of the window in the front dining room.

"I'm good..." My voice trails off as I stretch my neck. Jesse's slowly pacing back and forth on the front porch, hand in his pocket, grin on his face.

Probably a girl. Why else would he jump like that? It's the only thing that makes sense.

I feel like Fia would've mentioned if he was seeing someone, but that's only if she knew. Maybe he's keeping it hidden. My heart lurches like it's dropped into my stomach.

It wouldn't be the first time he hid something from me.

22

Jesse

NOW

My bed is significantly cooler, and as I turn the light off, I find myself wishing I were under a pink quilt instead. Not that I got much sleep last night, considering I stayed awake most of it, glancing over to remind myself it wasn't a dream.

Maybe I had been afraid to shut my eyes because it *was* all a dream—she only invited me in because she was drunk.

I toss the covers back, feeling hot in the cold house, even as I lie here in just my boxers.

It's been five whole days since Penny walked back into my life, and I don't feel much closer to cracking her open. I thought I was a patient man, but my heart isn't on board with my head right now.

Logic is fading quickly when she's around me.

I don't know what I expected when I came back to North Carolina. I showed up without a real plan. What I didn't expect was to get tangled up with these two sisters again.

Or to make promises to my old best friend who's still behind bars.

She probably thought I didn't notice how distant she was when I came back inside from the phone call—the one I couldn't risk her hearing. I have no idea how she'd react if she knew I still spoke to Danny. Betrayed, maybe? But the phone call plays in my head as I lie here fully awake at midnight.

"I have one more visitation before Christmas, what's the verdict man?" he asked. His voice was full of desperation, yet so hopeless that I did something stupid. Again.

"I think I can get her to come," I said and immediately bit my fist.

In the dark of my room, I run my palms down my face.

Fucking idiot.

That's what I am.

It's not like I completely forgot about the visitation or the promise—I didn't. But there's been a lot of shit going on. And it's never felt like the right moment to bring it up with her. Not when I've just been trying to keep her from biting my head off.

I can't throw her over my shoulder and drive her to the prison. I can't wave a magic wand and heal a ten year wound that I still don't fully understand between her and her brother.

Logically, I know that. It's not my place. But at the same time, I'm a confident fool, feeling like maybe I'm the only one who *can* mend this family.

Because no matter what Penny says or thinks, we are still a family.

And you do stupid shit for your family.

I wake up with my heart racing as Tank barks, palms sweaty, and fumble for my phone in the dark room.

It's 1:30 a.m.

"Tank, knock it off," I grumble, squinting in the dark.

Tank barks again, sharp and loud, and it echoes through the hallway outside my door. I close my eyes, hoping whatever spooked him is gone, and set my phone back down, steadying my breath.

But then he lets out a low growl, one I've never heard from him, and all the hair on the back of my neck rises.

"Fuck." I grunt as I throw back the sheets, my bare feet hitting the cold floor.

His growls intensify along with my blood pressure. Something's not right.

Before I can even find the light switch, there's pounding on the front door that shakes the whole house. My breath quickens, and I'm fully awake as I nearly rip the bedroom door off the hinges, darting into the moonlit hallway. In sync, two more bedroom doors open, and Penny and Fia groggily step out.

"What's going on?" Fia's green eyes are wide, while Penny's chest is heaving, her hair messily toppled on her head.

"Who is disrupting my beauty sleep?" she snaps, with a stare that could cut glass. She looks like she's ready to fuck someone up.

That's my girl.

Three more loud bangs on the front door come before I can answer. Tank barks, his hackles raised as he barrels down the steps to the front door.

"Stay here," I instruct the girls, eyeing the only one stubborn enough to follow me.

Penny crosses her arms but doesn't move. I'm not playing around.

"Fia, I know you're in there! Open the fucking door!" a deep muffled voice bellows, the sound carrying up the hall.

"You've got to be kidding me right now," Penny growls, ripping past me, but I grab her waist, tossing her back up the stairs.

"Don't you fucking move, Penny. Stay upstairs," I bark, and her eyes harden, but she clenches her jaw and turns around to stand next to her sister.

Fia pulls her robe tightly around her frame, her lips parted in shallow breaths.

I'm going to kill this guy.

"Grab the baseball bat!" Penny hisses at me, but I walk past the coat closet. I don't need a bat.

"Heel, Tank," I command, and he reluctantly sits behind me, but his eyes remain locked on the door.

I open the front door and step out into the freezing cold night with nothing on but sweatpants.

A guy about Fia's age leans against the porch pillar with a baseball hat low over his eyes and a UNCW sweatshirt on. A luxury white sedan is parked haphazardly on the street in front of the house, and I choke back a scoff.

There's only one person this could be, and if I'm right, they've got about three seconds before they're swallowing their own teeth.

Fuckboy snaps his head up, and his bloodshot eyes find mine in the dark. The single functioning outdoor light barely illuminates the porch, but the neighbors' Christmas lights twinkle behind him, almost making this look like a peaceful moment.

It's not going to be.

"You looking for something?" I ask. Not the words I *want* to say, but I have to play nice.

His glassy eyes scan my body, sizing me up. "I'm here for Fia. *Who* the hell are you?" He cocks his head back, and I fold my arms across my chest.

So this is how it's gonna be. I have to laugh, shaking my head ever so slightly.

"It's the middle of the night, *buddy*." I'm not going to lay my hands on him, but I'm also not letting him anywhere near the house. "Let me guess, you're Brett?"

His eyes narrow, but I hold up my hand before he can get another slurred word out. "Want to talk to Fia? Come back when it's not the middle of the goddamn night."

In the daylight, I'd let Penny rip into him. He wouldn't be left standing.

Brett laughs, shaking his head. He takes a step toward the door, and I put my arm up, blocking him.

He's close enough to smell. Shitty liquor on his breath and weed clinging to his clothes. Bile rises in my throat as I realize this is who Fia was with for the last few years.

"Try again." I nod at his car. "Here's what you're gonna do, turn your ass around and leave before you do something you'll regret."

Or I do.

Every muscle in me begs for the old ways—clenched fists and broken noses. My jaw's tight enough to crack a tooth right now, but I don't move.

Not because he doesn't deserve it—and more. But because I have someone who might still believe I'm worth a second chance. Someone whose trust I already shattered once. This is my second chance—and I'm holding on to it with every fucking thing I've got.

"*Bro*, I don't know who *you* are, but my girlfriend's in there. I've been trying to fucking reach her all day. She blocked my number, and I want to talk." His finger's wavering, but he's pointing at the house. How the fuck did he even drive here?

"And I'm telling you that you need to get off my front porch." My voice is low and cold because I'm just about over this thick-skulled pretty boy.

"You gonna make me?" he sneers.

"I'm giving you an out, man, just go home," I say it slow and steady, every syllable a warning.

He moves.

Brett lunges forward, head down, all brute force and zero thought—trying to shoulder past me toward the door.

I pivot, grabbing his wrist mid-charge, and twist his arm behind his back so hard something might've popped. I don't care.

He grunts, body collapsing down, his knees buckling until he's kneeling on the sagging wood porch. My other hand grips the back of his hoodie, dragging him lower until I'm huddled over him.

You don't get through three years in prison without learning how to deal with guys who have pent-up aggression.

Tank snarls on the other side of the door, and this shit head looks like he's regretting a few things.

Good.

"Jesus, fine! Let me go!" he says through gritted teeth.

"I'm going to say this one more time." I let his arm go, only to grab the front of his hoodie and yank him upright until we're eye-to-eye, gazing right into those deadbeat eyes.

"You have never been, and never will be, good enough for Fia Hanson." I spit out every word, making sure they're ingrained. "So erase her from your memory. Burn the idea of her out of your mind."

His jaw clenches, but I don't care.

"If I see you anywhere near this house again, I will take you apart piece by piece. You think you've hit rock bottom? Try me, and I'll show you what hell actually feels like."

I shove him hard, and he stumbles back, arms flailing, nearly tumbling down the porch steps. The last of his cocky smirk falters as he catches himself before hitting the pavement.

"Stop calling her. Stop texting her," I yell, sure everyone in this neighborhood can hear me now. I want humiliation to seep into his bones.

He staggers toward his car, throwing a middle finger over his shoulder. "Fine! Fuck—she's not worth it anyway!" he slurs out.

I watch him fumble with his keys, hands shaking. I give him exactly two seconds after the engine turns over before I pull out my phone and tell the cops there's an inebriated driver heading east down our street.

My heart is pounding so hard, I'm not sure I'll be able to sit down until sunrise, and when I step back inside, both anger and relief flood me simultaneously.

Fia's standing at the base of the steps, biting her lip, eyes brimming with tears.

"You heard all that?" I ask, but it's a dumb question. Old houses have thin walls.

"You almost killed him," Penny says, and I laugh, a bit maniacally.

"He'll be fine," I reply coolly.

Fia steps toward me, wrapping her arms tightly around my torso. I hug her back.

If that's the guy she's been dealing with, I can only imagine the shit she's been carrying.

"Thank you." Her voice wavers as her small frame rests against me.

"What good are big brothers if they don't get to beat up their sister's trash boyfriends?" I reply, and Fia chuckles, wiping her nose as she steps back. "That was on my bucket list," I add with a shrug.

That's when I feel her eyes on me.

I glance over, and Penny's still standing at the base of the steps, one hand resting lightly on the banister, the other stroking Tank's head. He's still alert, ears twitching, panting heavily, but even he's leaning into Penny, calmed by her touch.

She's gnawing gently on her bottom lip, eyes fixed on me like she's trying to see something she's never let herself look at before. There's a softness in her expression.

She nods once. It's slow and meaningful.

Then she turns to head up the steps, pausing a few stairs up to glance over her shoulder. "Fia, you can sleep with me if you want," she says gently. "We'll put on *Gilmore Girls* until you fall asleep." Her tone is soothing, almost maternal. Though I know she'd scoff at that notion. "Come on Tank, you too." She pats her thigh, and Tank glances quickly at me before obediently prancing up the steps right past her.

Fia follows close behind, but Penny lingers, an unreadable expression on her face.

I pause. I was headed to the kitchen—planning to grab some water, calm down—but something about the way Penny stays there, her eyes meeting mine, makes me wait.

"Thank you," she says softly.

I stand frozen for a beat, warmth creeping back into my chest. I nod, a small smile tugging at the corner of my mouth as she turns and disappears up the stairs.

It's another hour before I finally make it to bed.

I grab the pillow and clutch it to my chest, trying to let go of the tension still in my body. My heart's still beating like the fight's not over.

But it is, and they're safe. I repeat it to myself over and over.

When I finally drift off—somewhere between the muffled sound of the television and the steady hum of the heat—my last thought is her.

It's always her.

23

Penny

Now

"You sure you don't want to come in? I can get you a free drink," Fia offers again, resting her hand on the inside of the car door as I stop at the curb outside Good Grinds.

I shake my head, eyeing the business she works at. It looks busy in there, considering it's Friday morning, and I woke up in the mood to be alone today.

Not unexpectedly, we all seem a little worse for the wear today.

My sister's sporting puffy bags under her eyes; she tossed and turned next to me all night, and this morning, she pretended like nothing happened.

She was quiet as she got ready for work, and when I offered to drive her, she said yes, instead of insisting she walk.

I'm not going to force her to talk about it, though. She will when she's ready.

"Thank you, but I promise I'm good. There are a few things I need to do this morning." I smile, and Fia gets out of the car, name tag in hand.

I roll down the window, and she turns around, her red braid slung over her sweater, cheeks rosy in the chilly morning. "I'll pick you up when your shift's over."

"Thanks, mom." She sarcastically waves.

Maybe she just needs a little distance from last night. Work will be good for her today.

As for me, I *do* have a lot of errands to run.

Usually on Friday mornings in Raleigh, I go to my favorite café downtown to treat myself to a fancy latte, pop in my headphones, and work on business admin stuff. Friday nights usually involve dinner out with friends, cocktails on Audrey's front porch, or even a date with some guy whose name I forget by the following Monday.

But this town is smaller, and there's not as much noise to hide behind.

And now that I have a stretch of alone time, I do the thing I should've done when I got here. Something I can't avoid any longer.

Even if doing it breaks my heart.

I take the long and windy road to the cemetery, slowing down because the parking lot always creeps up suddenly. My tires crunch the gravel as I pull in. I park and turn off the car. I'm in no particular rush to walk through the maze of gray headstones.

I've shown up empty-handed, unlike most people who visit their loved ones' final resting place.

Then again, I don't really see the point in putting flowers on a grave site. Something about it always felt unnecessarily mournful to me. Maybe because I know in a few days, those flowers are just going to wither and die, and the groundskeeper will collect them with all the other bouquets.

My calves burn as I trudge up the grassy knoll, taking a shortcut to avoid other people. When I finally spot Nan's granite headstone at the end of a long row, a sigh of relief rolls through me. Perhaps I needed this more than I realized.

It's silent here, save for the sound of the wind gently blowing the evergreens that surround this place. But a tightness crawls up my throat—the same one that always greets me when I come here. I ignore it and I kneel at her grave site, rubbing my palms on my jeans.

"Hey, Nan," I start, glancing around and biting my lip. I never know how to address her like this. "It's been a while."

A chilly wind blows my hair in my face, and I notice a few bundled up people in the distance carrying flowers. I pull my attention back to the gravestone.

Still so new looking.

Nan was only sixty-eight when she was taken from us, and it seems cruelly unfair. She only retired a year before, and we were all so excited for her to finally get a break and enjoy a slower life. She deserved so much after giving everything she had to raise me and my siblings.

"I'm sorry I didn't bring flowers." A pitiful laugh escapes me. I scoot closer to the stone and turn around, resting my back against it. It feels steady and strong, like her. This is how I used to sit against her chest when I was younger. Even before my mom and dad left, Nan was always the one I ran to. She was the family pillar. When my parents decided a new life somewhere without their three children would be better, Nan didn't blink an eye. She stepped in, taking their place and showing us all true strength.

She was always smiling, too. And usually decked out in her favorite color—yellow.

"I don't know where to start, so I'm just going to update you," I begin, playing with the stack of gold bracelets around my wrist. "Fia's pregnant, and Jesse's back." It slips off my tongue and keeps pouring out of me. "I could use some of your strength right now."

A single tear, hot and thick, rolls down my cheek. I curse at myself, wiping it on my coat sleeve.

I hate crying.

I hate it so much, yet the tears are leaking from me, and I'm defenseless against my own body.

"Fia's going to be a mom, and I don't know how to help her." I inhale a rattled breath. "I'm trying, but I'm ill-equipped for this. I want her to sell the house, because that seems like the right choice. Is it?" I ask, waiting for an answer that won't come.

"I'm trying to get through to her, Nan, I really am, but she won't listen to me." I pull my legs in closer to my body, so small you wouldn't be able to see me on the other side of the stone. "She's stubborn." I hiccup a small laugh. "She acts like everything's okay, but deep down I know she's scared, because I'm scared, too. I know it's all going to come to a head, and I don't know what to do when it does." The confession is heavy on my shoulders, and they shudder.

I turn my head, feeling the cool granite stone on my cheek, bringing myself back to her.

"There's something else." I gulp, feeling like a child as I wring my hands together. "There's something I never told you." I peer up toward the gray December sky. "Jesse wasn't *just* my best friend. He was the first boy I ever loved."

A moment goes by, and I wait for the effect of talking about Jesse to feel burdensome like it always does. But the feeling doesn't arise. "Actually, I think he's the first, last, and only boy I've ever loved." I sit up straighter, like she's listening, like she can talk back to me.

"But he broke my heart that summer when he left me to do life alone. I know you said I was never the same after him and Danny got locked up, and you were right. I wasn't. I cut them out, because it hurt too much. My twin brother and the boy I loved with my entire heart were both ripped from me because of their own stupidity, and suddenly, I was alone." Shaking my head, I squeeze my eyes shut as they puff up from the tears.

"I always know what to do. *Always*. But right now, I am more lost than ever."

Footsteps approach in the grass behind me, and I wipe my eyes quickly, trying not to smudge my makeup. Not that I care what a stranger thinks of me, but I don't want someone to flash me looks of pity as I sit like a child in the grass.

Anyway, I'll be fine. I always find a way to be okay.

However, the footsteps don't belong to a stranger.

I'd know those black boots anywhere; they're worn in all the right places, familiar in a way that makes my chest ache. As they land next to me, I stay sitting on my butt, feeling safer down here, pretending I don't already feel the weight of his presence pressing into me.

"I didn't know you'd be here this morning, I'm sorry." His voice is an unexpected comfort.

"It's fine, I was just about to leave," I reply, and I don't know if that's the truth, but I feel stupid now, so I stuff the tissues in my pocket and spring up, wiping the dead grass from my legs. I'm sure he can tell by the red rimming my eyes that I wasn't here having a jolly good time.

"Don't leave because of me. I just haven't been here yet..." His sentence trails off, and I glance up. A black helmet is propped under one of his arms, dark jeans are tucked into his motorcycle boots, and a worn leather jacket sits on his broad shoulders.

But my eyes are immediately drawn to the small bundle of flowers in his other hand.

My gut drops, the tears pressing against the wall again.

Do not let him see you cry.

I take a step back, and Jesse fills in the space, squatting down to place one hand on the gravestone. He gently leans the flowers under Nan's name. A bundle of daisies.

"That's kind of you." I gesture, unsure what to do. A fidgety sensation takes over my limbs.

He doesn't peel his stare away from the stone.

"Daisies always reminded me of her. She used to wear that daisy necklace," he replies with a tiny grin.

I can't believe he remembers.

I bought her that necklace when I was ten. The metal was cheap, and it was definitely a necklace meant for kids, but anytime we had somewhere nice to go, she had it around her neck.

"I remember it. She was sweet like that," I reply.

He shifts back on his heels. Jesse's face tilts toward mine, eyes squinting in the sun. His face has lost all boyishness, and I'm still uneasy about just how beautiful he is.

"You're a lot like her, you know that?" he says, studying my face.

Warmth creeps up my throat. "I don't know about that."

"No, you are. You take care of people like she did. She was a saint."

Nan *was* a saint, but not me. I seem to make messes worse these days. But I don't bring this up, I just nod, biting my lip. "Hey, about last night. You didn't have to do that."

He stands, facing me, brows furrowed. "Of course, I did. You really think I was going to let something happen to you two?"

"I don't think it would've been that serious," I say, but I doubt my own logic. Brett has always been a loose cannon.

"I wasn't going to risk losing anyone else," he replies, and the words sink into me.

I rest a hand on the headstone to steady myself. I still remember the day we buried her—it was just Fia and me, Nan's cousin, and a few friends from the hospital she worked at for decades. It was small; even Danny's furlough request was denied, so he couldn't attend.

"I'm sorry we didn't tell you when it happened. It was so sudden, and my whole focus was on my sister and taking care of the legal stuff, but that's no excuse."

Maybe it's the tears, maybe it's the damn bouquet of daisies, maybe it's seeing him defend me and my sister last night, but something in me cracks open. A tiny piece of myself willing to meet him halfway.

Willing to give him the apology he deserves.

Jesse chews his lip, hand shoved in his pocket. "I would've been here in a heartbeat, you know that, right?"

"I know." I nod, absorbing the hurt I know he felt. He *feels.* Right here—right now.

Jesse blows out his cheeks, his tough exterior softening. If he cries, I'll lose it.

"She loved you like you were her own, she never stopped thinking about you," I offer. "I hope you know that."

She really did. Jesse became one of us so quickly, and Nan had a soft spot for him. When he moved to California, she was so worried. She didn't bring it up to me, but I knew he was on her mind.

He laughs, but it's the kind you do when it hurts, when words can't suffice. I want to hold him, to tell him it's okay. But I just smile, locking in on the ocean of green that stares back at me.

"It sucks to not be able to say goodbye to someone you love," he replies.

My heart slams into my rib cage, the air stolen from my lungs, because those words land like thunder—echoing and sudden.

I'm caught somewhere between a memory and this very real, raw moment. I never got to say goodbye to him. He was out of my life in a split second, just like Nan.

"It's a pain I wouldn't wish on anyone," I say, pulling my arms across myself as the wind picks up.

The space between us hums with everything we haven't said—and somehow, it's all there. Every word. Every goodbye we never got to give.

With my heart still racing, my words slip out without second thought.

"What are you doing after this?"

I guess I really don't want to spend this day alone, after all.

The smile that follows could light up the whole world—just like it lit up mine, once upon a time.

Jesse grins. "What did you have in mind, princess?"

24

Jesse

NOW

"You know you can look at me." It's like I barked a command to one of my dogs, the way her eyes snap to mine, startled. I *almost* feel bad.

"I know, but you have to admit, this is weird," she replies, easing the slightest bit into the driver's seat as I watch my motorcycle grow smaller in the rearview mirror. I'd much rather have her arms tightly around me as she straddled the back of the bike while we cruised into town, but there was no way I was winning that battle.

It's winter, I am not getting on a bike, Jesse Rivers!

"What's weird?" I grab onto the oh-shit bar. I wonder if anyone's ever told her that she drives like she's fleeing a crime scene.

"That we're driving through Wilmington...together... in my car!" She laughs, stealing a look at me. My whole body gets a shiver from one look.

"I feel like you're not *real*," she adds.

Something in Penny shifted at the grave site, and I just hope I can keep her open, keep her talking. I need this version of Penny, the one who's beginning to show herself to me again. The one who makes me think that maybe a second chance isn't completely impossible.

"I think that's what it's like..." I pause, wondering how she'll react if I say what's really on my mind.

But *screw it*, I'm done dancing around the truth with her.

That's what I came back for, didn't I?

"I think that's what it's like when you're seeing someone for the first time in a long time." I finish my thought, and she tilts her head side to side.

A song comes on the radio, interrupting us. It's an angst-filled love song by an old emo band I haven't heard in forever. Penny quickly reaches out to change it, but I grab her hand.

"Keep it, I like this song."

She pulls her hand back, fingers wrapping around the steering wheel tightly, like I stung her.

I stretch back, avoiding touching her, desperately needing more leg room in this tiny car. Testing if she'll listen to me, I turn up the stereo a notch and glance over at her.

Penny's hair isn't sleek and styled like it was when she first got here earlier this week. It's wavy and wild, cascading down her back, like how she used to wear it when we were teenagers. Like she just got off the beach. Or like I just finished running my hands through it.

"Why'd you go to turn it off anyway?" I inquire, and her pale cheeks redden as she whips the car sharply into a parking lot.

Yeah, I should've driven.

"I didn't want to hear it," she replies promptly, parking roughly between two spots and turning toward me.

I crack a small laugh and lean my head back, peering at her. "Or was it because you remember when I fucked you in the backseat of your car on graduation night to this song?"

Penny's jaw drops, and she shoves my shoulder with all her might.

"You're unhinged!" She feigns offense, as if she doesn't have a much dirtier mind and mouth. She might fool everyone with her sweet appearance and wardrobe of pink, but I know the real Penny.

"I'm just wondering." I shrug, unable to hide my cocky smirk. "I mean, that's what I think about when I hear it."

A little grunt sounds from her, her lips pursing as she fidgets with her seatbelt.

I give her five seconds to come up with an insult to hurl back at me, but she remains flustered. Out of mercy, I crawl out of this tiny vehicle.

Penny steps out, too, and the tiniest scowl remains on those pink pouty lips.

"Don't make me regret inviting you along for my errands," she says, pointedly looking at me over the top of her toy-sized car.

I glance up to see that we're at a store called Sunshine Baby. "I think I'm the one who might be regretting saying yes."

Penny rounds the car to grab my arm roughly, her touch startling me. "Let's go. I want to see if they have a crib."

"Wait—" I stop in my tracks, and Penny sulks, pulling on my outstretched arm. My mind short-circuits from the warmth of her hand on my wrist. "I thought you were totally against this whole Fia having a baby thing."

"I'm not *against* it." She pops her hip, free hand resting on it. "I simply want to make sure she is as prepared as she can be."

"And that means..."

"It means if Fia won't prepare, then I will do it for her. I'm going to surprise her with a crib for Christmas and a few other essentials."

I crinkle my brow at her, still not getting it. Sounds like my stubborn girl is having a change of heart.

She huffs. "Anyway, *when* I sell the house, she can take a crib with her. I'm *not* helping her nest."

"Right." I let her continue to pull me to the front doors.

It's like walking into a lullaby—soft music, the smell of flowers, pastel everything, and aisles lined with labels that scream *organic baby* and *Montessori-approved*. I'm completely out of place, and from the stares I'm getting, I can't tell if the women want to climb me or call security. Either way, I trail behind Penny like I'm on a leash.

She stops short in front of a crib, and I catch her too late, bumping into her. My hand lands on her ass—snug in those tight jeans—and I don't move it fast enough. The heat spikes between us, but she doesn't say a word.

"This is it!" she says matter-of-factly, spinning to face me. "This is what I want."

I reach over to lift the display tag and get a better look at the crib model. Though I have no clue what I'm supposed to be looking for.

The tag may as well read *organic sugar-free vegan wood*.

"Is this a good one?" I scratch my head, and Penny nods.

"It's a convertible bassinet, which means she can keep it near her bed until the baby starts rolling, or is about four months, and then it converts to a full crib, then a toddler bed. It's really the Rolls-Royce of non-toxic infant beds."

I tilt my head. "Huh. You know a lot about this."

"Is it a crime to want my niece to have the safest crib? I'm never having kids, so this is my chance to spoil one."

I throw my hands up. "Whatever you say, Aunt Penny."

She leans down to look at the tag, and her hair gets caught on a display of wooden rings. *Teethers*?

"Shit, my hair is tangled!" she whispers, but before she can full-blown panic, I step behind her and attempt to free her locks.

My belt buckle brushes up against her shoulder as I lean over her. She glances up at me, silent, and I'm close enough to see her lips part slightly, her breathing hitch as I roughly whisper, "Stop moving, Pen, you're making it worse."

My biceps are boxing her head in when I finally get it un-stuck from her hair...and right in time for an employee to round the corner.

"Can I help you two?" The worker plasters a dramatic smile on her face. "My name is Linda!"

Without missing a beat, I pull Penny to her feet and nod toward the convertible crib or whatever the hell she said it was. "Do you have this one in stock?" I ask.

"Yes, we have one left in the backroom, but it's in birch, not walnut like the display."

Penny grins. "That's perfect. That's the one we want."

The woman takes out a scanner and types in a few things.

"Can you deliver it by Christmas Eve, assembled?" Penny asks, and Linda makes a face.

"Oh no, I'm so sorry. We can't assemble it by then. But we *can* deliver it in the box first thing Monday morning."

Penny's smile falls slightly. "Oh dang—"

"Monday's good," I cut in before she could change her mind.

She looks up at me, eyes narrowing just a fraction, her wild hair brushing against my chest.

"I can build it, *sweetheart*," I assure her, and Penny's brows rise.

Monday is Danny's visitation day—the one I'm supposed to magically bring Penny to. Maybe building this crib will buy me points with her.

"Oh, how sweet!" the saleswoman practically squeals. "I love seeing couples working together before the baby comes!"

Penny shudders.

To add insult to injury, I ruffle her blonde hair.

She's going to murder me, but she made it too easy.

"Let me go check on that, but feel free to shop around and I'll meet you up at the checkout when you're ready," Linda says.

I wrap an arm protectively over Penny's chest from behind and pull her close, landing a kiss on the top of her head. "We appreciate it, Linda."

As soon as we're alone again, Penny whirls around, ducking under my arm, pink lips hanging open.

"Did you hit your head last night?" she hisses at me.

I grin. "Come on, Pen, you're telling me you don't like a little role play?"

She nudges my shoulder hard. "Yeah, sexy role play, like a slutty *librarian*. Not mom and dad," she replies, and my body clenches in all the wrong places.

"Noted." I wink at her.

She smirks. "Well, jokes on you, *sweetheart*, because you're going to spend your Monday night building that crib for me."

I shrug, unbothered. "Cool, I had nowhere else to be."

25

Penny

NOW

My stomach growls loudly as we exit the drugstore I dragged Jesse into after the baby store. Even after that little scene in Sunshine Baby, he's still sticking close, seemingly happy to go where I go.

It's weirdly comforting in ways I'm not yet ready to unpack.

"I'm kind of hungry..." I have my eyes on a café straight ahead, already imagining the warmth inside.

"I never say no to eating," Jesse says, easy as anything. My mind goes straight to the gutter, and I clear my throat fast.

"Good, let's grab lunch over there, then I'll take you back to your bike."

Inside, the café is toasty and almost romantic, a soft amber glow spilling from Edison bulbs strung along the ceiling. The scent of cinnamon and roasted espresso clings to the air, and people are packed in tight, bundled in winter coats, their conversations overlapping in a low, holiday buzz.

We order at the counter before finding a small table near the front, one of those half-table, half-booth situations. Jesse pushes in my chair as a server sets our plates down quietly, and I wait for my nervous system to go into fight mode because this is too *normal*, but it doesn't.

Our food is brought to the table quickly, and as I take a bite of the crusty, delicious sandwich, Jesse leans back in his chair like this is the most natural thing in the world—like we are old friends who do casual lunch all the time.

"So, tell me about your life in Raleigh." His voice is low and steady, but it still jars me every time I hear it.

I take another bite of my sandwich, buying time. "What do you want to know?"

"You like living there on your own?" he asks, eyes intensely focused on me. "I found LA to be isolating."

"Yeah, I enjoy it." I tuck my hair behind my ear. "I bought my condo two years ago, and my best friend, Audrey, lives nearby. It's home." I fidget with the paper wrapper from the straw.

"Is that why you want Fia to move with you?"

"She told you that?" I ask, my heart racing. Fia really *does* trust him.

"She did," is all he says.

"I just don't want her to be trapped here. I want Fia to get everything she wants, a career, a family, her youth." I set down my sandwich, a lump creeping up my throat. "I don't want to leave her here to drown."

"You know I'm not going to up and leave her hanging, right? I care about her, too."

I lock eyes with him. "You don't know what's going to happen. You could...meet someone and leave. It's normal. People do that." The words feel horrible coming out of my mouth. But I have to consider the truth—a guy like Jesse isn't going to stay single for long.

Jesse stares at me pensively, letting out a humorless chuckle. "I'm not interested in *meeting someone*."

My heart lodges in my throat, but before I can reply, a blur of movement catches my eye, and a woman stops at our table.

"Oh my gosh, Penny Hanson? I thought that was you!" She smiles, shopping bags slung over her arm.

I blink at her, dazed, before standing abruptly as recognition sets in. "Holy shit, Krista? Wow, how long has it been?" I grip her arms, doing my best to summon a smile that feels real.

I feel Jesse's eyes on me, two feet away.

I gesture between them. "This is Krista. We lived together junior year when we studied abroad in Paris."

Krista unabashedly rakes her eyes over his body, and Jesse smiles, dimples and all, standing to shake her hand.

"Nice to meet you. I'm Jesse," he says, enveloping her hand in his large one. We exchange a glance that I can't decode fast enough. "Family friend," he adds.

He sits back down, and my stomach twists. Family friend is technically accurate. So why does it sting?

Krista, oblivious, launches into flirt mode. "I love all your ink!" she gushes. "You know, the only reason I have this"—she moves her ponytail to reveal the tiniest Eiffel Tower tattoo behind her ear—"is because of this girl."

I barely remember being involved in that decision, but it sounds like something twenty-one-year-old me might've hyped up after one too many cheap glasses of wine.

"Penny was a wild time in college. I don't know how we even survived." She laughs, loud and unbothered, placing a hand on my shoulder. "This girl *knows* how to live."

The last thing I want to do right now is discuss the years I was partying it up while Jesse was in prison.

"By the way, I've been following you on socials. Girl, you are literally everywhere. I mean, do you ever rest? And your photos were featured in that huge magazine. Can we trade lives?" Krista says with another shrill laugh.

The café air thickens around me. The hiss of the milk steamer, the scrape of forks against plates, the clink of ceramic—it all blurs together. My cheeks flush, and my cashmere sweater suddenly feels like it's clinging too tightly around my neck.

"It's a busy life!" is all I manage to come up with in reply.

"And how's your little sister doing? She must be so old now!" she asks. I can't believe she remembers meeting her at siblings' week all those years ago.

"Oh—she's great!" I smile tightly, feeling Jesse's eyes on me.

Fia's great, and my brother who you don't know exists is still in prison, but I'm going behind my sister's back to see him and sell our family home in a few days! It's all grand, babe!

"I'll be in Raleigh in a few weeks, let's grab drinks!" she offers way too enthusiastically.

"Of course," I reply quickly.

We hug goodbye, and I sit back down the moment she's gone, feeling like every pair of eyes in the room is on me.

Of course, only Jesse's are.

"Why are you looking at me like that?" I ask, scooting my chair in.

He scrubs his jaw. "You okay?"

"I'm fine." I smile tightly.

"I have to say, you're pretty humble for being such a *big deal*," he says, but it's not sarcastic. It's genuine, but either way, I'm done talking about me.

"Because none of it is a big deal. It's just my work." I take another bite of my sandwich, eyes down.

He doesn't argue, just studies me quietly. "You made it to Paris, though...and it looks like you got to work around the world. That was your dream."

Heat blooms at the back of my neck. Jesse was the only person who truly ever understood how badly I wanted that—wanted everything I have now. He believed in me more than anyone back when it was just ideas on a pinboard in my bedroom.

"I did," I say softly, eyes dropping to my plate again. I study the pattern of seeds on the bread crust, like it might open a door to another topic. One that doesn't leave me feeling exposed.

"I'm proud of you."

My heart skips a beat, and I lift my head.

He leans forward, resting his elbows on the table, one hand dragging slowly along the edge of his jaw. And just like that, the rest of the café fades away, blurring into the background.

Jesse has always had this gravity to him. This way of pulling me into a quieter space where it's just us.

It's a feeling you can easily get addicted to if you're not careful.

"You did it. You made it big, got everything you wanted from your dream board." His lips pull into a tiny smile, and I know he means it to be nice, but it does nothing but break my heart.

How could he think that?

"I didn't get everything I wanted..." I shake my head, my throat tightening as I lift my eyes to his, holding them there. "I didn't get you."

26

Penny

THEN

Age 18, Fall Semester at UNC

The smell of cinnamon and fresh-baked rolls overwhelms me as soon as I step inside the house. The music's loud—some symphony playing on the radio—and I only make it three steps into the foyer before it sounds like a herd of elephants is rushing down the staircase.

"Oh, thank god you're home!" Fia flings her body onto mine, unruly red hair and long arms flying everywhere as she smiles, flashing shiny new braces.

"Hey, Fi." I squeeze her back before she twirls down the hallway leading to the kitchen. It's only been four months since I left for school, and two months since I saw her last, when Nan brought Fia to Chapel Hill for parents' weekend, but to a twelve-year-old, I guess that's forever ago.

"My college girl is home!" Nan dusts the flour onto her yellow apron and rushes over to pull me into a warm hug. She smells like a mix of sweet apples and spicy nutmeg, and there are bits of flour in her pale-blonde hair that's piled high on her head—her signature style.

"Hi, Nan." I smile softly, guilt gnawing at my core for not having been back since the day I left.

This weekend is Thanksgiving, though, and I wasn't about to stay on campus and miss out on Nan's famous dinner. She goes all out with a feast, making everything under the sun—*from scratch with love*, she says. Cooking and hosting people is something she doesn't get to do often, but it's her love language.

Even if the act of stepping into this home feels suffocating for me, I did it for her.

However, the state of the house is undeniably jarring. I've only been home for ten minutes when I realize that every TV is on, but the blasting music drowns out all the voices coming from them. Dozens of wooden utensils, ceramic bowls, and baking sheets cover every open inch of the kitchen counter, and all the lights are turned on, even though it's a sunshiny day. Fia dances around the living room like a ballerina, blissfully oblivious to the stacks of library books and crafting supplies strewn about the floor around her. Nan always kept an orderly house. Even if it was crammed full, it was *neat*.

This is a tornado.

If it's their attempt to fill the empty void, distracting from the fact that Jesse and Danny are spending their holiday in prison and not at home with us, it's not working on me. No amount of clutter and stimulation can make this feel right.

Frustration simmers in my chest. *Why did I come back? I can't handle this yet.*

But Nan's eyes find mine, just as I feel myself start to come undone. Her expression is soft, knowing. A small smile pulls on her rosy lips.

She knows.

She knows what I'm thinking. And that breaks my heart a little more.

"Why don't you get all settled in, honey, and come join us? We're about to start on the pecan pie, and I could use your precision blending skills." She winks, and I let out a little chuckle.

"Oh, can I make something, too?" Fia flitters over, observing everything Nan has going on.

Thanksgiving is tomorrow, and Nan doesn't like to leave anything to the last minute.

"Grab an apron, wash those hands, and grab a spoon. You can stir the caramel," she instructs Fia, who listens without hesitation.

I'm worthless in the kitchen, but a little piece of me feels better knowing I can busy myself with a task.

"I'll be back soon." I head upstairs with my duffle bag slung over my shoulder, fighting the urge to look at the room across the hall from mine.

Luckily, the door is shut.

I decide then and there that while I'm home, I will not set foot in Jesse or Danny's rooms under any circumstance. I have to keep that door shut and bolted, or I will rightfully come undone the moment I leave this town again.

I quickly toss my lightly packed bag onto the bed and drop my phone beside it. On my way out of the room, my gaze falls on the pinboard hanging on the wall, collecting dust. It's full of magazine clippings and photos of my planned-out dream life.

The pictures of Jesse and me are no longer there, replaced with empty spots. I make a mental note to bring the board to my dorm and fill it with new photos.

The moment I step back into the messy kitchen, Nan hands me an apron, and I swallow down the feelings budding in my throat and smile. I can pretend everything is completely normal. I can pretend like I'm not living with a shattered heart.

"How are your classes going, Penny?" Nan passes me a wet plate, and I mindlessly dry it, stacking it on the counter next to me.

We're both tired, the house recently emptied from the Thanksgiving dinner guests. Nan's cousin, who we only see once a year and never seems to remember me and my siblings' names, came from Jacksonville. She brought her husband and their little dog, whom Fia obsessed over the whole time. Usually, the house is busier for Thanksgiving with Nan inviting people from her work who have no plans, but this year, she kept it small.

I wish it had been full.

Pleasantries were exchanged, and our guests asked how my first semester of college was going. I answered politely and truthfully. My classes were interesting, I was doing well in my courses, and I loved my roommate.

The food looked like a spread out of *Southern Living* magazine; enough Turkey for a small army, stuffing, cranberry sauce, four different pies, and all the sides you could possibly dream of. The house was also clean—thanks to Fia and me working all morning to shove every random item into a closet and dust every nook and cranny of this old home.

During dinner, I found myself glancing at the chair across from me every few minutes. Muscle memory, perhaps, because *he* should've been sitting there. My Nan's cousin, who was seated there, started giving me concerned glances.

Her husband waited until dessert to address the thing no one wanted to talk about—asking Nan if she had plans to visit Jesse and Danny in prison anytime soon.

They were at the same facility for now, but in separate buildings, which made it hard for Nan to visit them both on the same day. But Nan said yes—she was going to visit them on Monday, her day off. He had more questions, none that I thought were appropriate, so I excused myself from the room.

No one came to ask me if I was okay.

No one asked me if I was riddled with guilt that my twin brother got addicted to drugs and took my best friend down with him, while I was off partying, and studying, and moving on with my life.

·❤·❤·❤·❤·❤·

A light knock sounds on my door before it swings open, and Nan peeks her head into my room. She has on a white robe and slippers, with a healthy serving of pumpkin pie in her hands.

"You didn't eat dessert, and I don't know a *Penny* who skips out on her Nan's pumpkin pie." She grins, and I can't help but return the gesture. The lamp in my bedroom casts a soft glow as I remain cross-legged on top of my paisley bedspread.

She steps all the way in to hand it to me, but lingers, readjusting her hair clip. "Classes don't start again 'til Tuesday, right?" she asks.

I swallow a bite of pie, and it gets lodged in my chest. I know where she's going with this, and dread fills me as she continues.

"Fia will be in school on Monday, so I can't bring her, but I know it would cheer the boys up greatly if they could see *you*." Her brown eyes are hopeful, and I hate that I'm going to crush her spirits.

"Nan...I can't," I reply, and she nods, but her mouth is ajar. Ready to convince me otherwise. "I need to get back and study." It's an easy overarching excuse.

She exhales a little puff, sitting on the edge of my bed, studying me. I put the pie plate down, suddenly not craving it anymore.

"Baby, I know you're upset with them, but they love you."

I peel my eyes away from hers, unable to handle the hurt in them.

"No one can force you to go, but I want you to think it over. Maybe by Christmas, you'll feel ready." She pats my knee and smiles, and I give her a little shrug. "That'd be a nice surprise for them!"

"Yeah, we'll see," I say to appease her.

When she shuts the door behind her, the silence in my room is deafening.

Nan doesn't know about the drawer full of letters I wrote to Danny—unfinished, unsent—half-drunk and heartbroken, the ink blurred by tears until the words dissolved into nothing.

She doesn't know about the ring Jesse gave me, the one I lost somewhere in this house, like so much else. Or the old black shirt I stole from his room before I left for college four months ago, worn thin from time and sleep, the one I still pull over my head on the nights the sadness won't loosen its grip.

She thinks I'm just angry that they're gone, locked away from us.

But it's more than that.

I can't live in this in-between—half holding on, half trying to breathe.

Most days, letting them go feels like breaking my own heart, but if I don't, I know I'll drown in the weight of what could've been.

27

Jesse

NOW

The thing I love most about riding my motorcycle is that it's just me and the open road. A place to let my thoughts sort themselves out.

Some people do that in the shower. I do it on my bike.

After Penny dropped me off at the cemetery, I didn't go straight home. I kept riding.

How else was I going to process what she said?

"I didn't get everything I wanted... I didn't get you."

God, it just keeps replaying in my mind.

So I ride.

Straight past the tiny urban grocery store I spent my summers working at just to save enough to get out of this town. Past the gas station we'd walk to get 99-cent slushies together as kids.

The cold air numbs my face. She was right, it *is* too cold for a ride, but I needed it. I needed to feel something other than the chaos in my head.

Today was more than I expected, though every day has been since she arrived.

The apology for not telling me about Nan's death caught me off guard. Not because I was seeking it, but because it was a breakthrough. A mending of the past, and because it meant she saw me. The version of me that still misses Nan, who is still lost in some ways without a family.

And then there was lunch at the café.

The way she smiled at strangers, warmer than her normal self. The way she played with her straw wrapper, a nervous habit, as she talked to me. The way she looked at me when I laughed at one of her jokes about my gray wardrobe—like maybe she remembered the boy I used to be. The boy she loved once.

It didn't feel forced. Not today.

It felt so natural to be there with Penny. Like we were just two people who'd figured out life together, like we skipped all the heartbreak in between. I let myself imagine that life for a second while I sat there at the café.

I pictured her curling up against me on the sofa, take-out dinner on the way. Because I know Penny hates cooking. Sunday mornings in bed, her golden hair tangled in the sheets.

But that's a dangerous daydream.

Because the reality is, I broke something in her ten years ago. She said it herself. She wanted me, and I left her.

I didn't know the extent of how much I broke her until this week. And that kills me. But it's not something I can quickly patch, at least not all of it, not at once.

There's no instruction manual on how to rebuild trust from scratch. If it were as simple as saying *"I won't hurt you again,"* those words would've been out of my mouth already, when I kissed her a few nights ago.

But even if I had said it, would she have believed me?

Trust takes time.

Time is something I don't really have.

She's leaving in a week—that's not enough to rewrite the ending of our story, no matter how much I want it to be. Not enough to prove I'm a man now, not a scared eighteen-year-old kid. Not enough to unpack all the years she lived without me.

But maybe it's enough for something—a start, a second chance, a *maybe*.

It's getting late, and the wind is picking up, so I finally turn around and go back home. At a light near the house, I glance down at my bare hands, red and stiff from the cold.

HOPE inked across one set of knuckles, *HURT* across the other—fading a little now.

It was the first tattoo I got in prison, and I got it retouched in LA. I got them in a moment when I didn't know which one I felt more, always toggling between the two.

Some days, I still don't know which one wins.

Neither Penny nor Fia has asked what they mean, though I notice Penny looking at them a lot. Maybe she's afraid to find out.

I grip the handlebars tighter, my hands freezing cold, but I don't mind. I like the way the ache reminds me I am still alive. That today had been real.

I want more of today. I want to remind Penny of the boy who loved her.

And maybe, just maybe, show her the man who still does—the one who loves her enough to wait for trust to come back around.

28

Jesse

THEN

Age 18, End of Senior Year

"Are you sure you want to do this?" I ask, my voice low, rough with restraint. "I don't want you to feel rushed."

The room is stuffy and warm, and only lit by the moonlight leaking through the slats in the blinds, leaving silver lines across her face. She touches her collarbone, nervously pulling on the hem of her T-shirt.

It's just us at home tonight.

Fia's at a sleepover, and Nan's working the night shift. Danny even miraculously picked up an evening stock shift at the grocery store. It's the first time we've been truly alone. Not stolen moments or whispered touches behind closed doors.

I can't let it go to waste.

Penny nods, her forehead brushing against my chest. I can feel her breath, warm and unsteady against me.

"Yes, I'm sure... I've been wanting this for so long," she replies.

I lean my head against hers for a second, needing her to know, *really* know. "I love you so much, Pen...I need to know you feel safe before we do this."

She melts into me like those words were all she needed. And hell, I mean them. Every syllable. I've never loved anyone like this...never wanted to *protect* someone like this.

I'd never let anyone hurt her.

Her fingers tremble slightly as she lifts her shirt, and I meet her halfway, pulling it over her head and dropping it on the floor next to me. I press a kiss to her forehead, then her temple, her cheekbone, and finally her lips. I hook a finger under her chin, gently tilting her face up so I can kiss her deeply.

"I love you, too, Jesse," she whispers against my mouth.

I pull my shirt over my head, too, and suddenly, we're chest to chest, the heat between us too real to go back now.

The pink lace of her bra cups her softly, delicately, and catches the low light. She steals my breath. I'm the luckiest guy in the world.

"Fuck, princess," I murmur without thinking, my voice strained. "You are so damn beautiful."

Her cheeks flush a deep, rose pink, blooming down her neck. She dips her head like she can hide from me, but I won't let her. I tip her chin back with a finger, and then I do it—scoop her into my arms. She gasps, instinctively clutching my shoulders, and it sends something deep and protective clawing up inside me. I've imagined this moment a hundred times.

Her hands are shaky, and mine aren't much steadier, but I catch the glint of the silver condom wrapper I put on the nightstand earlier, and then I look at her again, making sure. Her eyes don't waver.

She's sure.

But when I trail kisses down her neck and press my body against hers, I feel the shift. Her breath catches, and when I pull back, her eyes glisten. A single tear spills out.

My chest tightens. "Hey." I swipe my thumb over the tear, over her damp, parted lips. "What's wrong, baby?" I hover over her, worry clawing at my throat.

"Nothing," she whispers.

I trace circles over the soft dip of her collarbone, grounding her, grounding me. Her skin is warm beneath my fingertips. I've learned you can't rush with Penny, she does everything in her own time.

My eyes flick back and forth as the silent beats seem to painfully stretch on.

"Promise me...." she whispers, biting her lip, and I lower myself another inch closer to her. "Promise me you'll always be mine?"

Time fucking stops.

I smile—softly, not cocky, but the way only Penny draws out of me. I pull her close and cradle her head in my hands like she's the most precious thing I've ever held.

"I promise," I say. "What made you think of that?"

"It's just...everything is about to change. I'll be starting school in a few months, and you'll be working, and we won't live together and—"

"Hey, hey." I interrupt her spiral, grabbing both her hands in mine, holding them tightly. Penny's misty eyes find mine, and I wish I could just grab her heart and rewire her brain and make her understand I'm not ever going to stop loving her.

"I promise you, Penny Hanson, I'm yours. We've waited for so long to be together for real...and soon, we won't have to hide it. Everything *will* change, and it's going to be perfect. It's going to be just like we always planned."

29

Penny

NOW

I'm halfway to the door, keys in hand, when my phone buzzes. One glance at the screen, and my stomach drops.

Fia: I forgot this evening was the employee Christmas party at work. Oops! I will be here until 8ish, and Kayden said he can give me a ride home!

My fingers hover over the screen. This means I have three more hours alone at home with Jesse. And just like that, my stomach twists again. Not in fear, but in that tight, fluttery way.

Penny: Ok, have fun! Uh who's Kayden?

Oh my god, I *am* being a mom.

Fia: He owns Good Grounds.

That tells me nothing. But at least I don't need to worry about her getting knocked up.

The sun's nearly gone, casting long, amber shadows across the floorboards. I flick on the hallway light on my way to my bedroom. My feet are covered in ridiculous, fluffy Christmas socks Fia lent me, and the worn wood in the upstairs hallway creaks under each step.

But then I pause.

The door across the hall is cracked open—Jesse's room. I stare at it, contemplating what I already know I'm going to do.

It's been six days, and I haven't once looked inside. Not even a peek. He and Tank are out on an evening walk, and curiosity gets the best of me.

I have to know how he lives.

Did he pack light when he left California? Maybe he has weird shit hanging on his walls, or maybe there's a photo of him and a girl on the dresser.

That thought alone moves my feet the last few steps. I reach for the door and ease it open, wincing as the hinges squeak. I hold my breath as I step in, though it's not like it's illegal. Technically, I *own* this house and he's the tenant, so I have the right to enter.

Something like that.

Stepping over the threshold is like stepping through a time machine, and the memories hit me square in the chest.

If these walls could talk, they'd have quite the stories. Explicit stories.

Checking over my shoulder, I decide it's safe for another minute. My heart hammers as I tiptoe around the queen bed—still covered with the same green-plaid bedspread.

Nan truly didn't touch this room.

I run my fingers over the perfectly tucked bedspread. I spent so many hours lying here, staring up at the ceiling, complaining about school, about Danny, wishing away the days until I was graduated and free.

It smells good, too, like leather and cedarwood. I lean down to sniff the bedspread. He definitely uses a room spray or something. It's intoxicatingly masculine-smelling.

There's no suitcase on the floor, and when I open the closet door, his clothes are hung in even rows. His wardrobe couldn't be more opposite mine, but I'll never complain about the way his black jeans hug his ass.

That's my dirty little secret, though.

A pair of running shoes and leather tennis shoes line the wall next to the tiny closet. I never understood how men survive with fewer than five pairs of shoes.

I shut the door, moving along. There's not much to look at. It's all pretty tidy, and the only other piece of furniture in here is the long pine dresser.

My lips curl into a smile when I see the single picture frame sitting in the corner. It's a black-and-white photo of Jesse and Tank sitting on the beach—a rocky beach, the Pacific Ocean, presumably, in the background. Jesse with his signature smirk and Tank's tongue hanging out. Carefree and happy. I pick it up gingerly, running my fingertip over Jesse's face, lost in the moment.

"Penelope Hanson." Jesse's husky growl startles me, and I drop the frame on the dresser, jumping back, only to stumble onto his bed.

I clutch my chest like it will help settle my thumping heart. Heat rushes up my neck, covering my cheeks, but there's nowhere to hide—I'm caught.

Still on the bed, my mouth cracks open as I nervously glance up at Jesse. He's chill and coy as ever, leaning against the doorframe, arms crossed over his chest. His cheeks are rosy too—from the cold—and his forearms flex in a way that shouldn't be so sexy. A mischievous grin spreads across that perfect mouth when he notices me staring.

"You scared the shit out of me," I stammer, my mind running through a million excuses, but I come up empty as he watches me like a hunter stalking their prey.

He moves into the room, eyes tracking me in a way that feels seductive. Maybe it's just my racing heart telling me that. He stops in front of the dresser.

"I didn't take you as a trespasser. Tsk-tsk." His voice is low and smooth.

"I'm not." I bite my lip and mentally curse the pulse moving lower into my core. "I'm sorry. I shouldn't have come in here without asking."

Jesse picks up the silver frame I was looking at, studying it for a moment before his gaze catches mine. My lungs constrict in this quiet space. There's only feet between us, but somehow every inch feels thick with tension. I prop myself up on the bed, my arms heavy against the billowy comforter. My body has no intention of moving.

"It wouldn't be the first time you trespassed." He sets the photo down.

"We were pretty devious, weren't we?" I let out a quiet chuckle.

"It was one of the hardest things I ever had to do," Jesse says, his voice strained, sexy.

"What, keeping your horny teenage self under control?" I tease, cocking my head to the side, baiting him for an answer.

He shakes his head ever so slightly, a lock of dark hair falling loosely over his forehead. "Pretending every single day that I wasn't fucking *obsessed* with you."

My breath stutters. I stare at his mouth, afraid to believe the words that came out. Afraid to believe what they might mean.

We stay staring, and something silent passes between us. A dare. A plea. I don't even know what I'm asking for—but I know I need it.

I need his hands on me. I need to kiss him, in this room, where it all started.

Maybe just a kiss will heal what time hasn't been able to.

Maybe one kiss with his hands in my hair, one breath from him, will close the circuit that's been opening, hurting me.

It's the only rational thing I can think of as he stares at me like he wants to eat me.

"And now what? You still obsessed with me?" My voice is raspy, but there's no tease in it anymore. I lightly scrunch the bedding under my fingers, inhaling the smell of Jesse that surrounds me. If only to remind myself this is real. With my heart on my sleeve, I gaze up at the man who broke my heart ten years ago, the one who still holds every potential to break it all over again.

He takes three slow, torturous steps toward the bed. And then he inches onto it, and I don't move. My chest rises with each lessened inch between us until the lines of his jaw, the gold flecks in his green eyes, are visible.

Jesse moves forward on all fours, and like a scale, I fall back as he comes down on me. His elbows land next to my ribs, boxing me in, his large frame hovering over me, and I have no escape.

But there's nowhere I want to go.

Silence encases us as I lift a finger, tracing the ink on his throat up to the softness of his parted lips. His green irises stare right into me, like they see everything.

He kisses my fingertip, and I drop my hand to the side of his face, admiring the way his jaw fits in my palm.

"You want the truth?" His voice pulls my gaze back to him, and I nod. "I never stopped being obsessed with you."

His confession crashes into me, breaking down a wall with such force that all I can do is shiver under his touch.

Jesse trails kisses across my palm.

"Is this wrong?" I ask, worried I just ruined everything by asking. Worried that what we are doing is so wrong. That it's going to hurt me even more. That it's a temporary Band-Aid on my heart. That I'm treating Jesse like an easy fuck when the truth is he holds a piece of my heart I never got back.

His eyes grow darker, a small grin pulling on the corners of his delicious mouth.

"If this is wrong, I don't want to be right. I'm a good man, Penny, but I want to be bad right now."

"Show me how bad you want to be," I whisper back against all my judgment, and for a moment, he hesitates. Like maybe he thought I wouldn't agree to *this,* and he'll jump up and say "gotcha!" or that our time has passed, there's too much hurt, too many years between us. That doing *this* would be irresponsible.

But he doesn't do any of that.

Instead, he laces his strong hands through my wild hair, gripping me tightly, trapping me under him, and lays his lips on mine.

His kiss isn't soft and sweet, it's rough and needy. He sucks my lip into his mouth, and the breath in my lungs no longer belongs to me. I moan, and he releases my mouth, smiling against me. He smells like I remember, like leather and musk. His tongue darts into my mouth again, and I hold on to his neck.

It's thicker than it was ten years ago. He is solid and steady, and I'm filled with a desire to claim him right here, right now.

His biceps flex against the fabric of his shirt, and logic leaves my body—disintegrating into thin air, because all I want is to see what's under his clothing.

I want to run my fingers over every line of ink covering his torso. I want to kiss the column of his throat, I want to scrape my nails down the valleys of his back.

I want to remember, just for tonight, what it feels like when Jesse Rivers is all mine.

We strip down until there's only my lace panties and his black boxers between us. The air is cool on my skin, but the heat of his body makes me feel wild. Ravenous.

Jesse rakes his eyes over my body as I inch back on the bed. He grips my thigh, and I stare down at the tattooed hands wrapped around my pale, unmarked skin.

I love how we contrast, love how he still remembers where I like being touched. He massages my inner thighs as I writhe on the bed, bucking my hips, desperate for pressure on my aching center. But Jesse takes his time, studying me as he does.

"Fuck, you're so sexy, Penny." He growls, and I reach for his shoulder, yanking him toward me until his lips crash onto my neck. He kisses me slowly, his tongue swirling around the sensitive skin. Then his fingers dip into the band of my panties, and I gasp as he pushes two fingers inside me.

There's no space between us to think about what this is. Or how familiar yet different it feels.

I'm not the teenage girl he promised forever to and had stolen kisses with. I'm a woman who's been without him for ten years, who's fought off what-ifs and denied herself so much because of his betrayal. But he's not the boy I knew either. He's steady and sure, confident and strong.

"You're dripping for me." He bites my earlobe as his calloused thumb strokes me. His tongue ravishes its way down my collarbone until I'm arching my back.

Jesse's gaze drops to mine, his irises swirls of dark green, and he smirks. His lips part as he pulls my nipple into his mouth, and my eyes roll back in my head.

He is all man... He knows *exactly* what he's doing.

"I'm going to come," I breathe out, relishing his touch, but he pulls out, leaving me throbbing.

"Not yet...I want all of you." He growls, and there's no time to think about what this means—because right now, I want this. I want all of him, too.

"Jesse...fuck me. Now," I command, still bucking my hips into him, and he reaches for the nightstand.

I grab his hand. "No—I'm safe... I want to feel every inch of you. Please."

That's all he needed to hear, because in one swift motion, he yanks me up until I'm on my hands and knees in front of him. From behind, he presses his hard cock against my ass.

It's bigger than I remember, but his lips feather against my ear, and I all but come as he whispers, "Hold on to the headboard, *princess*."

I don't even have time to glance behind me before I'm forced to grip the headboard, my knuckles white as he slides into me, and I take all of him.

The moment he's inside me, it's like a puzzle piece shifted back into place. He's rough, palming my breast, squeezing my nipple, kissing my neck, and biting me as he fucks me hard.

But there's nothing quick and dirty about this.

Because every touch reaches in and finds places in me I've sheltered off, that only he could reach.

No one is Jesse, no one could ever be. He's sweet where it counts, but knows how to handle me. It's like no time has passed, like we fell right back into our rough and rowdy ways between the sheets.

My fingernails dent the pine headboard as I turn around and beg for him to be rougher.

He obeys me, just like I knew he would, wrapping my long hair in his fist and pulling my head back. He lies on his back and instructs me to straddle him.

"Turn around, I want you to watch yourself as I make you come." His voice wraps around me, and I do what he says.

Fingers tightly grip the swells of my hips, and he guides me over him. I meet my eyes in the mirror over the dresser, and they quickly fall to the place where he and I meet. I watch as he does as he says.

His fingers grip my thighs tight as he thrusts into me so hard I feel like I might split in half.

"Jesse! Fuck!" His name rolls off my tongue, and I tighten my hips, knowing I can't stave off this orgasm for another second. I ride out the wave of our ecstasy, watching his muscles strain and glisten, my pink nails raking down his hard chest.

But it's not until he slows down, still inside me, his hands running slowly down the sides of my body, that a dam in my heart bursts open. We're warm, and the air is sticky, but my body shakes, and he sits up, folding us together. He continues to kiss me, gently.

Jesse pulls out, and instantly, my body feels empty. I fall back, collapsing into the messy sheets that smell like cedar and floral together. Us.

As he stands, I don't hide my lingering gaze. His arms and chest bulge from the workout he just performed on my body, and it's not fair that anyone can look this good.

But he doesn't leave me alone for long; he drops back down on the bed after grabbing a towel, and I roll onto his chest, so we're face to face. I can feel my hair wildly splayed around me and his heart beating under my chest as Jesse runs his fingers over my cheek.

We hold each other's eyes in the low evening light.

"I think I missed you," I whisper, and the words hang in the air above us.

I can't take that back. It's the truth.

No matter how he hurt me, I missed him.

Jesse kisses my lips and rolls me over until I'm on my back and he's next to me. He then pulls the covers around us, creating a safe cocoon, just like he used to.

His arm wraps around my stomach, pulling me close.

"I'm here now, Pen." He brings my knuckles to his lips, and I let my eyes close to the sound of his voice.

Messy hair entangles me, Jesse's heavy arm draped over my body. The sky outside is completely black, but I don't need light to know what the man next to me looks like.

The profile of his nose, his strong jaw, and the dimple on his chin. And his full lips, which part as he breathes deeply; it's all ingrained in my mind. I could draw him from memory, down to the little scar above his eyebrow.

The rise and fall of his chest are more prominent than the last time I lay here with him, but I still trace the valleys and peaks with my fingertips. Gently, like he might disappear if I push too hard.

His dark brows are furrowed, and a piece of me aches. The same piece of me that ached the day I found out what his life was like at home, the same piece that wanted nothing more than to protect him.

Carefully, I prop myself up on my elbows. I don't want to wake him, but I can't stop myself from running my fingers lightly through his hair.

Now that I've touched him, I feel like I can't stop.

He's chipping away at my resolve, and it both enlivens and terrifies me. There's so much left unsaid, so much I still don't understand about our breakup.

I just know that after what happened tonight between us, there's no going back to pretending there was no *us*.

I can still be angry at him for what happened ten years ago, but a line was crossed. A very vulnerable, raw line.

When I trace his lips, his eyes flicker open.

"I'm sorry, I didn't mean to wake you."

He smiles, but then footsteps sound in the foyer, and I lunge over Jesse, grabbing his phone to check the time.

"Fuck, fuck, fuck!" I whisper, my voice hoarse from sleep.

It's almost nine.

Jesse's eyes trace my frantic movements, but he doesn't look nearly as panicked as I feel. My bare feet hit the wooden floors next to the bed, and the chilly air of the house quickly wakes me from my daydream as I search for my clothes in the dark.

"Hey, you guys up there?" Fia's sing-song voice travels up the stairwell.

Without another look at Jesse, I forfeit the search and dart out of his room, sliding into the bathroom just as Fia reaches the top of the steps.

"Penny?" Her voice is muffled behind the door, and my pulse steadies.

Way too close.

I hear the telltale signs of Tank's pitter-patter as he smooshes his nose into the door, sniffing loudly. I need to talk to Jesse about his manners, he is always trying to follow everyone into the bathroom.

"I'm in here, just about to shower!" I yell, shrill as hell. I hurry up and turn on the faucet.

"Okay! Well, I'm home! Where's Jesse?" Fia's leaning against the bathroom door.

This is what happens when you grow up sharing a bathroom with a sister. Privacy is a foreign policy.

"He's probably sleeping, I don't know, I just came home from a walk," I blatantly lie and jump into the shower, recoiling as the old pipes spew out lukewarm water.

Fia's footsteps fade down the hallway, and I sigh, leaning my head against the shower wall as water rushes down my face.

After a solid minute of deep breathing, I open my eyes.

Only to see handprint bruises on my thighs and hickeys lining my chest.

I exhale a chuckle and shake my head.

Audrey was right—*I am so screwed.*

30

Jesse

NOW

The next morning, I find myself shifting boxes around in the backyard shed. There's an extra pep in my step—something I literally never thought I'd say.

I guess that's what happens when you finally get something you've been dreaming of for so long.

It takes everything in me to focus on the dusty cardboard boxes, trying to remember which one Penny said to grab. She was brief this morning, but I noticed the sunshine returning to her face.

Scanning the stacks, I see one labeled *Christmas 98*.

Penny might have a point about getting rid of some of this stuff.

"Forget the boxes right now, let's start with the tree." Fia waltzes into the shed, startling me.

"Sure, sure." I turn and run a hand through my hair, grabbing the bag with the tree in it.

"I can't believe Christmas is in three days and we're just now putting up the tree." Fia sighs, hands on hips.

"You know you could've asked me to do this earlier?" I hulk it over my shoulder and walk past her into the yard.

She follows me, opening the back door so I can wedge the faux tree through. Tank gets one look at the seven-foot tree bag and scatters, letting out a low growl as he disappears into the dining room.

Fia shakes her head. "I know I could've asked you to do this earlier, but I was preoccupied with other things. Christmas snuck up on me this year."

Penny points to the empty spot next to the fireplace. "Right there."

It's the same place the tree went every year I lived here.

I raise my brows at her. "Bossy."

She swats my arm, but a small smile plays on those lush lips.

The lips I can't stop thinking about.

The girls get busy fluffing out the fake spindly branches, and Tank tiptoes into the room, eyeing the tree.

"I don't think he likes it." Fia tilts her head toward my dog.

"I'm not sure he's ever seen one, to be honest."

Penny freezes, head snapping my way. "You never had a Christmas tree all the years you lived in California?"

California comes out of her mouth like a foreign word, as if she's only now beginning to accept that's where I've been all this time.

"No, don't believe so. My studio apartment was tiny, there wasn't space for decorations."

"Yeah, but it's Christmas," Fia adds while intensely focused on getting the branches to stick out at the perfect angle. "It's not the same as hanging pictures on the wall."

This fake tree is on its last legs, like everything else in this house, but I don't mention it.

Penny's gaze lingers on me, her face fallen. "What did you do each year...for the holidays and such?" she asks, unable to hide the emotion in her voice. A mix of sadness and curiosity. Just like when we were teenagers, and she asked me about my father. She cares deeply, but she keeps it locked deep down.

I shrug and lift a box of ornaments off the floor, placing it on the coffee table so I can begin to unwrap them. The tissue paper is worn and thin, almost disintegrating at the touch.

"Sometimes I'd go out to eat, have a beach bonfire with friends, or go to the movies." I hand Penny a red bulb, and she takes it from me, her smile gone. "It wasn't a big deal," I reassure her, suddenly feeling like I need to cheer her up.

"Well, I'm glad you're here with us this year," she replies, and Fia glances at her sister, but neither of them says anything else on the matter. Maybe they don't know what to say.

I didn't think much of my uneventful holidays the past few years, to be honest. I'm used to not having family around; being a loner is encoded in me. I haven't spoken to my father since the day I left sixteen years ago. He saw me packing a duffel bag and told me no one would want me and that I wouldn't be welcomed back once I stepped out the front door. He could be six feet under right now, and I wouldn't know, or care.

Family isn't the blood that binds, but the hearts that open when you need it most. And right now, I'm here with two of the people who, at one point, loved me like their own.

Even if one of them won't fully admit that yet.

"See, I knew forcing you two to hangout would rekindle your friendship!" Fia smiles, reaching for a glass ornament from the box in front of me as I pause mid-unwrap.

Penny's face flushes, and she nervously laughs. "What are you talking about?"

Fia peers around the tree at her sister. "You two were best friends. There's history there. That's all—I'm just glad you're not trying to cut his jugular out anymore." Fia rolls her eyes at me, as if to say *can you believe how dumb my sister is?*

"We *really* were close, weren't we, Penny?" I chime in and grab a strand of beads to wrap around the tree. I'm sure I'll do it wrong and Penny will come behind me, adjusting every bead, but right now, she's too stunned, watching me like a sniper. "Funny how inseparable we were back then, hmm?"

"Mhm," she replies and repeatedly readjusts the same ornament.

I circle the tree with the metallic bead string and stop directly behind her, my chest pressed to her back, and tuck the end of the strand into the branches above her head.

Penny goes still.

"To think I used to know *everything* about you." I lay it on thick, my lips hovering right beside her ear.

Penny steps back, beneath my arm, nearly knocking the tree over to get away.

"Careful!" Fia cries out, but Penny hops over boxes on the floor and widens her eyes in warning.

"I knew all the buttons to press to make you *tick*...inside and out." I slowly drag my eyes up her body and watch her stiffen.

Then she claps once, loudly, making Tank jump up, alert.

"Who wants something to drink? To eat? I'm going to the kitchen. To cook. To drink." She beelines to the fridge, and I chuckle.

Fia passes a weird look at us both. "What's her deal?" she asks, throwing tinsel on the tree. It's really beginning to look like a hot mess, but I just go along with it.

"She's just worked up about *Christmas*, that's all."

After twenty minutes, the tree is done—a sporadic display of old ornaments, tinsel, beads, and half-working lights. So I head out the back door, followed by Fia and Tank, to grab a few wreaths. Onto the next task.

Nan always hung a boxwood wreath over the fireplace and one on each window on the front of the house—Fia reminded us. We might be the last home on the block to decorate for the holidays, but if I have any control over it, I'm going to make sure it feels like old times for the Hanson girls.

It's chilly and damp inside the large shed, and Fia pulls her green sweater over her fingertips, drawing her arms close to her body.

I hand her a trash bag with a wreath inside it. "Hey, while I have you a moment, I need to tell you something," I start, and she freezes, looking up at me.

"Sure, what's up?"

"I might've made a promise I'm not sure I can deliver."

Fia furrows her brow, cocking her head back. "Oh?"

I wasn't planning on confiding in her, but the clock is ticking and I can't do it without her. I need her help. She may be the quiet and softer sister, but she holds a quiet strength I don't think she sees.

"Last Monday at visitation, I told Danny that Penny was in town," I start, and she inhales sharply, waiting for the punchline. "And he asked me for a favor... He wants me to bring her to visitation. He said he needs to talk to her."

Fia drops her hands to her hips, her belly swaying back and forth as she gnaws on her bottom lip. "Damn, that's a big promise."

"Yeah, I know." I exhale my words, feeling the weight of reality. "It might've been the dumbest shit I've done in a while, but I can't break another promise."

"Another?"

I shouldn't have said that.

All I've done is break promises to Penny. To myself. And this one was a stupid one to make.

I'm sure Penny has her reasons for not visiting Danny, ones I'm not even aware of. But I know about all the letters he's sent her, and I've seen his face when I bring up his twin sister. Any animosity from his side is gone. He simply wants to talk to her.

"I know it's a slim chance..." I hate asking for help. Loathe it. But I'm desperate not to let him down, even if his hopes are low.

I need a win.

"It's Sunday, Jesse... You really think you can convince Penny to go in less than twenty-four hours?"

Well fuck, when she puts it like that.

"She wouldn't even listen when I suggested a phone call on Christmas..." Fia sighs. "My sister hasn't spoken to our brother for like...well, since the summer after graduation, I think. It's not something she'll talk about with me. And you know it's not easy to change her mind."

"I know." I steel myself. "I think everyone is just ready to start healing."

Fia peers down as Tank meanders in, nuzzling his white-and-gray snout into her thigh.

"Is that why you're back? To try and fix things or something?" She peers up at me, searching.

"Something like that, yeah."

"Okay." Fia nods, nostrils flaring. "I'll help you."

She doesn't sound confident, but I grab her small shoulder and give it a squeeze. Relief floods me.

"I can't even tell you what this means. Thank you."

She scrunches her nose at me. "I'm *not* saying she'll go, but I'll help your case." She grabs another bagged wreath and pauses before walking out of the shed, glancing back at me. "For the record, I think you're a really good guy, Jesse."

I smile at her before she disappears into the yard.

If only everyone thought so.

31

Penny

NOW

It's not *my* pink-and-white Christmas decor decking out the house, but the house is nonetheless decked. The tree, while a bit wonky, is covered in ornaments that remind me of my childhood. Homemade, vintage, and just a bit worn.

The windows have wreaths, the banister and fireplace have garland, and the lights are twinkling. Well, most of them anyway.

It took nearly all afternoon to get everything done, and while I may have been bossy, I'm not a complete monster. I decided to cook everyone a hearty dinner. When I told Fia and Jesse that, after they both fell back on the couch, exhausted, Fia threw a skeptical glance my way.

"You sure?" she asked.

"Yes! It's going to be cooked. Not gourmet," I replied, leaning into the fridge to see what I'm working with.

The key is to never promise good food. Then, if by some miracle you don't burn the living hell out of everything, everyone is impressed.

The only thing I can assure will be perfection are the after-dinner espresso martinis.

After much chaos in the kitchen, and probably too much salt, I serve dinner around the coffee table, since it seems no one is willing to move from their spots on the sofa. It's something Nan would've never allowed, and in a way, it feels rebellious, like we're all kids, home alone again.

Snagging a pillow from the chair, I sit between the coffee table and the sofa, exhaling a tired breath and digging into dinner.

The chicken bake turned out half decent.

I watch as Jesse and Penny take bites. No one's complaining.

"Hey, don't forget we need to wash those sweaters for our picture on Christmas morning," I remind Fia, and Jesse chuckles.

"Still doing that?" he asks.

"It's tradition, Jesse." Fia smirks.

"Do you remember the year the carolers showed up and your Nan was so excited she just decided to join them on the spot?" Jesse asks, laughing to himself, and I can't help but reminisce, too.

"I was so embarrassed, she just ran out the door and followed them, leaving us in our ugly sweaters on the front porch," I reply with a hearty laugh.

Fia's eyes dart between us, a small smile playing on her lips. No doubt happy that Jesse and I are *friendly* again.

"She was the best." Fia smiles to herself, and I know if we say one more word, someone's going to end up in tears.

So I stay quiet, looking up at the old, crooked tree, the strands of lights twinkling next to the crackling fireplace, and the two people across from me.

A wave of guilt simmers in my gut, one that's haunted me all damn week.

Guilt for trying to push Fia from this home, even if it's still what I think would be best in the long run.

Guilt for not visiting Wilmington often the last few years, for thinking I had more time, or maybe not thinking about the time at all.

And then there's Jesse.

He wasn't wrong when he said he knew every detail about me. The things that made me tick, my biggest hopes, my fears. There once was a time I shared that all with him. And if I'm being honest, I wonder what it would be like to share them again with him.

But that's where the guilt comes in.

I slept with him last night when I knew I had to leave again.

In five days, I'll be packing up my convertible and heading home.

He's not some one-night stand I met at a wedding. He's not an easy goodbye.

I've let myself slip into the cozy daydream that Christmas brings, but I can't let myself forget what lies outside of this bubble.

We have separate lives. All three of us.

"Thanks for making this again." Fia eats the last morsel off her plate, and Jesse pats his stomach.

I hold my fork, still chewing, deep in thought, because there's another thing I feel guilty about. Tomorrow, I might drive to the prison to see my brother. I can't go home, after all of *this*, without finding out if he'd be willing to sell the house.

Maybe he'll be thrilled to get a third of the money—he can use it to start life again in a few months. I doubt there's anything else we can talk about, if he'll even agree to see me.

"I need to talk to you both about something that's happening tomorrow." I abruptly interrupt Fia and Jesse's conversation about Tank.

They turn slowly to look at each other, and my stomach squeezes.

"Why are you two looking at each other like that?" I ask, feeling exposed.

"I actually wanted to talk to you about something, too," Jesse starts, and now I really feel sick.

"Okay...you go first," I reply shakily.

Fia clears her throat, and I drop my fork. It clinks off the ceramic plate. They definitely aren't telling me something.

"I wanted to ask you something," he starts again, green eyes meeting mine, and I see the nervous teenage boy behind them.

"Okay..."

"Christmas is Wednesday...and I was wondering if you could do something for me...uhm, as a favor." His elbows rest on his knees, his chin in his palms, and I wait with bated breath.

"Go on." My pulse is through the damn roof.

"Fia and I are going to the prison tomorrow afternoon."

It takes two seconds for that to sink in. I glance at my sister, who looks pale as a ghost, unmoving.

"I didn't know you were talking to Danny," I say directly to Jesse. There's a new sharp pain in my chest. Why didn't he tell me? But now isn't the time to address it, not in front of Fia.

"Yeah, I am." Jesse nods hesitantly. "And we want you to come with us."

I lean against the sofa, taken aback.

"I know this is really hard for you, but we'll be there. He gets out in five months, and maybe..." Fia starts, but it's like the fork is lodged in my chest. It's tight, and I'm cornered.

Fia doesn't know exactly why I haven't seen him in ten years. She just thinks it was a falling out of sorts.

She doesn't know I have a box of unread letters in a closet at home. And she doesn't know about the one drawn up by my lawyer that I'll be bringing tomorrow.

"Last week, after visitation, he told me he needed to talk to you. He's genuine, Pen." Jesse's talking directly to me. "I know he's hurt you. He's hurt us."

I swallow, tears pricking at the back of my eyes, immediately giving me a headache.

I'm not sure if this is the worst or best thing to do, but I nod. "I'll go."

Jesse's eyes light up, his head tilted, the firelight glowing off his cheekbones. "Really?" Disbelief coats his voice.

"Yes, but I want to do this alone," I add, feeling queasy. I hate lying to Fia. But there's no other way. "I *need* to see him alone."

They pause for a moment and collectively say, "Okay."

Jesse's foot finds mine under the coffee table, knocking into it playfully. "Thank you." He smirks, but I can't offer anything in return.

I'm not sure if it's a self-destructive desire or a complete lack of consciousness licking up my throat like a flame, but whatever it is, it pulls me straight out of bed. I can't be alone with my thoughts any longer tonight.

That's all it is, I tell myself as I tiptoe across the dark hallway, grip the brass doorknob, and push the door open while my eyes adjust.

Adrenaline courses through my veins, my ribs tight under my flannel nightshirt, and then, like a match dropped in kerosene, my body roars to life the moment Jesse looks up, a playful grin spreading on his face.

I shouldn't be doing this.

We already hooked up once.

That was supposed to be closure. It was supposed to be a release of emotions, of all the bottling up, to solidify that we no longer hate each other. An end to a long era of wondering.

But I'm not sure Jesse feels that way.

My knees hit the soft edge of the mattress, and as I crawl on all fours toward him, he reaches up, running his rough hands down my body until they stop, holding my hips in a perfect grip.

As I hover over him, my knees on either side of his tapered waist, he stretches up effortlessly to suck my tongue into his mouth, consuming my mind.

I shouldn't be in here right now.

It's decidedly wrong, but I am not a good girl.

All we are is two people who were once in love. Two people who gave each other all their firsts, all the pieces of each other to hold tight.

Two people who hurt each other and still can't talk about it.

So we just do what we know we can do right.

We kiss.

There's no sweet gentleness, just rough neediness. A neediness you have when you're parched, drinking water like you can't consume it fast enough, like every cold drop will save you, will heal a part of you that you can't even see.

So I take each kiss from him greedily.

The tightness of his fingers encasing my exposed skin makes me gasp, and I let out a wicked laugh.

"Quiet, baby," Jesse purrs, and I do as he says, forgetting time and space. His fingers work quickly at the buttons on my shirt until there are no layers between me and his hands. He cups my tits, squeezing my perked nipples, and I throw my head back, grinding my hips into his hard pelvis.

I want him to take away the pain that still sits in the center of me, threatening to spill out.

Because fuck closure.

Jesse Rivers ripped me right open, and I'm not sure what to do with that.

But he gives me no time to think as one hand leaves my chest, cupping my ass as I straddle him, and his hot tongue finds my chest.

The feeling of his hair between my fingers, his arms protectively holding me up, draws a whimper from my mouth.

I haven't spoken a word to him since I entered this room. No instructions. One look, and he knows what to do, knows what I want.

He once told me my amber eyes give everything away, and even in the moonlight of this room that holds so many ghosts of our past, I lock onto his eyes, begging him to chase them away.

Just for tonight.

He hooks a thumb in my panties, easing me up to my knees so he can rip them from me. His fingers expertly find the place I ache for him, and his mouth returns to my neck.

"I want to taste you, Penny..." he growls into my ear, and I buck my hips against his hand, needing the friction. He fills me with another finger, and I take it. I roll my hips into his touch, but Jesse snaps his hand away, leaving me empty and pouting in his face.

"Ah-ah, not so fast. Be patient, and I'll make you feel good."

The bulge of his length presses into me, barely contained by his black boxers, ink weaving into his forbidden fruit, and I snake a finger under the waistband and watch his dark pupils grow into the emerald field around them.

Jesse grabs my wrist with a quick cockiness. "You're not listening to me, *princess*." His voice is strained, white flashing under his lips.

He flips me over, and my head hits the pillow, eyes trained on him as he crawls back.

I writhe against his strong grip. Seconds go by before his tongue is licking up my center. My back arches at the hot touch of him.

He adds a finger, moving his tongue in a way that has me wondering how anyone could be this *good*, but I push the thoughts from my head, focusing on this man worshipping my trembling body.

I whimper as he adds two more long fingers, stretching me. Quickly, a hand clamps my mouth, his arm extended up my side. He pulls away, and desperation sears through me as I drip for him, his mouth hovering just over my core, not touching me.

"Be a good girl and stay quiet," he instructs, and every instinct in me to be feisty dissipates into thin air.

Falling silent under his hand, I nudge his head back down to satiate me, eyes rolling back as he devours me like I'm the most delicious treat he's ever tasted.

Nothing else exists while he's worshipping me, and it could've been seconds, or minutes, I have no idea, but his hand clamps down on my mouth as a wave of ecstasy rolls through me. My whole body shudders against the damp comforter, my muffled whimpers filling the air...his name on the tip of my tongue...his tongue torturing me as I continue to drown under his spell.

He releases me from his hold, sits up, hair messy, eyes full of lust, looking down at the puddle he's left me in.

It's impossible that *this* is the guy who broke my heart.

And yet, as I study his face, the curves of his glistening lips, tracing down the lines of ink, the magnolias that lead to my fucking name on his back, every piece of me hurts.

I didn't have to shut him out like I did.

I could've called him.

I could've looked him up all the times I was in California.

I thought I was protecting myself, but right now, I'm not sure I was.

Jesse runs his lips gently over my body, and tears prick at the back of my eyes, because all I can think about is what would've become of us if I chased after him that day.

If I took care of him the way he always took care of me.

I shut my eyes as his lips find mine in the dark and encase his jaw in my palms, holding him to me like my life depends on it.

I don't cuddle after sex. I don't sleep over.

My dating life has been loose, ruleless, and at times non-existent. I always lost interest quickly, because no one ever compared to someone I didn't want to admit I was still comparing them to. No one made me feel like this: Safe, wanting to stay up into the night just so I don't miss out on anything because the next day isn't guaranteed.

Jesse clears his throat, his rough fingers tracing light lines down my shoulder as the early morning catches up to us.

"What's next for you, Pen...for us?" The gruffness of his voice doesn't mask the raw vulnerability.

Pulling the covers up to my chin, I know he feels my body tense against his, but at least the dark acts as a shield. He can't see my face.

It's contorted and pained, and I don't want him to see me like this, so I clear my throat, too, waking from the sleepy state I was in. The room doesn't feel warm enough, even against the planes of Jesse's body.

"I can't stay here forever," I whisper and know it's not the answer he wants. "I have to get back to my life at home."

He doesn't reply.

"There's a lot going on right now. I have a really busy winter with my business, Fia's having her baby in three months...then Danny will be out. And then there's the house—"

"I understand," he says in a way that makes me believe he doesn't understand any of it.

"Can we just lie here a little longer together?" I ask, and he pulls me closer to him, until my body is inside the curve of his, not an inch between us.

We lie there for another hour, silent, until I get up to leave. Quietly, so no one knows our secret.

32

Penny

THEN

Age 18, High School Graduation

"It feels weird to be sitting alphabetically," I whisper, leaning closer to my brother as the cheap polyester scratches my bare legs. "I feel like Jesse should be next to us."

Danny glances up at me from under his crooked black cap. His eyes are not red for once—I begged him not to smoke before graduation, and he actually listened. Though he's been a grouch.

"All I know is that in ten minutes they're calling my name and I never have to step foot in this godforsaken school again," he mutters.

It's sunny on the football field as I drag my feet against the short green grass. The valedictorian is giving her speech, but I haven't really heard a word she's saying.

For the tenth time, I steal a glance behind me.

Three rows back, across the aisle. Our eyes meet, and warmth pools in my chest. His black gown sits handsomely over his broad shoulders, and the black cap makes his green eyes shine even brighter.

He winks at me, and I bite my lip to stop the smile as I turn my attention back to the stage.

·♥·♥·♥·♥·♥·

Twenty minutes and a million cheers later, we throw our caps into the sky. I throw mine so high it disappears into the blinding southern sun, but I don't care, because as soon as everyone starts moving, I'm looking for him.

I don't have to look very far. His eyes lock on mine, and he's rushing toward me.

"We're free!" Danny yells, intercepting Jesse from me, leaping onto his back like a wild animal. We all explode in laughter. It's a rare glimpse of who we all used to be together.

"I have no idea how you even got that," I shoot at my brother.

He holds his diploma up, shaking it. "By the skin of my teeth, baby! That's how!" he replies, jumping off Jesse, who's rolling his eyes but is all smiles.

I'm not sure how my brother pulled it off, but I'm mostly just relieved for him. And my Nan.

We all link arms, me acting as the middle anchor. I start pulling them toward the edge of the field. We're almost to the fence when a tiny fireball of red hair comes barreling toward us.

"Congratulations!" Fia beams, a small bouquet clutched in her hands. The pink carnations are slightly crushed, but they still make me melt.

"Fia!" I scoop them into my arms and hug her with one arm. "Thank you!"

She shyly hands flowers to the boys, too. Definitely her idea—it has Fia written all over it.

Jesse bends down and hugs her tight. Her face lights up as he ruffles her messy hair. "Thanks, kiddo."

I know Fia's going to miss us when we move at the end of the summer, and part of me feels bad about it. Nan assured Fia they'll visit me for all the special family weekends, and Fia already has a UNC shirt she's been sporting. It's adorable.

Nan stands a few feet behind her, blonde hair piled high on her head, a yellow cotton dress swaying around her ankles. She's blinking back tears, dabbing the rims of her eyes as an ancient digital camera she refuses to get rid of is neatly wedged under her arm.

"I can't believe you three did it." She sniffles. "You're so grown up."

Danny groans as she lifts the camera. "We can do this at the house, Nan—"

"Shut it." I grab his arm and pull him into frame. "You'll want these pictures one day."

I smile at Nan, a genuine smile on my face that I couldn't bite back if I wanted to.

Today is a good day—the start of a new chapter.

Jesse chuckles and steps beside me. His hand wraps around my waist, and he and Danny sandwich me between them. We have a hundred pictures like this as messy kids.

"Say cheese!" Fia yells from beside Nan—her mini-me.
Click. Click. Click.

We smile until our cheeks hurt, until it gets too warm under my gown, and I take it off to reveal my white cotton sundress.

"You three meet me at the car in fifteen, okay? We can't be late for the dinner reservation," Nan reminds us, putting her camera away and grabbing Fia's shoulder.

I nod and turn back to the boys.

"Hey, I'm gonna go find Sean," Danny says, rubbing the back of his neck. "He's got something for me."

I roll my eyes. "Whatever he's giving you, don't take it before dinner. Nan's taking us somewhere nice. Don't be an ass."

He runs his hand through his shaggy blond hair, smirking. "Okay, *mom*." He turns to Jesse. "You coming, man?"

"I'll meet you in a few, just give me a sec," Jesse replies without looking at him.

Once Danny's out of earshot, there's a shift in the air. I exhale.

It's just us.

But Jesse's staring into the crowd, scanning the bleachers. His jaw's tight, and I already know what he's looking for. Or whom.

"They didn't come," I say softly.

"Nope." He pulls his lips to one side and shrugs.

I never expected Jesse's parents to show up today. They haven't said a word to him in two years, and I don't think *he* expected it either.

But he still looks, and I understand it more than anyone.

The year after my parents left, I'd find myself looking out the window for them without even realizing I was doing it. I know what it's like to be forgotten.

My heart aches for him right now, and I wish I could fix this. I can't, though.

All I can do is love him.

And I do. So damn much.

"Hey, have you heard from any places yet?" I ask, bringing him back to me.

Jesse didn't apply to any schools. His grades weren't good enough for scholarships, but he's been saving and applying to jobs in Chapel Hill.

"Not yet, but I will," he replies, his hand brushing mine as we stand awkwardly. Always with enough space between us, always wanting no space.

We already agreed that once I get a grip on school fall semester and he gets a few months of work under his belt, we'll tell my family together.

We'll say it *just* happened.

Danny will probably flip out because he freaks out over everything, but I pray Nan will be okay with it.

My grades won't slip, and I have a plan. Everything will be perfect; she won't even be able to justify being mad.

But I can't spiral too far ahead. All I want to think about is the first night we are free in a place where no one knows us, where our relationship doesn't put anyone at risk.

That dream is what keeps me moving forward every single day.

"Hey," I say softly, getting his attention again. Jesse smiles at me. "We did it. Off to our next adventure."

His thumb grazes the top of mine.

Jesse studies me, something unspoken glittering in his eyes.

"Penny Hanson, you are my adventure."

My heart stumbles in my chest.

I bite my lip so hard it stings. I want to kiss him more than I want air.

"Wait—I actually got you something," he says suddenly, unzipping his gown.

"What?" I blink. "Jesse! You didn't have to—"

He rummages through his khaki pockets, and my heart races in anticipation. I selfishly wish I could freeze this moment.

Then he pulls out a ring.

No—*the* ring.

Green sea glass set in sterling silver. The one I saw at the mall, and never stopped thinking about.

My breath catches. "Jesse...you didn't."

"You worked so hard. I'm so proud of you, baby." His voice is low, and I don't know what to do. It's too much.

But he pulls my right hand up and slips it on my finger. It fits like it was custom-made for me. I stare at the green stone, and tears sting my eyes.

"I wanted you to have something to wear every day," he says softly. "To remember how far you've come. You're going to continue kicking ass."

My throat is tight, but I look up at him, holding his hand in mine.

"You...you really think so?"

Jesse cocks his head back, beaming at me. Then he wraps his arms around me like armor. I breathe in the scent of his cedar cologne and soap and let myself be held. His arms are the safest place I've ever been.

His lips brush my hair. "I know so, princess. I'll be right there with you, you'll be unstoppable, Pen."

I pull back just enough to see his eyes—clear and steady. "No, Jesse. *We'll* be unstoppable. Together. Always."

I hold out my pinky. He laughs and loops his around mine.

We kiss our hands and seal the promise.

33

Jesse

NOW

The black coffee's gone cold again as I stare at the gray clouds outside. It's the third reheat, which Penny always said was foul—but she's never tasted prison coffee. I'll take this organic roast, microwave reheated and all, any day.

Cold coffee isn't my problem; my focus is—or lack thereof. Nothing holds my concentration. Not the mug wrapped too tightly between my hands, not the emails from work that I should've replied to a day ago.

Fuck, I've managed to waste a whole morning doing absolutely nothing. And the morning slid right into the afternoon, in a house that's still and quiet. Too fucking still.

I almost miss when everyone was on edge, because now it's just polite words and a lot left unsaid. I feel like I'm going insane.

My foot taps the wood floor obsessively as I glance toward the front door. The girls took Tank for a walk. They invited me, but I declined. Not because I didn't want to, but because I have no self-control left.

I'm living on a prayer that I can gain Penny's coveted trust again, and yet the trust for myself has run dry. I can't imagine anything more torturous than walking beside her and not touching her. Not holding her hand or bringing her knuckles to my lips. The way her skin stuck to mine as we lay somewhere between sleep and awake, it's all that's looping in my mind. I can't stop seeing her vixen smirk when she showed up in my doorway, risking it all, knowing that whatever she asked me to do, I would say yes to.

I've always been defenseless against her.

Now that I've had her, I can't pretend I haven't. But that's not my choice.

The dining chair scrapes the floor, and I'm up.

An idle man is a dangerous one, and I'm right on the edge of losing control. I don't know what her long game is, but I went ten years without her, and the idea of going ten more is fucking terrifying.

But I know that's not what's on her mind right now. She's made it clear. It's *complicated*, she says.

Penny's a planner, a fixer, and right now, fixing *us* is too big a task to take on amidst everything else she feels she has to fix.

The door slams behind me as I grab the ax in the backyard. Something I've done all week when I feel like I'm on the verge of losing my shit. Picking up the ax, I swing it until the dead tree that's been lying in the yard is cut up into enough wood for every fireplace on this street.

The funny thing is, my friend in LA texted me last night, asking how I'm adjusting "out there in the boonies." I just laughed, because the Jesse I was in LA isn't the one I am here. I don't miss California, because everything I missed is *here*. So close I can almost reach it. And yet, it still feels just out of grasp.

Like it's still not mine to have.

Whack.

I carry a heavy load of split wood inside and stoke the fire. The flames flicker and crack, the heat kissing my hands.

The time flashes on my phone, reminding me that in a few hours, Penny's finally going to see her twin brother.

I know what Danny means to Penny, or once meant to her. That kind of sibling love might dim, but I don't know if it ever disappears. Below the stubborn anger and fortress she's surrounded herself with, she's drowning in hurt she doesn't let anyone see.

But I see it. I see all of her.

My gut twists, and I drag the mesh screen across the opening. It's not like I'm not happy that they will be seeing each other, but selfishly, I'm terrified. She might not come back as the same person.

Danny might be my oldest friend, a brother to me, but Penny is the love of my life. She always has been, and I would do anything to protect her. Everything about today has the potential to hurt her. The potential to reopen every scar she's tried to bury. I can't promise her it won't, but I can promise this: when she walks back through that door this evening, I'll be here.

It's a promise I broke once, without meaning to.

She might still be waiting for me to vanish.

But I'm not going anywhere.

My eyes shutter closed, the growing flames licking me in warmth. Releasing a slow breath from deep in my lungs, I stand, slipping on my leather boots and grabbing a jacket. The front porch is quiet, the city has slowed down with Christmas three days away.

I thought the fresh air and change of scenery might release tension from my shoulders, but it doesn't.

Then I hear her laugh, and it's genuine.

That soft, effortless sound that hits me right in the ribs. I turn my head toward it instinctively, my muscles melting when I see her rounding the corner at the end of the block in her bubblegum-pink jacket, cheeks flushed from the cold. Fia walks beside her, small round belly in a cream coat, one hand holding the leash as Tank trots happily beside them.

They're talking, laughing, lost in their world, and for a moment, all I do is stand there, committing it to memory.

Penny opens the little iron gate in front of the house. Her gaze catches mine as she closes the gap, walking up the steps toward me. There's something sly and knowing in those eyes.

"You guys want to grab brunch in town before Penny has to leave?" Fia calls out, unclipping Tank's leash before slipping him a treat from her pocket.

I nod without hesitation. "You two pick—I'll buy."

Penny pauses beside me, studying my face, eyebrows knitting like she can see all the things I've been thinking about while she was gone.

"You don't need to do that," she replies.

"I know." I shrug, turning to push open the front door for her. "But I want to."

"I'm exhausted, I'm going to take a nap."

Penny turns to her sister, concern creasing her face. "You sure? You barely ate anything?"

Fia shakes her head and gives a tiny smile. "I'm fine." She kicks off her tennis shoes in the foyer and waves her sister off. "This eggplant-sized baby is calling the shots. And right now, she wants to lie in bed and watch *Bridgerton*."

Fia trudges up the steps, leaving Penny and me alone in the kitchen.

She tosses her leftovers in the refrigerator, and I whistle for Tank. The afternoon sun is peeking through the white lace curtains above the kitchen sink, and we both stand without taking off our jackets. Penny leans back on the counter, her arms crossed over her chest, eyes darting around the space like she is trying to figure out what's next.

The sound of Tank's paws on the floor draws my attention down the hall. He waddles up next to me, letting out a loud yawn, stretching his legs out in front of him.

"I'm going to take him out." I don't know why I tell her this. Maybe I'm desperate for the conversation between us not to end.

Penny nods but doesn't move, so I follow Tank into the yard as he sniffs.

A tiny smile tugs at my mouth as I stand with my back to the house and hear the back door creak open. Penny appears next to me, her blonde hair curled around her shoulders, looking beautiful. She always does.

At brunch, all I could think about was how badly I wanted her all to myself, just us on a date. But I'm beginning to wonder if that's just selfish.

Maybe I'm meant to have a taste but never the whole thing.

Maybe that's karma for breaking her heart.

"Thanks again for lunch." She breaks my spiraling thoughts and smiles up at me.

"Don't mention it."

Tank shoves his nose in the bundle of logs leaning on the shed, but something startles him and he jolts. He glances sideways at me, stiff-bodied, waiting for permission.

"Go on, boy!" I holler, and he leaps into action, running in circles like a Tasmanian devil.

"We only had parks in LA, and I think he's still in disbelief about this yard," I tell Penny, but she's doubled over, laughing.

Her eyes are pinched shut as she clutches her stomach, watching my dog put on a show. He does an insane parkour move off the back steps, leaping through the yard, darting around like something invisible is chasing him.

My smile spreads.

"What the hell is happening?" Penny asks, trying to catch her breath.

"Zoomies?" I chuckle, gazing down at Pen. "You've never seen a dog do this?"

Penny shakes her head. "Not like this!"

Tank stops a moment later, catching his breath, his thick muscular chest heaving.

"Now he'll be ready to go inside and conk out on the edge of Fia's bed like he just got off a twelve-hour factory shift," I say, and Penny's just staring at me. The winter sun casts a soft light over her face.

A face I've dreamt about looking at in person for so long.

A face I've had to see on social media over the last ten years, hating myself for even looking.

"Why do dogs do that?" she asks innocently, snapping me back to the moment.

I run a hand through my hair, chuckling. "Uhm... It's their way of showing joy, I guess. They run around in bursts when they're excited and feel safe."

Penny bites her lips. "Huh." Her amber eyes lock on mine as I nod toward Tank.

"That's why I love working with them. They don't hold grudges. Even the dogs who were completely let down by people know when they're with someone safe."

Tank walks over to me, leaning on my legs as I squat down to scratch his ears. He closes his eyes, pointing his snout toward the sunlight.

"It took some time for me to convince him I wasn't going to hurt him. But then I became his safe person. He trusts me."

Penny shoves her hands in her pockets. "You've always had that effect, you know."

I crinkle my eyebrows at her.

"You become people's safety, Jesse," she says.

Those words squeeze the air from my lungs. "Oh."

She rocks back and forth, sucking her lips in before her words burst from her, straight at me. "So...when were you going to tell me that you and Danny were *buddies* again?"

I nod slowly, kinda shocked it took her this long to ask. "To be honest, I didn't think you'd be interested in knowing that."

"What? That everyone has forgiven and forgotten around here but me?" Her tone is sharp, but there's an undercurrent there.

"Penny, no one has forgotten, I promise you that." I stand back up, facing her.

"Promises don't mean much."

Ouch.

"Do you ever think about what life would be like if you didn't go out that night?" Penny asks, voice soft again.

All the fucking time.

But I shake my head. "I've thought about it, but I try not to live with regrets."

As soon as the words leave my lips, I wish they hadn't. She cocks her head back, and the walls I was slowly chipping away at rise back up.

"Wow. Okay...got it."

I reach out to touch her arm, to pull her into me, but she's already taken a step back, out of my reach. She quickly walks to the back door.

"Come on, that's not how I meant it, Pen. You know that night was complicated..."

She turns her head around to look at me, eyes cold. "I need to get on the road. Wouldn't want to keep my brother waiting."

34

Penny

NOW

The trees surrounding the prison parking lot are starting to morph together in a green and brown line. That's how long I've been staring at them. Loblolly pine trees. Tall, strong, fast growing—all of the things I don't feel right now.

My car is in park, but I haven't moved my fingers from the black leather steering wheel. It was so easy to say yes when they asked me to go see Danny yesterday. It seemed too good, actually, like the stars were aligning in my favor for once. I could go visit Danny and not raise the alarms for the "sudden" decision.

But on the drive here, I started to feel the weight of this decision weigh on me. To distract myself, I had called Audrey, asking about her Christmas plans. I listened to her recite her entire holiday menu, though I can't tell you a single thing she's making. I just needed a familiar voice, one that's far away, one from my other life. The life I have outside of Wilmington.

The one I can return to at the end of this week.

I didn't mention being on my way to the prison to visit Danny. She knows I have an estranged brother, but she's never pushed, never asked too many questions.

She certainly doesn't know he's been sitting in prison for ten years because the drugs he sold put his classmate in a coma. She doesn't know that I'm on his call list, but have never accepted a call. Or that four years ago, the phone stopped ringing altogether.

She doesn't know that Danny's been sober for a long time. That's what Fia told me, anyway. My Nan was so proud of him when he celebrated one year.

And no one knows that deep down, I'm proud of him, too.

It's clouded by anger and hurt and confusion about a night I feel I never got answers to. I never planned to cut Danny from my life; it just happened, slowly, over time. It got easier to pretend that part of my life didn't exist.

And now here I sit, twenty minutes early for visitation, my lungs burning with tightness, my eyes blurry. My first instinct is to turn this car on and slam on the gas, driving back to the house as quickly as I can.

I can't do that, though.

My next instinct is to call Jesse.

I'm still angry with him right now. He continues to hurt me, and I continue to hurt him—but I know he'll answer. Before I can dissect how shitty of a person this makes me, I dial his number.

It's a California area code—something I'll never get used to seeing.

"Penny?" His voice sounds on the other side as I rub my clammy palms against my jeans.

"Hey," I respond shakily and wipe my eyes.

"What's wrong, baby?"

There are dogs barking in the background, and I remember he was volunteering at the shelter this afternoon. "Shit, you're busy, it's okay, I'm okay."

"No, you're not." His voice is calm and steady, like an anchor at sea. "Talk to me"

I'd do anything to climb into his arms right now.

"I don't know if I can go in there." I rest my heavy head against the steering wheel.

"Yes, you can. You can do this, Pen," he replies, tone even.

I nod, sniffling. He sounds sure, but I'm not.

"What do I even say to him?"

Hi, remember me? Your sister. Sorry I haven't seen you in ten years, I've been busy pretending you don't exist.

"He's your brother, you'll know what to say. It might be shitty and uncomfortable at first, but he loves you. And I think you still love him."

Jesse possesses a gene I don't. An hour ago, I was storming out of the backyard, pissed at him for implying that he didn't regret ruining us. I walked away, like I always do. Avoiding the truth.

The truth that this week would've been really hard without him. The truth that a piece of my heart *does* trust him, wants him, while the other part is too scared.

Scared that our love story was only meant to exist in a tiny bubble, way back when.

But I *need* him right now. He's the only one who knows what I'm about to walk into. He's the only one who knows what calms me. And he is here, ready to listen.

He's the good one, not me.

"Okay," I choke out, feeling my eyes already puffing up from crying. Luckily, I brought my makeup with me. I can't walk in to see Danny after all this time, looking like this.

"You're still sunshine, Penny."

I shake my head because that's absolutely a lie. I know the monster I've been this week, I know the sister I've neglected to be to Danny. To Fia.

"How can you even say that?" I groan.

"Because I know who you really are. Just be yourself. It's going to be okay, I promise."

My tears render me a speechless, blubbering mess, but I nod, making whimpering noises that sound like an injured animal. I really need to pull myself together.

"Fia and I will be waiting for you at home after." His voice grounds me in my seat, and I close my eyes, soaking in the sound I have only heard in my head for years. "Take deep breaths."

"Thank you... I'm going to go," I reply softly and hang up. I pull down the sunshade, confirming what I was afraid of. I look like a hot mess.

Deep breaths.

I do what I can to look presentable and shove my possessions into the glove compartment. Everything must stay out here except a manila folder that I called ahead about—the printed-out papers from my attorney about the deed. I can't legally get Danny to sign them today, but I can show him the document, explain it all, and set up a date with the attorney for the finalization. I can e-sign from Raleigh.

The smell of rain hangs in the air as heavy clouds block the afternoon sun, so I speed walk to the entrance of the low brick building.

I tell myself this is for my family; a fresh start for them, closure for me. Selling the house, facing Danny...it *should* feel right. But my gut twists, and I can't shake the feeling that I'm walking blindfolded into a storm.

35

Penny

THEN

Age 18, Summer After Graduation

I grab a chilled Coke out of the fridge and skip out the back door. Danny's out here, too, but I don't let that stop me from dropping down into the green plastic lawn chair. I pop the can open and lean back, pretending I don't notice the bong sitting on the cracked concrete between us. He's got a lot of balls to smoke in the middle of our yard.

I glance down at my worn-out plastic sandals and sigh.

It's been a long fucking Saturday, working all day in the mall, dealing with rich girls from my high school. Every dollar I've made working through high school has gone to my college savings, but with my larger-than-expected scholarship, I'll finally have a little room to breathe soon. New shoes are at the top of my list.

Jesse's also been working nonstop—he even picked up a closing shift at the grocery store tonight. It sucks barely seeing him, but graduation is behind us, and now there are just a few short months of summer before we're free.

I sigh again, but Danny doesn't look up or acknowledge me. The buzzing of the cicadas fills the silence between us, and the stifling humidity is enough to make me not want to move. Inside isn't much better. It's been an awfully hot June, and there's only so much ceiling fans and a few used AC window units can do.

"Fia's still up." I break the silence, sipping the sweet dark cola as I tilt my head up to the black sky. "She never listens to me anymore."

Danny stretches his long legs out in front of him, his tennis shoes beaten to hell. He *could* afford new ones if he didn't spend so much on drugs. It makes zero sense to me.

"Whatever. She's eleven, she can fend for herself," he mumbles, lifting his eyebrows lazily at me. "We're not her keepers."

I pick at the broken plastic weaving in the chair beneath me. "When Nan's working, she's our responsibility. Not that you ever spend time with her."

"What do you want me to do, play Barbies all afternoon?" he spits back, and I roll my eyes. My brother is an ass most days. It's hard to believe I was born only four minutes before him. He's more immature than our eleven-year-old sister.

"She's going into sixth grade, she doesn't play with dolls any-more." I kick a rock near my feet. Danny doesn't reply.

"Maybe you could just *try* to be part of this family," I say, sitting up and leaning toward him, exasperated.

It's not fair that I had to grow up fast, and he gets to act like a child, doing nothing all day. Nan does the best she can to provide for us, plus Jesse. It's not her fault our parents left us. Danny has had all the same opportunities I have; he just doesn't see it that way.

He makes a *pshh* noise, kicking gravel, and slumps down deeper in the lawn chair till it looks like it's consuming his slender body.

I knock his foot with mine, *hard*. "Maybe if you stopped get-ting stoned every goddamned hour, you'd wake up and see what's around you." An ache grows in my chest.

"Penny, give it a rest," Danny grumbles.

I glare at him, my fingers tight around my sweating drink. "God forbid you have people that miss you, Danny," I snap at him, sitting on the edge of my seat. "You're my twin brother, I don't understand what happened between us. This isn't how it used to be."

He studies me with red-rimmed eyes and smirks. "Come on, be real. You and Jesse don't miss me." He shakes his head, and I furrow my brow, a pit forming in my stomach, ready to defend what's mine in secret.

"What the hell are you talking about? We ask you to hang out all the time."

Danny leans forward, head in his hands. His messy dark-blond hair swoops over his eyes. "The moment he moved in, you two shut me out. You don't need me, you have each other. Kinda shitty, you know, since he was my friend first," he replies dryly.

"Wait, are you seriously jealous?" I raise my voice and scoff. "You're the one who pulled away."

"Whatever. I don't know why you still bother trying," he mumbles, and I stand, grabbing my drink.

The metal base of the chair scratches loudly on the concrete patio, and red-hot heat throbs in my head as I march toward the back door. With my hand on the doorknob, I turn over my shoulder at my brother, who's not even looking at me anymore.

"Maybe because you, Jesse, and Fia are all that I have. We're family, in case you *forgot*. And in less than ten weeks, I'm going to be leaving this town, and you're going to be sitting here wasting away on drugs. One day, you'll regret this, Danny."

I don't give him a chance to reply, not that his brain could even keep up. I let the back door slam loudly behind me.

36

Penny

NOW

The prison staff look over my papers again, which only makes me more nervous to see my brother. He's in a minimum-security prison as of two years ago to finish out his sentence, but even *this* feels like too much.

I'll admit, when he first got arrested, I thought he deserved it. I hoped that it would turn him around, but as I walk through the several checkpoints, getting scanned and ID'd, I think about Danny; the blond-haired skinny kid who slept in the bunk bed above me for the first seven years of my life, until Fia was born. He was always a troublemaker, but he wasn't a bad kid. He was not a bad person. He got wrapped up in the wrong scene and made some poor decisions.

But sometimes I think competing with me was the issue all along.

I was little miss perfect—perfect grades, didn't date, and got a full ride to college, while he was barely getting by in school and spent his weekends getting high. He received nothing but discipline from Nan, while I got nothing but praise.

I thought I was doing the right thing, but maybe I should've tried harder to pull him up with me.

Maybe I'm part of the reason he's here.

After the final metal detector scan, the gray metal door outside the visitation room buzzes, that harsh electric sound signaling it's unlocked, but my tennis shoes stay planted on the speckled linoleum

226

floor. I glance down, half expecting them to actually be glued. An impossible prank from my brother.

My white leather sneakers, scuffed near the toes, under my faded blue jeans, stay put, even though my mind screams to move my damn legs. Nervously, I pull at the sleeves of my bright-pink sweater with white beaded bows and swallow hard. I chose my brightest, most cheerful sweater, because I thought a little color might soften the edges around here. I thought it would cheer him up.

As I stand, *stuck* in this hallway on the verge of a panic attack, that seems stupid now. The sweater suddenly feels too loud, too bright, like I'm trying too hard, and my lip throbs...I didn't realize how hard I was biting it.

"Ma'am, you can't block the door," an older woman's voice snaps at me, stern and tired, and I meet her eyes for a split second.

"Yes, sorry."

I step forward, arms instinctively folding across my torso. I feel like I'm about to walk onto a stage, ass naked, and tell everyone about all the ways I've fucked up in life.

As I enter the visitation room, I'm instantly overstimulated by the rows of hard plastic chairs occupied by families and couples, some leaning in close, whispering fast, others just...staring. My heart flutters, eyes snapping to the blinking clock on the far wall.

Thirty minutes is too much time to spend here.

The white cinderblock walls are streaked and chipped, like they're molting. Overhead, the fluorescents hum low and cast a sickly yellow glow. There are windows at least—high, narrow ones—but the light they let in is filtered through layers of grime and bars.

The rush of blood in my head is so loud it drowns everything else, so I suck in the deepest breath I can manage—air thick with disinfectant and coffee—and let it out slowly, praying I stay standing.

When I open my eyes, we catch each other's stare.

Across the room is Danny. My brother.

Sitting in the far corner, with his hands folded on the table, a small but nervously crooked smile wavers on his face, like he's been waiting for me forever. It feels like I'm floating as I move closer, like my feet aren't really hitting the floor, but before I can register everything, I'm standing beside the table. Probably paler than a ghost.

"Penny." His voice startles me out of the underwater cage my mind is in. It's deeper than I remember, and I study his face. His smile's the same—always mischievous, even if it's genuine, but now it's punctuated by faint lines around his eyes, and the shaggy blond hair he used to hide behind was traded in for a crew cut.

His face falters, just barely, as I blink hard at him for several seconds, the manila folder still clutched in my clammy fingers.

"Ma'am, you need to sit or move along," another guard mutters, appearing out of nowhere with a disapproving scowl.

I nod and force my rigid body to sit.

The plastic chair is cold beneath me as I settle into it, and the table between us wobbles when I lean, so I sit back carefully, arms tucked at my sides. Danny hasn't stopped staring at me.

He looks smaller. We *were* premature twins—always on the little side—but this is different. He's not the cocky kid from high school anymore. He's quiet and peaceful in a way that unsettles me.

Maybe I expected to come here feeling rage. Was it naive to think he would be the same asshole he was in high school? Decidedly, that would've made things easier.

But this?

This is unexpected and strange. Because instead of battling my brother, who should hate me, I just see a man. One who's been sitting in this place alone for ten years. That thought makes me want to scream. I want to sob. I want to throw my arms around him and apologize for everything. And I think he knows it.

"Hey, it's good to see you," he says quietly, placing his hand on the table between us.

I stare at it.

Are we allowed to touch?

I keep my arms at my sides, mostly because they feel like they weigh a hundred pounds. I can't hold his gaze for more than a second—it hurts too much. We have the same amber eyes. We got them from our mother, but that's someone Danny refuses to talk about, so I never do either.

"You cut your hair," I say, because it's the only thing I can think of.

He cracks a big grin, ribs shaking with laughter. It's familiar and strange all at the same time. "I did, yes." He runs a hand through his short hair. He looks handsome. "Figured the skater boy look doesn't fly when you're almost thirty."

I smile for real this time. I don't see the blue jumpsuit, I just see my brother.

"I didn't think you'd come," he says with a shrug.

"Yeah…me neither."

From the table next to us, a cough cracks through the air. There's a burst of laughter somewhere behind me, and it sounds easier for everyone else. They've probably been coming every week for years.

"How's Fia?" he asks, and I let out a small sigh of relief. I can talk about her, that's easy.

"She's good." I lean forward. "Well, I mean, she's six months pregnant, as you know."

I don't have to wait for a reaction, because Danny's shaking his head, though he's still grinning. How could someone who has no freedom smile so much? Danny didn't look this happy even when he had an easy life as a teenager with barely any rules.

"I can't believe our baby sister is going to be a mom. She better be finishing school."

"Oh, she is. Nan would haunt her if she didn't," I add, feeling my body loosen little by little. I play with my hair, and the papers are brought into view.

He quizzically nods at me. "What've you got there?"

I swallow, nervous jitters racing up my legs. "I wanted to talk to you about something, Danny..." I start, his name still feeling strange on my lips. "It's about the house and Fia."

My body braces in anticipation of a blow-up. It's not like I don't want to talk to him, I do. More than ever, I want to sit here and talk to Danny about everything. I want to hug him, I want to apologize, I want to hear what he's been up to, but we only have thirty minutes, and I have to remember Fia, too.

"Shoot," he says, and I blurt it out.

"I want to sell the house. I want to help Fia settle somewhere nice and safe, preferably closer to me in Raleigh. And we'll split the profits three ways, so you'll have a nest egg available for you when you get out in May."

My words hang between us, and Danny laughs.

"What's so funny?" I furrow my brow, and he partially covers his mouth.

"You're still doing that? Taking full responsibility for our sister," he says, and my walls rise immediately.

"I know you haven't seen the house in...a while..." I choose my words carefully. I need him to take my side on this. "But it needs so much work. The historical homes are going for a lot right now. We could get a huge amount, and I'd handle everything. Fia is resisting it, but if you agree to sell, she might reconsider."

He looks at me skeptically, but I keep going.

"I'm not going to pull the rug out from under her, or from Jesse. I just want to make sure she's set up for success." I nod, feeling strong in my convictions.

Danny is silent for a while, so long that I begin to wonder if something is wrong, but he looks up, eyes sharp and clear. Something I'm not used to—last time I saw him, he was stoned.

"If you think this is the right choice, you have my support. But on one condition."

I don't like *conditions*, but I eagerly wait.

"Give her one year. Let her have the baby and give her time. If you really think it's going to be too much, she'll come to that realization quickly, on her own. Then you can swoop in and get the ball rolling."

I consider this. I don't love it, but given how stubborn Fia is, it might be my only choice.

"Okay," I say slowly, inhaling and exhaling through my nose. "You'll sign in a year, I have your word?"

"You have my word." Danny nods, seriously.

"Thank you... So, will you live there with her when you get out?" I ask.

Danny laughs and shakes his head. "Yes, but only until I get on my feet. I want to help her any way I can. *But* I won't coddle her."

This gets a laugh out of me, and my shoulders relax. "Ha-ha. Have you ever done that?"

"Nah, I was a shitty brother. I own that."

I want to shrug and forgive him, but Danny holds up his palm, stopping me. We never had the twin telepathy thing that I always hear and am quite frankly jealous of, but he does seem to know how I feel right now.

"I actually should thank you."

I pause, holding my breath. "Thank me?"

"Yeah...you took care of us. And look, you still are," he says, and I blush. "Even though we were the same age, you assumed the role of caretaker. Nan did everything she could for us, but Fia's told me everything, you know? You never let her slip through the cracks all these years."

I expel a humorless laugh. "I'm no saint, Danny." I swipe at a tear I refuse to let fall. "I abandoned you...and Jesse. I didn't tell Nan how bad your drug problem was. And now Fia's pregnant and alone. I've failed everyone."

Danny reaches out, grabbing my hand, and it jolts my whole body.

"Nope, I'm not letting you say that shit." He releases my hand as a guard eyes us. "First, even if Nan knew the severity of the drugs, nothing was going to stop me from going down this route. I made my choices, so don't for a moment blame yourself for any of it. And Fia made her choices, too." He shakes his head, leaning closer to me, and I wish so badly we were at home on the sofa talking. This feels like too open of a space to let your heart out, but it's all we have. And I robbed him of it for so long because I was too scared. "Penny, you can't fix this family. All you can do is be there for us. You're doing that."

He smiles, but I pull at my sweater sleeves, flipping the paperwork upside down on the table, not wanting to look at the weight of it.

"Thank you... I just...I don't know how that explains Jesse." I sniffle and know I'm opening a floodgate. The truth has to come out, and there's no stopping it. I'm going to tell him what Jesse and I really were. I know it could hurt him, but I can't live with this secret anymore.

"What are you talking about?" Danny asks, and I crinkle the corner of the paper in my hand, too scared to look my brother in the eye.

"I need to tell you something about Jesse and me, and I know it might change everything, but you deserve the truth," I reply, glancing up with pause, but he's waiting patiently. "Jesse and I were dating from the time we were sixteen...until you two got arrested..."

My stomach goes stiff as I wait for a reaction, but Danny just crooks a smile.

"That bastard! I knew it." He laughs, and everything in me stirs in confusion. "I was right all along."

"You knew?" I choke out.

"I didn't know for sure, but I had my hunches. I mean you two were so close...neither of you dated anyone else, and he still gets worked up when he talks about you now."

"Wait... So, you don't hate me?" I ask with caution.

"Of course not."

"You know I couldn't tell anyone..." I start, and he nods.

"You were protecting him." Danny scrubs his stubbled jaw and catches my eye. "You really loved him, didn't you?"

I nod, eyes blurring. "I don't think I ever stopped loving him. But he chose to go to that party and get involved in that shit after he promised he wouldn't. Maybe I shouldn't be so angry about it, but we had a whole future planned, and that *one* reckless night changed everything."

Danny's forehead is wrinkled in deep thought, his eyes stay steady on mine. "Penny...he wasn't in prison because he chose something over you, or did drugs, or whatever you believe. If anything...his arrest is entirely my fault."

Blood rushes through my ears as my breath gets lodged in my chest. "What do you mean?" I stutter.

"I thought you knew by now," Danny replies breathily as I sit frozen in my chair. "Jesse came to the party because someone texted him and told him I needed help. He came there to save my ass."

My stomach drops, and it feels like the lights around me dim. "What about the possession charges?" I ask with a dry mouth.

"The drugs were mine—all of them." Danny taps his fingers on the plastic table. "Jesse told the cops half of it was his, just so I wouldn't get slammed harder. He said I saved his life, now he was paying me back. And he begged me not to tell you, didn't want you to hate me. I'm so sorry, Penny...."

I slap a palm to my mouth and lean back, unable to look at my brother. My throat tightens like a hand is wrapped around the column of my neck.

Jesse went to the party to save my brother.

He wasn't the villain.

Jesse was the hero.

"I don't understand... Why didn't he tell me?" I whisper.

Danny looks down and shakes his head. And for the first time since I arrived, I see how this place has worn him down. "You'll have to ask him that yourself."

Tears burn at the back of my throat, and my whole body shakes.

"He loves you, I hope you at least know that," Danny says softly.

"Five minutes left." The guard's loud voice startles me.

I grip the cold, hard plastic of my seat as my heart bounces in my chest. That was thirty minutes? I need more time.

"I don't know where to go from here. With him, with you," I admit, panic-stricken.

Danny shrugs, simply. "You go talk to him, about the truth. And you and me? We do this. You answer my calls. You tell me about your life—*your* life, not just updates about Fia."

I nod, rattled. "Danny," I say, and he snaps his head up at my voice. "I want you to know I don't hate you."

His eyes well for a split second, and he bites his lip, throat bobbing with a hard swallow.

We exchange a knowing look and both stand. I throw my arms around his shoulders, quickly squeezing him, even though we aren't supposed to.

Pulling away nearly kills me.

He starts to shuffle away when I call after him. "Hey... have a merry Christmas."

He turns, flashing his boyish crooked smile. "Merry Christmas... and Pen?"

"Yeah?"

"Don't wait ten more years to forgive him. Okay?" He smiles softly at me.

"I won't." I wave. "I'll see you soon, Danny. I promise."

37

Jesse

THEN

Age 18, August after Graduation

The music from the beat-up Honda Civic is so loud that my chest vibrates. If they don't drive away soon, someone on this street's going to call the cops. This is the nice part of town.

"You want to stop being pussy whipped and get in the fucking car, Rivers?" Sean asks, a cloud of smoke hanging around him inside the car.

"Dude, that's my sister. That's disgusting." Danny punches Sean in the shoulder, but then he stares up at me with red eyes, awaiting my answer.

"Fuck off." I pointedly aim my narrowed gaze at Sean. "And no. I'm good." I salute them both, grinding my jaw, as Danny flashes a peace sign.

"Alright, bro, if you change your mind, we'll be at Kel's. Just hit me up."

Danny barely finishes his sentence before the car peels off, puffs of black smoke sputtering from the exhaust before it disappears around the next corner.

The residential street is quiet again, besides the buzz of overhead power lines. My attention is drawn back to the house at the sound of the front door opening. Penny steps out in a short pink-and-blue sundress and bare feet—she looks like an ocean sunset. She's pure sunshine, and I can't help but stare.

Penny skips down the porch steps and sits, balancing a soda can in her hand. I shake my head, dropping next to her and stretching my legs out in front of me.

She holds the can up, offering me a sip. "You didn't want to go to *the* party of the summer? Half the graduating class will be there." She leans into me, her tanned bare shoulder bumping mine.

I laugh, locking eyes with hers. "Nothing says 'I'm cool' like a guy who graduated three years ago throwing a party for high schoolers."

There are three reasons I would never go to this party. First, the house is on the same block as my dad's house. Nothing could make me want to go to that part of town again.

Second, Danny and our "friends" will just be doing drugs the whole time and acting like I'm a loser for refusing. Not so much Danny, he's never pressured me. He knows why I don't even want to try weed. But the people he hangs with are total shit.

The third reason is because if I went, Penny would want to come, and then the whole night I'd be worrying and watching every asshole who comes within ten feet of her.

Luckily, we agreed to have a movie night in.

"Both Nan and Fia are already asleep." Penny winks at me before lowering the blinds in the living room, turning on the table lamp and bouncing onto the sofa excitedly.

I'll finally get to kiss her in peace. The Hansons sleep like rocks, and if anyone does wake up and comes down the steps, there's plenty of warning in this old house—everything creaks and squeaks.

"What do you want to watch?" I ask, and Penny lies back, resting her head on my lap as she looks up at me. I play with her fanned-out hair while she coyly smiles at me, humming like she is thinking of choices, but I already know what the answer is.

She smiles big, reading my mind.

"Again?" I groan, but truthfully, I don't really care. We always put something on and end up talking the whole time anyway. Or kissing. And tonight, I want to kiss Penny all over.

She sits up and plants a quick peck on my cheek, and I get a whiff of her strawberry lip gloss.

"Okay, put it on, I'll make popcorn," I tell her, never able to say no to that face.

We turn off all the lights until it's just the glow from the TV lighting the downstairs. Penny changed into her pajamas—a large t-shirt I think she stole from me—and now sits happily, hogging the colossal bowl of popcorn.

I don't even like popcorn, I just make it for her.

"I get why she stays, you know true love and all, but I mean, I could *never* live in a small town like that. I can't wait to have a city apartment with a view," she says wistfully, stuffing more popcorn into her mouth. I smile and nod, my arm dangling over her shoulder.

Sweet Home Alabama plays on the TV for the third time this summer, I swear. "A classic," both Penny and Nan claim.

With my arm around her and a blanket draped over our laps, I draw her back into my chest, and she leans her head on my shoulder.

It's my favorite fucking feeling in the world.

"Hey... I talked to the guy at the garage today," I start, and Penny pauses the movie, turning to look up at me. "He said he can bring me on for twenty-five hours a week. So that's something, right?"

I never really thought about what I wanted to do post-high school. Up until I moved in here, my future wasn't on my mind. I was just trying to survive. But I've always been into cars, so Penny suggested I work in a garage and see if I want to get into mechanics. It's a solid idea, and I'm actually starting to get excited about it.

Penny squeals and hugs my neck. "Babe, that's awesome!"

I smile softly at her.

"I'm still bummed that I have to live on campus for two years, but *you'll* have an apartment and we can finally have real sleepovers." She slides her hand over my crotch quickly, torturing me.

Penny feels guilty that she got a full ride to UNC and I have to live a bit out of town in a rented room, but I'm so proud of her. She was always going to go places. I'm just happy she wants me to come along for the ride.

"Don't be bummed, you'll have classes and I'll have work, but our free time will be *ours*. It's all going to work out," I reassure her with a kiss.

"One more week! I can hardly believe it." She does a little excited dance and grabs my face until I'm looking at her, her expression growing serious. "You know how much I love you, Jesse Rivers, right?"

I laugh. "I think I do. But I love you more. Now and always."

"Don't get mushy, or I'll tell everyone you're secretly a romantic." She kisses me hard, smooshing our noses together. I love when Penny is like this. Silly, uninhibited, just completely herself.

I wasn't raised to know what a healthy or normal relationship looks like. I don't always know how to communicate with Penny. I don't have the means to do everything I want for her. But she doesn't seem to care, always telling me I'm enough. I know all she wants is to get out of this town, to fulfill her dreams, and for us to be together through it all.

Penny presses play on the movie again, and her fingers lace through mine. As the end nears, I trace the lines on her palms and she begins to grow sleepy, her head heavy on my shoulder.

"Jesse?" She glances up at me, eyes tired but peaceful.

"What's up?"

"Promise you'll never leave me?"

I lower my brows and pause to take in her face. I trace the freckles across her nose that only come out in the summer. Her soft lips that pull into the most beautiful smile. Her eyes with flecks of gold, like honey. And beneath it all is a heart she so freely gives to everyone. Penny takes care of everyone. She seems older than any other girl our age, but then again, I know a thing or two about growing up fast. If you don't, you won't survive.

"Why would you think I'd leave you?" I squeeze her hand.

She bites her lip, eyes falling to her lap. "A lot is going to change soon, new town, new school, all that. I can handle change, but I don't want anything to change between *us*. You're everything to me. I can't do this without you, Jesse."

Penny doesn't talk about it, but I know her parents leaving in the middle of the night really fucked her and Danny up. They just show it in different ways. Penny needs to be reminded a lot that I'm not going anywhere. And that's the truth. I'm not.

I lean down until our foreheads are touching, my lips an inch from hers. "I can promise you, Penelope Hanson, we're going to be together no matter what."

She nods, a single tear quickly swept away, and I kiss her lips.

Less than fifteen minutes later, she's sound asleep on my shoulder. I quietly move the popcorn bowl from beside her and slowly stand to go to the bathroom. Penny slumps down, nuzzling into the tan sofa, so I pull the blanket over her. Even if it's still 90 degrees outside at midnight, she's always chilly.

My phone buzzes in my pocket as I make my way down the dark hallway to the powder room.

It's Tyler, one of Danny's friends. Someone he smokes with a lot.

Tyler: Dude I don't know where you are, but you need to come to Kels RIGHT NOW. Danny is majorly fucked up.

I exhale, annoyed. It's midnight, and he's seriously telling me now?

Jesse: Did he fight someone?

Tyler: Nah man...he is tweaking hard. He's not acting right...something is wrong.

Jesse: What happened to Sean?

Sean was supposed to drive him home, even though we both knew that was a horrible idea.

Tyler: He took whatever Danny was selling and passed out like an hour ago. It's fucked up here.

Fuck.

I grit my teeth and bang my fist against the door frame. Danny's gotten himself into plenty of shitty situations this past year, but he's always managed to get himself home.

I slip my phone in my pocket and walk swiftly to the back door, pausing next to the sofa. I know exactly what I'm about to walk into, these parties are notorious. But I know if I were in Danny's shoes, he'd drop everything to come get me. As weird as things have gotten between us lately, he's my brother for life. I can't leave him hanging.

Penny is still curled up, looking peaceful. She had a long day at work and made everyone dinner. She needs to sleep, so I decide not to wake her.

She'll just panic and want to come, probably making things worse. And there's no way I'm letting Penny go into that house. She doesn't know how wild these parties are. It's not safe.

She'll be asleep like this for a while, so I kiss her forehead softly.

"Be back soon. Wish me luck," I whisper, then curse Danny for being an idiot.

And silently pray he's actually okay.

I grab Penny's car keys and hope no one wakes up when I start the engine. I have no idea how I'm going to drag his ass out of there, but I do know that tomorrow I'm going to remind him how much he owes me.

Looks like I'm attending this party after all.

Sweat drips down my neck as I crank the windows of this old car down all the way. I drive as fast as I can, but there are cars lining the street a block away from the party and the heat is making me more agitated than usual. There's a random open spot, so I parallel park Penny's car sloppily, knowing damn well this isn't a legal spot. As I slam the car door shut, I don't look up at my father's house across the street.

I don't need to look to know there's nothing but rotting white clapboard and a yard that's never seen a lawn mower.

The absolute shit show comes to life before me as I sweatily jog down the street, pushing my hair back off my forehead, cursing under my breath. Colored lights flicker from every open window of the house like this is a full-on rave. It's not like I haven't seen this all before; there's been rowdy house parties on this street since my dad moved us here.

Pausing at the edge of the yard, I scan the yard for Danny or Tyler, but I don't see them. A can of beer rolls down the slanted front yard before hitting my foot, and a girl I recognize from school comes running after it, falling to her knees as she grabs it, holding it up like a trophy. Someone cheers from the front porch, and I quickly peel my eyes away, checking my phone for messages, but none have come through.

If Danny's inside chugging beer, I'm going to beat him up first... then drag his ass home.

Weaving my way through the crowd on the steps, I keep my head down, though it's hard to be 6'4" and not get noticed.

Everyone looks stoned, barely noticing me, though. Two kegs are tapped in the living room, and someone is guzzling beer straight from the hose.

The music is so loud I can't hear myself think, the bass rattling the bones in my chest. Some girl falls on me, and I gently nudge her back upright into her friend and keep moving.

Where the hell is Danny?

I see the staircase in the corner of the living room and shove my way through the sea of people reeking of weed and booze.

My pulse quickens as I climb the steps. But at the top, a fight breaks out, and I'm caught in between two guys who were on the varsity football team. It's a blur of arms and swinging fists, and someone knocks into my chest, hard. I gasp for air, purposely flattening myself along the wall, sliding down the narrow hallway.

They tumble past, thudding down the stairs.

"Oh my god, Jesse!" A girl from school claws at my shirt, and I take her by the shoulder, pivoting around her gently.

That's it, Danny is so dead when I see him.

And just as I feel a force behind me, and get knocked to the ground, I see him in the room at the end of the hallway.

The bathroom.

Slumped against the yellow tub.

Tyler's standing there, too. He catches my eyes, fear and relief flooding his ghastly face. "Dude, thank fuck you're here. I don't know what happened."

I stand and rush into the bathroom, shutting the door behind me, locking it. I squat down in the tight space between Tyler and Danny. This bathroom has carpet that looks like mud and smells worse.

"Danny, can you hear me?" I grip his shoulders roughly.

With barely the push of a finger, he leans back against the wall, amber eyes rolling up to mine.

"Jesse...you came..." His speech is slurred, but he's with it enough to know I'm here.

I glance up at Tyler. His eyes go wide, and he shrugs, twitching his foot back and forth.

"What did he take?" Between the music blaring, people scream-talking in every corner of this house, and my pounding heart, I have to yell to be heard.

"I don't know." He rubs the back of his neck. "He rolled a joint when we got here, but I don't think he even drank. Sean and him took a tablet together, maybe powder, I don't know, man."

"Where's Sean?" I stand. I'm going to beat his ass.

"I told you, he passed out in a bedroom like an hour ago. He was more fucked up than Danny."

Grunting, I pull on my hair, feeling like the peeling walls are closing in on me. I resist the urge to punch a hole in one of them. This is worse than I thought.

"Whatever everyone took was probably laced," I shout out of pure frustration.

Tyler mumbles something, then leaves the bathroom in a flash. I shut and lock the door again. I did not sign up to be a babysitter tonight.

"We're going home. Can you stand?" I ask, staring at Danny.

His chin drops to his chest, like his head is too heavy to hold up, and he lets out an empty laugh. "Dude, I can't even *feel* my legs."

Fuck! I bang on the wall so hard it dents.

Turning on the sink, I try to get the water cold, but it's no use, it's nearly 100 degrees outside. Inside, it feels hotter. Doesn't matter, I cup as much water in my hands as I can and splash Danny in the face.

I have to wake him up enough to get him out of here. I'm not sticking around to see how much worse this night gets.

"Is Penny here?" he mumbles, and my heart sinks. I have to get back before she wakes up.

I go to grab my phone, making sure Penny hasn't texted, but my pockets are empty. Against my better judgment, I drop to my knees searching the ground. "Shit, I lost my phone."

"It's fine, man."

"No, it's not," I spit back, losing my cool.

Danny peers up at me, his head lolling back against the wall, legs bent in front of him. He's wedged between the wall and the toilet like a sick child.

"I didn't bring your sister," I snap. "I'd never let her be caught dead in a place like *this*."

"Thank God." To my surprise, Danny smiles at me, his eyes half closed. "Penny's too good for this shit anyway. She's got a future."

I reel in my anger momentarily, squatting down next to my best friend. The one who talked to me when I was the shy new kid, the one who brought me into his house, literally made me his brother. The one who introduced me to his twin sister. I have her because of him.

"The fuck you talking about? You've got a future, too."

"Nah..." He closes his eyes. "She's the smart one." He shrugs, and my heart sinks. "I was always going to end up like this."

I bite my lip, shaking my head. "You're wrong." I grit my teeth. "Now shut up, because we're going home. Even if I have to drag your dumb ass through this house."

"Hey." Danny looks up, hooking his finger to call me close. He looks so pale. "Don't tell my sister how fucked up I am...okay? It'll break her heart..." he says before his eyes fully close.

I shake him, and he mumbles something.

Fuck fuck fuck. Danny's a lot smaller than me, but I can't carry him through this crowded house without a battle.

Someone bangs on the door just as I consider the options. "Cops!"

Several people scream, and all the blood rushes from my head.

"Motherfucker!" I scream, glancing at my friend. I can't leave him here like this.

Chaos ensues outside the bathroom, so I jump on the tub ledge to glance out the tiny window overlooking the backyard. People are drunkenly scattering as blue strobes light up the street. The music cuts abruptly downstairs.

I'm pretty sure almost everyone in this house is underage.

And on drugs.

I jump back down to Danny and slap his face, hard. His eyelids pop open.

"The police are here, and we have two minutes to get the fuck out," I shout, my limbs buzzing with fear.

He's in a daze, but he nods, and with every bit of adrenaline, I pull his arm around my shoulder and boost him up until we're both standing.

"Wait, wait," he slurs and nods back toward the tub. "Grab my backpack. My money and shit is in it."

Without thinking, I lean back and sling one strap of his backpack around my shoulder. I unlock the door and pull him into the hallway. Stern voices sound from downstairs.

"We're going to have to hide."

I shove the bedroom door open to the right of us and drag Danny in.

There's a huge bed in the corner of the room, and Sean's passed out face down. Next to him is a closet. Unless I want to throw myself and Danny out a second-story window, we're about to hide in a fucking closet.

But before I get to the doors, a blinding stream of light hits my back, and time stops.

"Freeze!" A commanding voice fills the room. "Put your hands up and turn around slowly."

"Danny, you have to stand on your own," I grit out between my teeth.

Danny doesn't say anything.

I spin slowly, my hands up, and he stays standing beside me, swaying but sobering up quickly.

I look straight into the eyes of the police officer, but a buzzing glow pulls my attention to the floor right behind them.

It's my phone, and it's ringing.

Penny's face lights up the screen.

She's calling me, and I can't answer.

My heart splits in two, bleeding out, and everything after that doesn't matter.

38

Penny

NOW

Breathing in the crisp winter air, I stare at the swaying pine trees as I walk toward my car.

Am I more like them now?

The woman I was when I entered the prison is miles away. She's a version of me I will never get to be again, not after learning the truth. But maybe that's how it's meant to be.

I feel like I've slipped into a parallel world—one where nothing makes sense, where my past isn't haunting me but suffocating me.

And I want to blame Nan for not telling me, given that she even knew the whole truth. But I'll never get that answer from her, I know that.

I reopened two decade-old wounds I kept buried, and logically, I know that's going to take time to heal, to process, but patience is a language I've never spoken fluently.

My heart hammers, and I fumble for the key in my pocket and lean against my baby-blue car.

All I can think about is all those years I let the phone ring, skipped visits with Fia and Nan because I thought I was protecting myself. Now I'm not sure I was.

A swell of sobs catches in my throat, and I grip the cold metal of my car door. I clamp my eyes shut, fighting the tears. There's no way I can drive like this.

Over my shoulder, I glance at the building where Danny's kept, and my heart pulls in my chest. I feel raw. Flayed open and numb at the same time.

"We go from here."

That's what he said. But where is *here*?

I can't plan this. I can't lay out a perfect schedule of healing, of how Danny is going to reintegrate into our mess. I can't map out what happens when Fia's baby arrives, or when Jesse decides to stay, or when I have to pack up and return to the life I left on pause.

I don't know what any of it means.

I sit in the car, oscillating between being completely numb and feeling too much, but I reach for my purse in the glovebox, knowing I can't sit here all evening.

Three missed calls from Jesse light up my screen. And a text.

Jesse: Call me ASAP

My heart plummets, and my fingers fumble as I attempt to dial him back. It takes three tries before the call connects. I start the car, click my buckle, and count my ragged breaths.

Every worst-case scenario flashes before my eyes.

"Pick up, Jesse, come on." My palm presses into the steering wheel as I peel out of the lot. On the final ring, he answers—winded, like he just sprinted to the phone.

"Jesse, what's going on?" My voice cracks as the sky opens and rain starts to fall, sharp and cold.

"Penny, are you driving?"

His question knocks me off balance. "Yes, of course, I am! And you're scaring me. Is Fia okay?" Dread pools in my stomach. Tank? *Oh god, what if something happened to precious Tank?*

"First, slow down. And I mean the car, too." I hate how calm his voice suddenly is.

I glance at the speedometer and release my lead foot from the pedal. He knows me too well.

There are muffled voices in the background.

"Listen, I'm at Coastal Way Hospital, in the emergency room."

I go to open my mouth, but nothing comes out.

"I came home about thirty minutes ago and found Fia passed out in the kitchen. She regained consciousness in the ambulance and is back with the doctor now."

The car suddenly feels too small, the air thick and unbreathable. The pine trees blur past, enclosing me in a tunnel of green.

"Penny, talk to me," Jesse says, sharp and grounded.

"What... Is she..." I can't form a coherent thought. I shouldn't have left, I should've stayed home. She was looking pale after breakfast, she didn't even touch her french toast. I should have rescheduled with Danny.

Oh my god. The baby.

"Breathe, Penny. I'm here," he says again.

I try, but the sound of my own breathing is jagged, desperate.

Jesse keeps talking. "She's going to be okay. Do you hear me, Penny?"

"You don't know that." My chest is a fist closing tighter by the second.

I can't speak. Tears stream down my cheeks, tracing the same path as the rain sliding across the windshield.

"I *do* know it. Because Fia is just like you. She's a fighter."

I nod instinctively, forgetting he can't see me.

39

Jesse

NOW

I've gotten up to stretch my legs no less than twenty times since they took Fia back an hour ago. In the bathroom, I splash my face with water, purple circles forming under my green eyes. My stubble has grown in, and I feel as crap as I look, but Penny is going to be here any moment, and I have to hold it together for her.

When I told her I knew Fia was going to be fine, I actually meant it. She *is* strong as hell. But that doesn't erase the worry lingering in every corner of my mind.

Just an hour ago, I was crawling into the back of the ambulance with the EMTs, eyes glued to Fia. Her red hair was coming out of her ponytail, wrapping around her face, and it felt like I failed her.

Big brothers are supposed to protect, right?

"What's going on?" I asked the medic twice, trying to make my body small and stay out of the way as they administered a shot.

Blood sugar's dangerously low is all I heard, and I stared helplessly at Fia's pale face as she stirred, near tears of relief when her eyes fluttered open. She was groggy, but there was barely time to explain anything before they rushed her into the ER.

I exit the bathroom in no less of a daze and decide on a second cup of shitty coffee.

As I'm waiting at the vending machine to fill my small paper cup, emptying granola bar wrappers from my pockets—my dinner—a small blonde tornado flies by. The machine finishes sputtering out the hot brown coffee just in time for me to spin around and call out to her.

Black streaks stain Penny's face as she clutches the counter at reception, her pink sweater bright in this beige waiting room. The small woman at the counter meets her with an apathetic expression. Penny's chest heaves up and down.

I glance at my watch. There's no way she got here this quickly without doing a hundred.

"My sister is here...Fia Hanson...I need to see her," she stutters out, and the woman starts rifling through papers, but I swoop in, resting a hand on Penny's shoulder.

She jolts but looks up, and her face scrunches. Penny throws her arms around my shoulders, leaning all of her weight on me.

I pull her into my chest and nod at the receptionist.

"Let's sit..." I murmur into her hair, holding her hand and leading the way to the green vinyl chairs. My limbs are restless, but I'm afraid that if I don't get her to sit, she will run laps around this place, or bust the doors down to locate her sister herself.

"Sit, Penny," I instruct, and she does. I hand her my black coffee, and she takes a sip, eyes glazed over. She drinks half the cup before breathing.

She hates black coffee—that's how I gauge her level of distress.

I'm almost afraid to ask if her car made it here in one piece. Pretty sure there's a chance that if I went outside right now, it'd be parked on the sidewalk.

Chaos stirs around us, but I focus on her, holding her hand in my lap.

"We'll find something out any minute," I whisper, and it's not a lie, but a hope.

She leans on me as I wrap my arm around her, feeling the softness of her sweater, of her hair. I hate seeing her red-rimmed eyes.

She grips the white cup, gulping the remaining coffee, and turns to me, sniffling. "Tell me everything, from the beginning."

Exhaling, I recap what happened, leaving my fears and dramatics out of it. Just facts. "I came home from the shelter, walked in, and Fia was lying on the floor next to the kitchen sink. She was on her side, she didn't land on her stomach, not that I could tell."

Penny nods, and I don't even think she notices her fingers digging into my arm.

"Tank was lying next to her, pawing her. He knew something was wrong." I scrub my jaw, my five o'clock shadow pricking my palm. "She texted me a few minutes prior, telling me she was going to take him for a walk, so she wasn't out long."

Penny isn't talking, so I squeeze her hand.

"The medic said she had a small cut on the back of her head, might've hit it on the counter. She was breathing, so I didn't move her, in case of a neck injury. Paramedics were there less than five minutes later. I rode in the ambulance with her, and they gave her a glucagon shot for low blood sugar, and she was becoming alert when we got here. They rushed her back immediately."

Penny drops her face into her hands. "I can't lose another sibling." She sobs into her hands, and I pull her in tighter.

Just then, the doors open and out walks a nurse, searching the faces until she sees me. She nods, and I nudge Penny.

Penny shoots up next to me as my chest constricts, trying to read the nurse's face before she speaks.

"Is she awake?" I ask.

"Yes, she is awake." She offers a tired smile, and Penny sighs deeply. "But right now, only family can come back."

"We're both family," Penny replies hastily, already three steps ahead. She's ready to run down the hall, so I reach for her hand as the nurse motions us back through the door.

"Is she okay? What's happening?" Penny starts talking a hundred miles a minute.

The nurse pauses outside the room, glancing down at her clipboard momentarily.

"Your sister's blood sugar dropped dangerously low. It appears she passed out from a hypoglycemic episode, which can be very serious yet not uncommon in the second trimester. We administered a glucose shot, she is on an IV drip for hydration, and she needed a few stitches in her head."

Penny nods, tears rolling down her face. She wipes them quickly. It takes everything in me not to wrap my arms around her.

The nurse looks at me. "They said you found her within minutes. She's very lucky for that."

Penny gazes up at me, eyes welling, and the nurse slides the clipboard into the pocket outside the door and pauses.

"She'll need to monitor her sugar levels for the remainder of her pregnancy. And we'd like to keep her overnight for observation, to ensure the baby is okay before discharge."

We both nod, Penny still speechless.

"Thank you. May we?" I ask, and the nurse leads us into the room.

"Your family is here," she says more brightly to Fia as Penny rushes to her side.

"Oh my god, Fia, you scared the living hell out of me!" She throws her arms around her little sister, and Fia cracks a tired smile.

She's leaning back in the bed in a blue gown, with a beeping monitor and an IV drip next to her. Her hair is messy, from the stitches, I'm guessing, but her eyes shine when she sees us.

"Hey, kid. Glad you're okay." I walk to her other side.

Penny's hands are cradling her sister's face. "You need to eat. I'm not leaving your side; you're going to eat every ten minutes. You cannot scare me like this." She kisses her head.

"I promise you, I will. I'm sorry for freaking everyone out," Fia apologizes, and I shake my head, nudging her arm.

"Don't apologize. We're just glad you're okay, Fi. I think you scared Tank more than anything." I rest my hands in my pockets, shrugging.

Her head whips my way. "Oh my gosh, the poor baby, is he okay?"

"He will be once you're home." I smile at her, my chest tight.

Fia yawns, reaching for the water cup on her side table.

Penny won't take her eyes off her sister, and I can't take my eyes off Penny.

As I watch her stand here, selflessly giving everything she has to her sister, all I see is the Penny I fell in love with, the Penny she still is. The one who's generous and kind, the one who holds everyone else up. The one who forces you to be the best version of yourself.

She doesn't see it; how lucky we all are just to have her in our lives.

After ten minutes of fluffing Fia's pillows and triple-checking all the papers the doctor left, Penny glances at me, then back at her sister, whose eyes are barely staying open.

"We should probably let you rest, huh?" Penny asks.

"Yeah, I'm exhausted." Fia rouses, flashing a tiny smirk. "Just don't forget to pick me up tomorrow."

"I'll be back first thing. You sure you don't want me to sleep here? I can drop Jesse off and be back in thirty minutes. I just—"

Fia reaches for her sister's arm. "Penny, please go home. I'll be okay."

She slowly reaches for her purse on the chair next to me.

"Hey, how was Danny?" Fia asks, her breathing shallow as she fights to stay awake.

Penny's eyes go wide, and she turns away from her sister. "Oh, fine, it was good." She waves, avoiding eye contact with both me and Fia. "We'll talk later. Get rest and call me if you need anything, okay? Anything at all, I'm here. I'll see you at 7 a.m. sharp, okay?"

"Okay." Fia nods, and we both take turns hugging her goodbye for the night.

"Thanks for saving my life. You're a hero, Jesse," she whispers to me.

I shake my head. "Just the right place, right time. Love you, kid." I ruffle her hair, and Penny stares at me blankly.

I have a feeling we have a lot to talk about, but it will have to wait till we're home.

"Get some rest." I place a hand on Penny's back, gently guiding her out of the room and down the corridor. People walk by us, busy with their own purposes, but my eyes stay on the back of her head.

She doesn't walk in a straight line, digging in her purse, clearly shaken, and I wish I could reach out and steady her, tell her to breathe. But something stops me.

Something happened at the prison, I can feel it in my bones. And I need her to talk to me about it, because I can handle a lot, but being shut out by Penny is something I don't think I can live with.

Not again.

40

Penny

NOW

The sun is setting in the evening sky as we leave the hospital in silence. We don't speak during the ten-minute drive home—music plays low through the speakers, and I stare at the lines on the road, grateful Jesse remains quiet.

As we pull in the driveway, my stomach rumbles, and I clutch it. My last meal was brunch, but I can't even think about making food right now.

I'm stuck in a whirlwind of fuckery.

One moment, I'm flooded with relief that Fia's okay, and the next, I'm back in that visitation room hearing Danny spill the truth. Then I remember how Jesse held me in the ER waiting room. It's too much.

"You're a good boy, you know that?" I squat down, scratching Tank's ears as we silently go inside. He was waiting just on the other side of the back door.

Jesse watches me with his dog, and it takes everything in me to stand and face him. I'm a shell right now, and I desperately want to scrub this day off me.

My stomach gurgles in protest, my head starting to get a dull ache.

"Hey, can we talk a moment?" Jesse breaks the silence, and I look away from his gaze.

I'm not ready to tell him I know everything. I'm not ready to tell him how wrong I was, how *fucked up* everything that happened was.

Because after we have that conversation, everything is going to change between us. Everything is going to change within myself.

There's going to be an after.

And I haven't decided what that means yet for us.

Whatever semblance of *us* there is.

"Can it wait?" I exhale, and he bites his lip but nods. "I desperately need a bath and to get food."

Jesse steps up, his brow lowered, but when his hand swoops under my chin, lifting my face to his, my heart does that little flutter thing it does every time he touches me. Without fail.

"Go take a bath, and *I'll* figure out dinner." His voice is smooth and strong.

Flutter.

"I can do both," I insist, but he grabs my waist, spinning me toward the staircase, and pats my ass.

"Yeah, see, that wasn't a suggestion. It was a command."

I turn with my mouth wide open, but his jaw is tight, his eyes locked on mine.

"Go. Now," he instructs, and I shut my mouth, silently heading upstairs toward the bathroom. I can't recall a time when someone told me "I got this" and I got to go relax.

The stress of the hospital slowly melts off my shoulders as I plug the drain of the clawfoot tub and start the hot water. Steam fills the small, tiled bathroom immediately, and I shove my clothes into a pile in the corner of the room.

I rummage through the bathroom cupboard and find the bubble bath soak packets I sent Fia for her birthday.

There's no point in pulling up my hair; I want every inch of me to be submerged in the scalding hot water. For just a few minutes,

I want to feel like I'm ten feet underwater, far, far away from this reality.

Only the dim vanity light remains, casting the bathroom in a golden glow from the retro fixture. I prefer my candlelit bathroom at home, but I *need* this.

Gripping the sides of the tub, I settle into the frothy, milky bubbles. My long hair floats on the surface, and when I lean my head back, I expect them to come, the tears. The ones I couldn't yield off all day. Now I feel safe enough to let them out, and they're trapped in my throat.

I close my eyes and try to focus on the smell of citrus and eucalyptus.

But Danny's words intrude my thoughts, and I snap my eyes open again.

He loves you, you know that, right?

"If he loved me, why didn't he tell me the truth?" I whisper to myself, mindlessly rubbing the oily bubbles into my slick skin.

If he did, would I have listened? Would it have changed everything?

I swallow and clear my throat, like that will ward off intrusive thoughts.

I don't *want* to answer those questions.

But then my heart jumps in my chest, and I jerk up. The water sloshes around me as the hinges of the bathroom door squeak.

"Tank, you can't come in here," I whisper grumpily. This old house needs all new doors—ones that latch—because Tank learned that all he has to do is nudge them with his nose and they'll open.

But it's Jesse who steps in, taking up half the bathroom with his frame. His eyes find mine, and I freeze.

The water is creamy white, hiding most of me, but the way he looks at me makes me feel like I'm standing here naked, dripping wet in front of him.

He doesn't wait for my allowance or dismissal—and I'm not entirely sure which one I'd give him—before he shuts the door behind him and steps toward the tub, kneeling down on the floor next to it. Even on his knees, I have to look up to him.

"What are you doing here?" I ask him, but he doesn't answer.

Jesse leans forward, cupping the back of my neck, capturing my mouth with his. It's delicious and soft, and when he pulls away, I blurt out the words I can't hold in any longer.

"He told me, Jesse... Danny told me." It comes out choked, and my eyes burn as they gaze up at him. "Why didn't you tell me the truth about that night?"

His eyes grow dark and pained. He drops his hands to the side of the tub. "I thought it was the right choice..."

I shake my head. "You left me... And for ten years you let me believe that you chose everything else over me." A sob rips through me and I sit up, my chest now exposed, and I half expect to look down and see my heart bleeding. That's what it feels like to look into Jesse Rivers's eyes and tell him the truth.

That he broke my heart, and it's never quite healed.

"We were supposed to do this together," I say louder, anger and hurt on my tongue.

He drops his head slightly, dark locks falling over his forehead. I place my hand over his, gripping it hard, using him as my anchor.

"Jesse, you broke my heart." My vision blurs as I stare at him.

"Penny..." He cocks his head back, saying my name like it hurts him. "I know I did. I know I left you." He pauses, and my breathing shallows.

"Three years had passed when I was released... I stayed away, because I didn't want to ruin *your* future." His voice cracks, guilt carved into every line on his face.

He lets out a soft laugh, almost bitter. "Look at you." There's a ghost of a smile on his lips. "You did it, baby. The dream school, you made something of yourself. I was just a lucky guy who got to be in your orbit for a bit."

"Don't say that." I shake my head, squeezing his forearm. "Do not say that. Please." His haunted green eyes meet mine. "You deserved *everything*, too. I believed in you," I say with as much conviction as I can, as my voice wavers.

"It's okay..." he murmurs, leaning toward me. "I took the pain and moved on. I loved you enough to let you go."

"Then why didn't you come looking for me?" The question cuts through the air, sharp and aching. He could ask me the same question.

Jesse lets out a hollow laugh. "The day I got out, I *wanted* to find you. God, how I wanted to run to you, Penny." He pauses. "Nan picked me up, and the whole car ride home, she talked about *you*. I'll never forget the way she radiated with pride."

The room feels darker, and my chest constricts.

"You were studying abroad, in Paris." He looks at me knowingly. My dream. "I knew then there was only one choice: to let you go. So I moved as far away as I could. I removed temptation, because you weren't mine to hold on to."

A lump as heavy as steel forges in my chest, and I shiver in this steaming hot water.

Every puzzle piece, every moment from the past ten years, suddenly clicks into place. It's like a ripple effect on my heart, smoothing over all the lines and jagged edges until it's whole again. Even if it's messy, even if I want to refuse to understand, I do.

We broke each other in different ways, at different times.

The water collects on my eyelashes, clumping them together as I look up at his tortured face, still focused on me.

Jesse lived in my head as a different guy for a decade.

The villain, the reason I'm jaded.

He was my secret, my scapegoat, the person I couldn't bear to think about, yet couldn't erase from my mind. And now here he is kneeling before me, in my most vulnerable state, and there's only one question left.

"Do you still love me?" I whisper.

He gives me that sad, crooked smile. His green eyes shimmer like rare sea glass. "I never stopped."

I curl my knees to my chest and press my cheek against them, trying to make myself smaller. "What does this mean? I don't know... I don't know what to do now," I say.

It's still and silent in the bathroom, and I tilt my head so I'm looking at him.

"About what?" he asks softly, fingers trailing up my spine. It's gentle, and I shiver under his touch.

"Everything," I breathe.

He waits patiently, strong, unwavering.

"I don't know how to be here for Fia, I don't know how to build a relationship with Danny, I don't know how I'm supposed to go back home in a few days. I don't know how I'm supposed to sit here and pretend that I'm okay with leaving you."

"You don't have to pretend." Jesse's hand finds my neck, gently massaging it. "You take care of everyone else, but who takes care of you?"

I'm unable to give him an answer, but he doesn't wait for one.

He lowers his lips to mine, capturing a soft moan from my mouth.

"Let me take care of you." His voice is velvet against my neck as his supple lips mark me. Calloused hands reach into the water, cupping my wet breasts as he leans me back against the tub.

I cling to him in return, taking, taking, taking. But he keeps giving.

My core clenches as he parts my thighs, slipping a finger inside me.

I inhale the sweet scents still wafting from the hot water and push every worry from my head. Jesse's other hand wraps around the column of my throat, possessive but gentle, while water drips off his corded, inked arms.

"Stop thinking, stop trying to control, just let yourself feel," he demands, biting my neck, licking and sucking down to my hard nipple, drawing it into his mouth as I arch my back into him.

Tears pool in my eyes as he takes away my pain, one touch, one kiss at a time.

His thumb expertly and gently strokes my center, his eyes steady on mine, not letting a single wall form between us.

"Jesse..." I moan as he adds another finger, filling me, kissing me gently, taking his time. I want to pull him in with me, but I lose all will when he smiles against my mouth, strumming me faster, and I tighten around his hooked fingers.

"That's it, good girl."

Fuck.

I grip the sides of the tub as he applies just the right amount of pressure to make me come undone. I roll my hips up into his hand. "Oh my god..."

He holds me while I ride out the wave of ecstasy, running his hand from my tits to my collarbone until he's holding my jaw tightly, forcing me to look at him.

"Jesse Rivers, I never stopped loving you either." I lean my forehead against his, catching my breath.

"Then promise me something," he replies, husky and low, and I look up, still in a dreamy ecstasy. "You have to stop hiding everything that's in there." He lightly jabs a finger to my chest, right over my beating heart. "Even if it scares you, even if you think it's going to hurt me, tell me. You understand?"

I nod, and he kisses me, biting my lip and pulling away quickly.

"Whatever's happening in that mind of yours, I can handle it. Got it, princess?"

It goes against everything I've held true for the last ten years.

Run and don't tell the truth.

Keep things light, keep things fun.
No relationships—once they say they love you, they're out.
And never, *ever* think about Jesse Rivers.
These were the rules I lived by.

But everything *has* changed. I couldn't forget him if I wanted to; it's worthless to try. He's a part of me, and like the ink etched on his ribs, I'm part of him.

41

Jesse

NOW

Dinner arrives in a brown paper bag, because ordering greasy food from an app on my phone seemed like a much better idea than delivering Penny a cold sandwich on a plate.

She comes downstairs as I'm plugging in the Christmas tree—an effort to give this place as much cheer as I could. With all this shit happening, it's almost hard to even fathom that tomorrow is Christmas Eve.

Her hair is blown dry, her face bare, and sweatpants sit low on her hips with a threadbare sweatshirt on top. I don't know if she's ever looked so beautiful.

She lifts her nose and sniffs before her eyes go wide when they land on the fast food bag. "You are my savior! Please tell me you got french fries, too?" She opens the bag, and the smell of burgers fills the kitchen.

"I did." I nod, and she grabs the paper-wrapped food, clutching it to her chest with a grin.

"You remembered?" She pulls my dinner from the bag, too, arranging it next to hers like we're at a restaurant. We slide onto the kitchen island stools, and she pops a salty fry into her mouth.

"How could I forget that?" I tease, and Penny laughs sweetly. "I know you're into health and eat green smoothies that look like seaweed...but I had a hunch that underneath it all was still the six-teen-year-old who craved a bag of fast food on rough days."

Her smile softens, and she tucks her hair behind her ear, taking another bite. "Well, thank you. You're not wrong."

We take a few bites, both ravenously hungry.

"I know you're tired, but I was wondering if you wanted to stay up with me for a bit?" I ask.

Penny turns to me, nodding with her mouth full. "I'd love that. What do you have in mind?"

"I thought we could catch up." I shrug, knowing that sounds trivial given today.

Tank plops down next to me at the same time, waiting for a french fry to drop. Fia has ruined him.

"Catch up?" Penny asks in between bites.

"Yeah, you know, since I haven't seen you in ten years."

She covers her mouth, laughing.

It's a sound that's as beautiful as she looks. I don't even know what we'll talk about; all I know is that her holiday break is coming to an end soon. She has to go back to work, and I don't want to face that. Not yet.

Tonight, Fia's in the hospital and in good hands. There's nothing we can do but show up tomorrow morning with her favorite bagel in tow.

But right now, in this empty house, it's just Penny and me. The walls are down around us, and there's nowhere left to hide.

And all I want to know about Penny is *everything*. I would stay up all night if it meant she just kept talking, laughing, and being the girl I fell in love with.

Penny's laptop stays straddling her sweatpants-clad lap as she leans back against my pine headboard, pointing at a picture on the screen and turning to me, wide-eyed.

"That's you?! I thought Fia was just fucking with me."

Somehow, after barely ten minutes of lying in bed together, talking about only good things—Penny's rules—we've landed on a website with my modeling pictures.

"I wish she was." I sigh, running a hand through my hair. "This was for the LA Dog Benefit. But let's move on to you. Show me your business." I try to pry the laptop from her, but she death grips it, eyes glued to the screen.

"You dirty little whore." She smirks, clicking through the topless photos of me posing with shelter dogs.

"It was for charity!" I gasp. I need to get these pictures erased ASAP.

"Charity for your dick?" Penny scoffs. "I bet you had dates lined up every night after this calendar went live."

Smart-mouth.

This time, I manage to grab the computer from her hands. "Alright, you got enough." I close out of the embarrassing pictures. "And yeah, I did have dates lined up. But I didn't take any."

Penny crawls over, sitting between my legs, and I fight my own body. Just the feel of her ass in my lap is making me get hard.

She is oblivious—or purposely ignoring it—and taps her nails on my hand. "It's okay if you did. You can tell me."

"I swear." I cross my heart. "Unfortunately, I dated this girl in high school, total drama queen," I say, and Penny swats at me. I grab her wrists and swivel her around to lay a kiss on her soft lips. "No one ever came close to her. It's been a real curse."

"I can relate." She rolls her eyes, biting back her smile. "And fine... Two minutes of my life. That's it," she says and leans back into my chest as she swiftly flicks through pictures.

"Don't skip things. I want to know everything. I want the crash course on Penny Hanson."

She sighs, but I see the grin on the corner of her lips.

"Fine, fine. The interesting edition," she starts, and I relax, listening to her talk. I could sit here forever if it meant hearing her voice. A voice I've dreamt about for the past decade.

She pulls up a picture of a pretty brunette with her arm around Penny. They have tall flutes of champagne in their hands.

"This is my best friend in the entire world—Audrey. She owns a bakery, the best in the state, probably the country. She's really talented. She'd probably love you, unfortunately."

I smirk, and Penny closes the laptop, crawling out of my lap so she's facing me now.

She pulls her knees to her chest, and I rest a hand on her legs. Penny stops fidgeting when I do, a splash of pink on her cheeks.

"I got my degree in business," she continues, running a hand through her hair. "But I fell in love with photography when I went to Paris junior year. I got lucky." She shrugs. But I know that's not true. I know she worked incredibly hard for everything she has.

"My Lucky Penny." I smile, and Penny rolls back into my arms.

One thing hasn't changed about her, she's always restless, always squirming around. I pin her in with my arms, and she exhales, melting into me again. Her fingers lightly trace idle shapes across my forearm, then they drop down and she laces her fingers through mine.

"Can I ask you something?"

"Anything," I reply steadily.

Her thumb brushes across my knuckles, and my heart skips a beat.

"Hope. Hurt," she says softly. "What do they mean?"

I glance down at our hands intertwined, the black ink staring back up at me. "Yeah..."

Turning my hand palm-up and curling my fingers through hers, I exhale, and she moves with my chest. "I got it years ago. My cellmate gave it to me. After I thought maybe I'd already lived the only good parts of my life."

She doesn't say anything.

"Hope was what I wanted to believe in. Hope that by some miracle, everything would go back to normal. That I could right my wrongs. That maybe one day, you'd forgive me." I pause. "Hurt was how it actually felt most days."

There's a long moment where neither of us speaks. She's still facing away, her back against my chest, but I know she can feel it—my heartbeat pounding against her ribs.

"And now what?" she finally asks.

I tighten my hold on her hand. "And now...you're here in my arms."

I hope it says enough.

She doesn't answer, not with words. She simply lets herself be held. Then, like a switch flipping, her voice is playful again.

"Okay, it's your turn. Any more topless modeling pictures?"

I bark a laugh, letting the weight in my chest lift for just a second. Penny does that. She finds ways to lighten the load, to make everything okay again.

"None," I say, sliding the laptop out of reach just in case she gets any ideas. I slip a hand under her sweatshirt, unhooking her bra, hungrily kissing the side of her neck. "If you want to see me topless, you're going to have to make it happen yourself."

Penny doesn't miss a beat, and before I can get out another word, she spins around, grabbing my neck with both hands.

Little vixen.

"I can do that." She smiles wickedly, and I pull her under the sheets, ready to show her just how full of *hope* I am.

42

Penny

NOW

I normally hate everything about hospitals. The beeping machines overstimulate me, the smell of antiseptic cleaners is enough to make anyone ill, and the sterile white environments are painfully void of cheer. Who designs these places anyway?

But this morning, as I walk through the hospital's main entrance doors, none of that bothers me. My sneakers squeak almost joyfully on the polished linoleum floor as I clutch my coffee, heading straight to my sister's room.

Don't get me wrong, I'm not on top of my game. The greasy fast food probably wasn't a wise idea, and neither was the mere four hours of sleep I got last night. But there's a clarity in my head that hasn't made an appearance since I set foot in Wilmington.

And it's Christmas Eve.

Almost my favorite day of the year.

Though nothing about this holiday season has led to a normal Christmas celebration—then again, it's fitting in a way.

It feels like I've gone through a war since I left my condo in the city eight days ago, but as I see movement in the room at the end of the hallway and take a sip of my hot peppermint latte, there's a little glimmer of hope.

The glimmer glows brighter when I stumble through the door and Fia's sitting up in bed, a smile stretching across her face when she sees me. The IVs are removed, a hand rests on her belly, and her long hair is braided.

"Good morning, merry Christmas Eve!" I give her a light hug.

"You're right on time!" She yawns, then her eyes go wide at the sight of the twenty-four-ounce coffee mug in my hand. "Wow...rough night?"

"Yeah, I didn't sleep well." I brush it off, not wanting to go into details, like Jesse keeping me up until two in the morning, his tongue ravishing every inch of my body.

Once he drifted off to sleep, I found myself caught between worry—that my sister would keep being stubborn and making reckless choices—and a sudden wave of gratitude, knowing the man beside me would keep watching over Fia when I couldn't.

"Yeah, me neither." Fia eyes the machines beside her. "I hate hospitals, I can't wait to go home and sleep in my own bed."

They should be discharging her any minute now, so I sit on the edge of her bed, the thin sheet wrinkling under my dark jeans. "Seriously, Fia, you have no idea how relieved I am that everything is okay with you and the baby. I don't know what I'd do without you."

Fia reaches for my hand. "Me neither. We're lucky to have you."

My heart bounces off my stomach, and I gasp, remembering the crib. The crib that was delivered and has been sitting on the front porch since yesterday afternoon. The crib that was supposed to be her Christmas surprise.

A quick knock draws our attention to the door, and a peppy young nurse steps in with Fia's discharge papers. I stealthily send Jesse a quick text.

Penny: Hey...feel like being a hero again today?

I hold my breath, glancing over my shoulder at Fia. It's not the end of the world if I don't get it built. But I really wanted to pull this off.

My phone buzzes a second later.

Jesse: Does this have something to do with the crib we forgot about?

We. I begin to type, but he beats me to it.

Jesse: I already have the box open. Shouldn't take me long.
Penny: I owe you
Jesse: I can think of a way to repay me for my good deeds

I roll my eyes, but a mischievous smile slips onto my face. I try to wipe it away, but Fia notices, standing at my side. She scans me up and down.

"Is that Audrey?" she inquires like a pesky little sister as I drop my phone into my coat pocket.

"Yeah..." I stop myself from lying. I can't do it anymore. Fia is an adult, and I'm not protecting anyone by keeping this a secret.

"Actually, no, it's Jesse," I admit, and Fia shoots me a side-eye. "I actually want to talk to you about him."

She fidgets with her sweater. "Oh, okay. What's up?"

A doctor and nurse walk by, chatting loudly, and even though there are phones ringing and machines beeping, it feels too quiet for *this* conversation.

"I'll tell you in the car." I pull her arm, but Fia grinds her boots into the ground.

"Is everything alright with him? Did he faint, too?"

God, Jesse is right. Us Hanson girls really are drama queens.

"No, he's good." *Actually he's great.* "I just want to get out of the hospital. Plus, I got you a bagel, it's in the car."

This gets her legs moving.

The sun is just peeking in the sky as we meander through the parking lot. I stare at my car, hoping it's actually further away than it appears. I'm chickening out, but I can't walk back into that house without Fia knowing the truth. She might vomit, she might be pissed, I have no idea. But she deserves to know.

Plus, Jesse is wearing a navy-blue sweater today that accentuates his forearms and thick tatted neck, and there's no way I can get through the day without kisses. And ass grabs.

The car is heating up, and I pretend to fidget with something on the dash, but Fia sighs loudly beside me.

"Dude, spit it out already!"

"Fine, fine." I stop touching the car and put my hands in my lap, twirling the stacks of gold rings on my fingers. Looking everywhere but my sister's face. "You know how I acted *odd* when I found out Jesse was back?" I begin.

Fia jeers, peering out the window. "By odd, you mean you were a raging bitch?"

I snap my gaze to her, narrowing my eyes, even though she's not wrong. "Yes. Okay, yes. I was really mad at him. And you deserve to know why."

"I mean, I think I understand," she says, her eyes softening as they meet mine. "He was your best friend, then he and Danny got themselves arrested, abandoning you essentially." Fia checks out her nails like this conversation is already boring.

She won't think so in a moment.

"Yes...but also..." I bite my lip and start to choke up. "Jesse and I...we weren't just best friends. We were together, like *together* together." I press my lips shut, waiting for her response.

Fia's brows raise, and her mouth hangs open, but then she lets out a loud laugh.

"Why are you laughing?" I shove her shoulder, but she keeps laughing.

"I thought I was having stress hallucinations." She covers her mouth.

"Explain yourself," I say sternly, and Fia leans her head back, looking over at me, green eyes twinkling.

"I didn't want to say anything, because if I was wrong, that would've been really awkward. But I had my suspicions. I've seen you around other guys, Penny, and you've never acted like *that*."

I gape at her. "Like what!"

Fia hesitates for a minute. "So, don't take this the wrong way..."

That doesn't help my shoulders ease, but I continue listening.

"You're usually relaxed, an easy flirt. But with Jesse, you were so worked up. So awkward. And mean."

"I wasn't awkward. Or *that* mean."

"No, it all makes sense, honestly," she continues. "I might've had no idea when I was a kid, but you do realize I'm twenty-one now?" She raises her eyebrows.

I sigh a little breath of relief. She's not mad, at least she doesn't seem like it.

"Well, now you know.... I told Danny yesterday, he kind of had the same reaction as you. Nan never knew, though."

"First, that's a miracle you kept it from Nan. But also, I can't believe you felt like you couldn't tell me. You know I wouldn't judge you. That's part of our *sisters rule*, remember?"

I nod, a stinging in my throat. "Honestly, Fi, I didn't know how to feel when he just reappeared in my life. I was so angry at Jesse for *so* long. It was all part of my life plan—we were supposed to be together."

"You and your life plan." She rolls her eyes.

"I'm serious!"

"I know you are. But I see the way he looks at you. He almost had a stroke when you wore that miniskirt to Rebel Tavern, you know. I think I was just in denial that someone I consider a big brother was into you like that. But it all makes sense."

My face blushes, and I toss myself forward, resting my head against the steering wheel before peeking up at my sister and her smug smile. "Okay...but you have to stop referring to him as your brother. It's creeping me the fuck out."

Fia scrunches up her freckled nose. "Yeah, I'll stop, promise."

"So this isn't weird for you?"

"Oh, it's totally freaking weird, but who am I to stand in true love's way?" she says, pulling out her bagel and taking the biggest bite I've ever seen.

"I never said it was true love," I mumble, feeling my face turn red.

"Hey, I'm the one who reads all the romance books, remember? I think I know true love," she says, and I don't argue. "Wait—since I invited Jesse to live with me, that kind of makes me a matchmaker."

"Not even close, Fi," I reply.

The tension in my shoulders unspools, slowly but surely, as I crank up the heat, turn on Christmas music, and leave the hospital parking lot.

I didn't expect it to be this easy to let go of a secret I've carried for ten years. Or that she'd receive it with such grace.

Maybe I underestimated my sister after all.

43

Jesse

NOW

Tank quickly got bored with the whole crib-building thing and fell asleep in a slump on the floor next to me. This bedroom's already too small for a guy my size, but add the thirty pieces of the birchwood crib lying around my snoring dog—splayed out like he's deliberately trying to take up every inch of floor space—and this quickly became an impossible task.

Well, almost impossible, because my determination to get this done is stronger.

I know nothing about babies. I grew up an only child, and for a while, I thought it would've been cool to have a sibling. By the time I was a teenager, I stopped believing that. It wasn't hard to walk away from the only home I'd ever known, because it was never a home.

But now, as I sit here, building a flipping *crib* for Fia, I know how detrimental a sibling would've been. I would've wanted to protect them from my father's wrath and probably wouldn't have left when Penny and Danny invited me in.

The only good thing my dad ever did was cease to procreate after me.

"How can anyone be small enough to fit in here?" I scratch my head, asking myself in this empty house. I toss the tiny mattress pad out of my way, looking for more bolts.

Twenty minutes later, and there's an oval structure of sorts. It looks like the one we saw in the store, so I wheel it into the corner of the room.

I have no idea how Penny plans to surprise Fia, but I'm sure she'll be excited. It seems like a nice crib? I haven't got a clue, I just hope I tightened all the bolts enough.

I stare at it, and visions of the baby falling through the bottom flash through my mind. "Tank, are you laying on the wrench?" I breathe out, squatting down to lift my dog's back leg. The wrench is underneath, and he doesn't open an eye.

"Just to make sure," I mutter, tightening every bolt again.

A little flutter of knocks sounds, and my head snaps up to the door.

"It's me," Penny says in a hushed voice. "Can I come in?"

I stand, stretching my cramped limbs, and glance at the clock. I was so obsessed with making sure no screw ever loosens, I didn't even hear them get home.

"Come in," I reply gruffly.

Penny's face lights up when she sees the crib in the corner. "It's so cute! Thank you!" She hops over Tank, who proceeds to yawn and roll on his back, gazing at Penny with sad little eyes.

I pull Penny into my side with one arm, roughly kissing her temple. She rests a hand on my biceps—something she's done a lot in the last twenty-four hours.

"I think it's right."

We both stare at it for a moment.

"I mean, it looks like the one in the store. Fia's going to love it," she reassures me.

"Cool, cool." I run a hand through my hair and catch the way Penny's eyes are heavy. There's a small flicker of guilt for keeping her up all last night—but then again, ten years without that laugh, that mouth, that body? I don't feel *that* bad.

"You're a straight-up daddy," Penny teases.

I grin and grab a handful of her ass, pulling her against me. "You know I'm good with being Uncle Jesse," I murmur into her hair, letting the words settle between us.

She stills slightly, not pulling away.

"I mean it," I say. "I love kids—working with them at the shelter's the best part of my week. But I don't need one of my own to feel fulfilled. I just want to be the uncle who shows up, spoils the hell out of them, then sends them home high on sugar."

Penny pulls back, just enough to look at me.

"You don't want kids?" she asks, her voice soft but curious.

I shake my head. "No, and I want you to know that. I never want you to second-guess it around me. And you don't have to explain or apologize for not wanting to be a mom. I love you for exactly who you are. You're enough for me."

She blinks, like she's letting the words soak in. Then, slowly, a smile spreads across her face—not her usual smirk or flirt, but something quieter and genuine.

"Uncle Jesse," she says flirtatiously. "Kinda has a sexy ring to it."

Penny stands on her tiptoes to lay a breathy kiss on my earlobe, and though it sends a shock of electricity straight down my body, I decide to be the good guy. Not the depraved sex god she claims I am.

I step back, head to the closet, and pull out my favorite black hoodie—soft, worn in, definitely going to hit mid-thigh on her. I toss it her way.

"Here," I say. "Go put this on, get in bed, and take a nap. I think you're delirious."

Penny gapes at me, feigning offense, but she takes the black hoodie anyway.

"Fine. I'll listen, but only because I need energy for later." I see her sniff it, thinking she's being sly. "Why do I need to wear this, though?"

"You've had your eye on it all week," I say, watching the way her lip catches between her teeth.

"Go sleep," I add, softer now. "You won't miss anything."

She steps back to the door. "Oh, you should know that Fia knows about us."

I nod, letting that sink in. "She knows about the past *us*?"

Penny nods. "And us *now*."

"Okay... That's good, right?" I nervously stretch my arms.

"Yeah, it's good." Penny shrugs a little and leaves the room, my hoodie draped in her arms, leaving me standing there with a stupid grin on my lips.

She's a wildfire that I've never quite been able to contain. Every time I think I have a handle on her, the wind blows and she goes in another direction, still taunting me to chase after her. And every time I get close, there's a threat of being burned, but now, as I stand here alone in this room, only a few days left before she's gone from this house, I yet again know there is only one choice.

I have to let myself get hurt so she can keep burning.

"Where did your father find you...heaven?" Fia's voice travels through the hall as I come down the steps.

She's sitting on the wood floor, being attacked by my dog. Ferocious slobbery kisses and whining like he hasn't seen her for years.

"How you feeling, Fi?" I grab a drink from the fridge, and she gets quiet, not taking her eyes off Tank.

"Better. Happy to be home." She must be tired, too.

"Your sister's taking a nap, she was exhausted," I add, taking a sip of sparkling water. Penny filled the fridge with this tasteless shit, and

I keep finding myself cracking them open, hoping they are better the next time. They aren't.

Fia purses her lips and pulls herself off the floor, going over to the sink to wash her hands.

"So, you're dating my sister, huh?" she asks casually, but the words twist my gut.

"We're not really dating..." My heart starts racing. "It's complicated. We have a history."

I'm not lying, I honestly have no idea what's going to happen. She's never going to be the woman who just warms my bed on the weekends. She's Penny, the girl I fell in love with when I was eleven years old, and who has outshone every other person I've ever met.

Fia turns around, arms tightly crossed over her chest, leaning back against the counter. "Let me get this straight. You're hooking up, but you're okay with Penny going back to the city and seeing other guys?" Fia tilts her head, testing me.

Fuck that.

The idea of Penny with anyone else makes me see red.

I groan, shaking my head, suddenly aware I must look like a complete idiot who can't even string two words together.

"You better do something about it, then," Fia snaps at me. "She's leaving in a few days, you know that, right?"

I've never seen her so serious, so protective. She's going to be a good mom.

"You two deserve each other," she adds, quieter now.

I chuckle. "Damn, Fia, I can't tell if that's meant to be an insult or not."

This makes her crack a grin.

"It just means don't fuck this up."

"Roger that," I reply as she mumbles something about going to take a shower, leaving me alone in the kitchen.

I gaze into the living room at the Christmas tree, noticing a few neatly wrapped gifts under it. Penny and Fia's gifts to each other, I'm assuming.

I close my eyes as it dawns on me—I didn't get Penny a gift.

But maybe it's not too late.

I take a sip of the tasteless sparkling water and wonder on a level of one to ten how much she'll freak out if I give her the gift I have in mind.

Possibly an eleven.

The afternoon drags by slowly, until suddenly, I look up and it's almost dinner time. I think about making a protein shake or something easy, but Penny's already busy in the kitchen...with a smile on her face. A sight I'm not sure I've ever seen.

She insisted she had it all handled, though, as she skirts around, still wearing my black hoodie, apologizing after a string of curse words when she spilled gravy down the front.

"I'm not Martha Stewart, but I think this is going to be okay," she says as three separate timers go off.

This meaning the three-course meal she made.

Fia sits with her feet up, completely lost in a book on her Kindle, but glances at me nervously. We both know there's a possibility that none of it's edible and we'll be eating frozen pizza.

"It smells good, I can't wait." I drum up enthusiasm from the living room.

Penny points a wooden spoon my direction, hand on hip, looking like her Nan. "No really, it's decent, not great. Lower your expectations."

I can't help but laugh.

"Okay, the roast has five minutes left." She ticks off her fingers. "I got a bottle of white wine, we have cookies. Fia, can you pull the Christmas records from the stash and get Nan's player going?"

Fia looks up at her sister, and without replying, walks to the cabinet.

Andy Williams's voice fills the first floor of the house minutes later as Penny pours the wine, handing us each a glass stem—Fia gets a pour of sparkling juice—and we cheers.

"To all being under one roof," Fia says, and my gaze meets Penny's.

A soft smile tugs at her lips, her hair messy on top of her head, and there's more food on her clothes than the kitchen counter, but she looks at peace.

"Well, let's dig in," I say, smiling at them.

Penny was right, it's decent.

Not great.

But we eat every last spoonful. The house is warm from the fire, Tank lies under the table, getting scraps from Fia that she thought I wouldn't notice. It feels good, like really good.

Halfway through dinner, Penny puts down her fork, stealing a look at me before turning her focus to her sister.

"Hey, Fi, I wanted to talk to you about the house."
She stops chewing, peering up at Penny, bracing for bad news.

"I never got a chance to tell you what Danny and I discussed yesterday. But the house was brought up, and…" Penny sighs but nods to Fia. "I'm giving it a rest. I'm not going to try to convince you to sell the house. Not yet, at least."

Fia lets out an audible sigh, and tears fill her eyes. "Thank you. What made you change your mind?" she asks, her fingers wrapped around her glass.

Penny clears her throat. "Danny, actually."

She twists her hand on the sweating water glass. Talking about Danny is still uncomfortable for her, but she's doing so well. I place my hand on her back and rub small circles.

"He said he wants to move back in until he's on his feet again. And Jesse's paid rent through May, so Danny and I thought that in a year, when the dust has had a chance to settle, we'd revisit the topic together. We'll collectively decide what's best."

My heart swells, and I lean over, laying my lips on the side of Penny's head.

"Okay, I can live with that." Fia offers Penny a soft smile. "So, does this mean you're talking to Danny again?"

This time, I look at Penny, waiting for the answer I don't know.

She considers it, nodding slowly.

"There's a lot to repair there..." She swallows. "And since I don't live here, it won't be that easy to visit him until he gets out. But the lines of communication are open." Penny wears a hopeful look, and as much as those words stitch a piece of me up, selfishly, I know that if Penny can't visit Danny often, that means I also probably won't see much of her either.

It's a cut that I have to learn to live with, and it also makes the Christmas gift I got her even more vital. I don't want to waste any more time.

The three of us all help clean up dinner, washing, drying, putting away dishes. Like old times. Fia lies on the sofa with Tank, *A Christmas Story* on the TV, and Penny curls up in the chair next to the fire.

"Penny, want to take a walk? Look at the lights?" I ask before she gets too comfortable. It's cold and dark out, but this might be my last chance.

My heart thrums loudly against my ribcage, and I sigh a little relief when she agrees.

"Yeah, sure. Let me grab a coat."

Fia snuggles down deeper under her blanket, and Tank wiggles up closer, exhaling loudly.

"We're not moving," Fia states the obvious.

I slip on my boots and coat, too, making sure the gift is still safely in my pocket, before following Penny out into the crisp night.

The street is full of parked cars, porches lit with lights and wreaths, silhouettes in the windows of Christmas Eve festivities.

Penny rocks back and forth on her heels at the gate, her face tucked into a red scarf, her cheeks rosy pink.

"This way." I nod to the left.

Penny remains quiet but reaches for my hand as I lead her down the sidewalk.

44

Penny

NOW

I'm almost afraid to blink, wondering if this will all disappear. I squeeze Jesse's hand harder, testing my reality as we walk down the street we traversed so many times as teenagers.

Our breath is cold, fogging the air around us, and lights twinkle on every house we pass. At the corner is a stately brick home, where guests file out the front door, hugging goodbye on the porch, breaking the silent bubble around Jesse and me.

"Did you want to circle the block?" I incline my head toward the street sign above. "The homes on 2nd Street are always beautifully decorated," I suggest, but he shakes his head.

"Let's keep going this way," he replies softly.

Jesse adjusts the navy-blue beanie on his head but keeps his green eyes locked ahead of us. His chiseled jaw isn't tense, but it's working, like he's mulling over something in his mind. There haven't been many moments between us lately that were this quiet—we've either had a lot to argue about, spewing off distrust that was rooted in a murky past, or it's been needy touching.

But now there's this.

"Where are you taking me?" I let out a small laugh, glancing nervously at the stop sign as we pass another block.

With his free hand, he points forward. "There's a little park just up ahead I wanted to take you to." He's coy, like I don't know which park he's talking about.

"Oh," is all I manage to say, biting a smile that's both nervous excitement and sadness.

I don't want this to end, not when it's just beginning.

Last night, I tossed and turned in the same bed Jesse slept in.

I stared at the ceiling, the same one I used to stare at dreaming about getting out, about escaping this town, the people, the situations, just wanting to start somewhere new.

But I stared at it, ten years older.

I stayed up, not thinking about what I was going to do after college, or where Jesse and I would live, or what cities I would explore. Instead, I wondered if, as the people we are now, could we still share each other's dreams?

Ten unknown years sit between us, ones where we led different lives, and that's such a daunting thing to think about.

What if I'm not the Penny he really remembers? What if I can't make him happy like before? What if he doesn't even want that?

"Hey." He shakes my hand, still gripped in his. "You good?"

I glance up—we're across from Magnolia Street Park. It's empty, but the streetlights still illuminate the best parts. The city even hung wreaths on the gazebo and lampposts.

"Yeah, sorry. Jesse...I think we need to talk."

I don't know where I'm going with it, but if I ramble, if I spew out all my jumbled thoughts and tangled heartstrings, maybe I'll figure it out.

"Okay, but first I need to show you something." He pulls me behind him across the grass. Straight toward the worn bench under the bare magnolia tree.

My eyes are drawn to Jesse's back as he walks a step in front of me.

Over the last few days, I've studied the ink across his body, and my heart aches remembering the magnolia tree tattooed right over his heart.

He sits on the bench and gently pulls me down next to him. I swivel so I can look at him.

"Our bench," I say softly, running my cold fingers over the wood slats beneath me.

Jesse's legs sprawl out in front of us, long and sturdy, and his arm rests on the back of the bench behind me. I'm cocooned in him.

"When I came back to North Carolina, *this* was the first place I stopped," he says.

My gaze snaps up at his admission.

"Really? Why?" I breathe out.

Without breaking eye contact, he narrows his eyes like the answer should be so obvious. "It's the place where my life changed," he replies, the corner of his lips pulling up.

I nod, understanding. It feels like everything big that happened to me as a teenager happened right here. Meeting Jesse for the first time. Realizing I loved him. Asking him to move in. It's where I ran away to when I found out about Danny and Jesse's arrest. It's where I sat for hours after Nan's funeral.

"I brought you here because I wanted to give you your Christmas gift." Jesse's hand fishes into his pocket. Deja vu comes over me like a veil.

I kick the dead grass under my feet with the tip of my black boot. "I didn't know we were exchanging—"

But he cuts me off, placing a large, warm hand over mine. "We weren't." He pulls his hand from his pocket, but his fingers are clenched in a tight fist. "But...this is...well, you'll see..."

My heart is doing weird things. If he doesn't show me soon, I think I'm going to end up right back in the hospital.

Jesse hooks a finger under my chin, tilting my face up. He places his lips on mine, kissing me slowly before pulling away.

"Last week, when I was certain you hated me, and I didn't know if there was any chance in hell of redeeming even an ounce of what we once had, I found this in my room."

I look down as his fist opens, and in his palm sits a silver ring with a green sea glass gem. My eyes widen, and tears well on my rims, but this time, I don't try to hide them.

"What? You found it…" My voice is scratchy as I look up at him through misty vision.

He holds the ring up, and it looks tiny in between his inked fingers. "I saved for a month to buy you this, and I made a promise of forever with it. You made me feel like the luckiest guy alive the day I slipped this on your finger. Do you remember?"

"Like it was yesterday," I breathe out.

It's a memory I've long pushed away, but here it is, replaying right before me.

"Penny…I know life is really messy right now," Jesse begins, still holding the ring up. "I know showing up here threw a wrench in your plan. And you love your plans." His arm on the back of the bench snakes around, his hand cupping the back of my neck gingerly. "You don't owe me anything, not a moment of your time. But when you asked the other day if I lived with regrets and I said I try not to—that's the truth."

It feels like if I even draw a breath, I'll miss something. So I stay incredibly still, watching him fumble over words in his head before speaking again.

Jesse bites his lower lip, voice strained. "I don't regret saving your brother's life. I don't regret falling in love with you when we were too young to know what that meant. And I don't regret coming back either. But, Penny, I will regret it if I don't ask you something."

I stay still, stuck on this bench like glue as he slips off it and onto his knee in the grass in front of me. The drumming in my ears gets so loud, all I can do is focus on him and the eyes that feel like safety.

"We've changed a lot since we were eighteen. But one thing hasn't changed for me. I still want forever with you. I still want the chance to be the man you deserve."

His words hit me square in the chest, and I suck in a breath, inching forward until we're close enough to touch.

"Jesse, I don't know what to say..." Tears run down my face freely, and my heart splits open in a way I didn't know it could.

In a way I haven't let it for ten years.

"I know we live in different cities and lead separate lives," he rasps out. "And I see how hard you've worked to build yours, your career, your independence, everything. I would never want to take any of that away from you. What I'm asking is...is there space for me in that life? This ring doesn't come with expectations or conditions. It's just a symbol of something new. A fresh start. You and me, together."

There are few times in my life when I've found myself at a loss for words.

But this is one of them.

Pushing off the bench, I fall forward into him, anchoring my arms around his neck. He holds me tight against his body.

I'd be lying if I said I didn't need him, didn't want him the same way he wanted me.

Life is really messy right now, and I have no idea what the future holds, what it will look like to keep this relationship going.

But there's one thing my heart won't let me lie about.

I nod, tears rolling down my face, the cold air biting my cheeks, and kiss him longingly, like it's the first time all over again. Jesse pulls us up to our feet and holds me in his arms.

"What do you say?" he whispers, and I glance down at the bench with our initials still carved in it.

"Yes."

There's no need to find space for him to fit in—there's been an empty gap in my life, in my heart, where Jesse was always meant to be. I just needed him to come home to realize that.

I stare at the green sea glass as he slips the ring on me.

It fits, like I never took it off.

45

Jesse

NOW

It looks like she's leaving for an international three-month vacation. The foyer's lined with overstuffed leather luggage, and every time I see it, something deep in me aches. I try to keep myself moving, busy, not thinking about the fact that in mere minutes, Penny's going to drive away from this house.

This isn't right, my heart screams, but this is how it was always going to be.

Penny has a life outside this bubble. Outside of me.

Two weeks ago, I wasn't sure what it would be like to see her, I half expected her to treat me like I was already dead, and now I'm reeling with the idea of her absence.

There's going to be a definite void of sunshine that only Penny Hanson can supply.

Fia's misty eyed, too, so I decide to be the strong one here.

"I'm not sure how this all fit in your Barbie car to begin with, but let me help you." I pick up two bags, and Penny tightens the belt around her long wool coat. My eyes catch on the ring.

She looks sophisticated and beautiful, like she's about to jet off to London or Paris. Another reminder of the promise I made to her: I'd love her no matter where she was, and I'd never get in the way of the life she made.

"Thank you—just lodge that one in the back." She points to the trunk, and I chuckle, but it rattles my chest.

Penny doesn't meet my eyes as we walk back in for more bags, more polite words between us.

Words that just reach the surface when all I want is more depth, more time. I know our relationship will be different, not ideal. But it's a sacrifice I'm willing to make for her.

I went ten years without so much as breathing the same air as Penny. I can go six weeks before she's back for Fia's baby shower.

"Got everything?" Fia asks, and Penny nods, wrapping her arms around her sister.

"Thanks again, for the crib...for trying to mend me," Fia murmurs, and Penny sniffles but plasters on the biggest smile.

"You're not broken, Fia, I'm just your big sister. I'll always have your back. Remember what the doctor said, frequent small meals."

"I know, I know," Fia reassures her.

Penny then squats down, eye level with Tank, and scratches his ears. Tank gives her a big kiss, and Penny makes a face but plops a light kiss back on his head.

"I might even miss you, mister Tank. Keep guarding the house, buddy," she whispers, her fingers lingering on the side of his head.

Well fuck, rip my heart out.

"I'll walk you out." I push open the door and follow her onto the chilly porch. I hold Penny tight from behind like a leech as she shuffles toward the car, laughing.

That's what I wanted, to wipe that frown from her face.

When we reach the driveway, I spin her around, pinning her against the side of the car. Penny flashes the same flirty gaze she always does when I focus all my attention on her. It's like she's under my microscope, and I wonder if she knows how spectacular I find her.

Three soft kisses. Then I bite her lip, and Penny hangs on my neck.

"I'll miss you," she says seriously.

It's only two hours from here to her condo in Raleigh, but between our work schedules, there's only a handful of days that we can actually make the trip to see each other.

"You're always going to be my girl, you know that, right? No matter how much time passes between us," I say, nuzzling my nose into hers.

Penny's amber eyes fill with water, and she nods, clenching her trembling lip. I lift up her chin.

"Hey, no more tears. I'll be seeing you soon. FaceTime me when you're settled in."

"Of course." She kisses me three more times. "I love you," she whispers, then places a hand on my chest. "Then. Now. And always."

Fuck.

Whatever part of my heart I thought I still possessed no longer belongs to me.

Penny reached in and pulled it out. And I let her.

I'd let her have every last part of me.

When she's in the driver's seat, typing in directions home—to her *home*—I reach over my back and pull my black hoodie off, handing it through the window.

She stares at it in silence for a moment, then takes it in her arms and smiles.

"Drive safe, princess."

46

Penny

NOW

4 Weeks Later

A sigh of relief rushes through my body when the paved road turns to dirt and I know I'm only minutes away from my best friend. A year ago, Audrey traded in her life in the city for a hundred-year-old farmhouse—and a man who she never saw coming. Every time I see her, she's unmistakably happy, falling more and more into the version of herself she was always meant to be.

I've never been envious of her, only happy she found the love she deserved. But as I turn into her driveway today, driving past the large oak trees, I wonder if maybe I missed my chance.

Maybe only certain people get to have it all.

The blue front door opens, and out flies Mabel first, their bloodhound and the official greeter of the property, then Audrey. Always elegant in her cashmere sweaters. And always with an apron on, even on her days off from the bakery.

"You're right on time." She smiles brightly, beckoning me up the porch steps and into the warm farmhouse. "I just pulled lemon scones from the oven, and Rhett put on a fresh pot of coffee."

Maybe I'll just move in with them.

Rhett's sitting at the kitchen table with his back to me as I enter the kitchen.

"Good morning, Red," I tease, touching his shoulder. It's an inside joke.

"Penny." He sets down his enormous cup of coffee and stands to wrap me in a big bear hug, always smelling of fresh-cut wood.

I plop myself down at the table across from him and pull my knees to my chest, sighing dramatically. Mabel races over, placing her heavy, slobbery head in my lap. I don't protest.

Peering down at her droopy brown eyes, I think of Tank. And I miss him.

"What's up, did the wedding go okay last night?" Audrey asks, placing a plated lemon scone with drizzled icing in front of me. I take an enormous bite, my eyes rolling back in my head. Because like everything she bakes, it's the most scrumptious thing I've ever had.

"To be honest, I was ready for this one to be done from the moment it started," I admit.

It's not that I don't love my job. I created this business from the ground up. I get paid to be witness to couples' happiest days, documenting once-in-a-lifetime moments. I see the look on the groom's face before anyone else usually notices. I see the nerves of the bride as her mother zips up the white dress, and I'm always there to reassure, to make the best of the moment, to give a little pep talk.

But last night was different.

"Oh no...what happened?" Audrey inches closer.

"The wedding was stunning, and the bride was a joy to work with." I start on a positive note. It was over the top, a winter wonderland at a boutique hotel downtown. No detail left untouched. There were smiles and tears all around, and I snapped my camera from muscle memory, capturing a thousand snippets of joy.

"But..." Audrey says, grasping her coffee mug, and even Rhett is leaning in, listening.

"You know I take my work seriously." I inhale deeply. I put every ounce of myself into building my business with the utmost professionalism. I never let my emotions get in the way, well not until last night. "But something happened last night. I was capturing the first dance, and I froze."

Audrey crinkles her brow at me. "You froze?"

"I froze," I say again. "I had to run to the bathroom, leaving my assistant to do the job. I couldn't handle it."

I spent ten minutes splashing cold water on my face, pushing the only thought from my mind.

Will that ever be Jesse and me?

"I *cried* during the first dance last night." I punctuate every word.

Audrey gasps, brows raised. It's the appropriate response. I don't even mention how, afterward, I drove home in a daze and curled up in bed without even calling Jesse, too ashamed of how much I missed him.

"I'm lost—that sounds like a normal reaction?" Rhett says, and we both turn to glare at him.

"Rhett, why are you eavesdropping!" Audrey gapes at her boyfriend, and I drop my head into my palms.

"I *never* cry during the weddings I shoot. Ever." I groan. "There's something wrong with me, guys. I'm going to have to quit and come work at the bakery. I can work the mixer."

Mabel nuzzles her nose into my side, clearly worried I'm in distress.

I am, girl.

My gorgeous best friend places a hand over mine.

"Did you talk to Jesse about this?" she asks, and I shake my head side to side, lifting it pathetically.

"No, no, definitely not." I inhale sharply. "I don't want him to think that I can't handle this. We're only four weeks in." Cradling the warm coffee mug in one hand, I pet Mabel with the other. "The thing is—it's not even the distance that bothers me. I can drive two hours in my sleep. It's that I waited ten years for *this* relationship. And now it feels like I only get bits and pieces of it."

Bless Audrey, she stands to bring the entire scone tray over. This calls for copious amounts of sugar and carbs, so I grab another one.

"Look at me!" I throw my hands up, crumbs falling out of my mouth. "I barged in on your lovely idyllic Saturday morning, and I'm a blubbering mess."

Rhett laughs. "Penny, you're family." He stands. "But also, I'm going to go to the workshop so y'all can chat, because you already know my advice."

"Red, we can't all just leave the city for our man," I grumble, but he laughs and skips out the back door.

"I want what you two have." I flash a tiny smile at Audrey.

She stays quiet, hesitating. Probably overanalyzing every word I said until she comes up with the perfect solution.

When she opens her mouth, her voice is soft but firm. "You know, Rhett's not wrong."

I furrow my brows, and she exhales, tracing her fingers over a groove on the farmhouse table.

"What I'm saying is...you could move there, and almost nothing would change with your business. You already travel for most of the weddings, but your home base could be there. With him. And Fia. Your family."

The idea is like a shock of cold water to the chest.

"But I built my life *here*. I have my classes, my condo...you."

Audrey shrugs, her hazel eyes kind. "Sometimes the best things in life can't be planned."

Thirty minutes later, I'm hugging my best friend goodbye on her front porch.

"You sure I can't just stay here, and avoid everything?" I ask, only half-jokingly, but she shakes her head.

"Nope. You're going to go home, shower and change, and drive to Wilmington. You're going to spend the day with Jesse, and you're going to tell him the truth about how you feel. And have some amazing sex. You need to get laid."

"First, you're not wrong. Second, I suck at dating." I'm getting better, but a committed relationship is still new. I feel like a fish out of water.

"You do not, it's just new for you. Now, go on," Audrey replies, a little twang in her voice.

I pause and look her over. "My god, Audrey, you sound like Rhett's mother."

Audrey gawks at me, and I smirk, waving goodbye.

I leave feeling full, buzzed on coffee, and warm. She has that effect.

I check myself out at the red light in the sun visor mirror. My hair is messily knotted on top of my head. I didn't even have a chance to put on makeup this morning. There's a dollop of lemon zest icing on the front of Jesse's black sweatshirt that I've worn for three days straight, and the pink rainboots I slipped on are obnoxiously bright.

It's fine. It's all fine.

If I'm really fast, I can shower, change, pack an overnight bag, and be in Wilmington by noon. Well, noon-ish. Jesse has a training seminar tomorrow, so I'll hang out with Fia. If she's not working.

It'll give me less than twenty-four hours with him, but I don't care. I just need to hold him. I need to see his face, to know this is all still real.

There's a coveted street spot outside my building, and I snag it, parking haphazardly, but I'll be quick. My heart pounds in my chest as my limbs carry me straight to the elevator. Floor three. I press the button hard. Then again, three more times for good measure.

Is this crazy? Maybe I should give him a heads-up that I'm coming. I thought it was romantic, but what if he's busy and then I'm a burden? I pull out my phone, staring at a photo of him as my background. I can't get myself to text him.

Fuck.

This isn't a good plan. I can't go. We said we'd do things casually, and this is borderline neurotic.

But then again, I threw casual out the window when I told him I loved him.

The elevator doors ding open, and I start down the hallway, my boots squeaking as I speed walk down the polished cement corridor, still unsure what I'm going to do.

My throat's growing hot and tight with each step. Why do I have to be like this? Why does love have to be so complicated? Why did he have to move back and steal my heart and consume every fragment of my mind?

I fuss with my purse, digging for my keys.

"Penny?"

My head snaps up at the sound of my name, and I stop right in my tracks.

Leaning against my front door, tall, brooding, and impossibly handsome, is Jesse. A smirk softens his beautifully chiseled face.

My throat stops restricting my breath as I take slow, cautious steps toward him. His stare is relentless, never leaving me as I near.

"What are you doing here?" I ask, embarrassingly winded.

Jesse smiles, his green eyes glistening. That's when I look down and notice a small black duffel bag by his feet. My lips start to pull to the side.

"I missed you." His voice is husky, vulnerable. He says it so matter-of-factly, no shame in it.

"Oh..." I take another step forward, mindlessly touching my messy hair.

"I know we have a whole weekend together in two weeks, but I figured I had"—he holds up his wrist, pretending to look at a watch that's not there—"the next eighteen hours free."

"And you wanted to spend them with me?" I ask, taking another step forward, closing the gap between us.

Jesse leans down, lifting my face to his with a tattooed knuckle. "Princess, I thought I made it pretty damn clear. I want every hour of every fucking day with you."

My heart lurches in my chest, and I want nothing more than to push that door open behind him and strip every layer off between us. But I shake my head.

"But you said...we could do this...this long distance thing."

Jesse throws back his head and lets out a throaty chuckle. "Yeah, I said that because I thought I could do it. But you've sunk your claws into me. Maybe that makes me a weak man, Penny, but I hate not being with you. I hate coming home and not hearing your laugh. I hate not seeing the house full of random pink items. I'm *trying*, but I'm not sure how to do life without you anymore."

"It's only been four weeks," I reason, even though every word out of his mouth is making my knees buckle.

Jesse bites his lip. "I told you, you've fully messed me up, and I've let you."

I laugh now, and Jesse's smile comes back. The most beautiful smile I've ever seen.

"I have a confession. I was on my way home to pack a bag and come to you," I whisper, scrunching my nose, and he grins wider.

I push Jesse aside to unlock my front door and grab his hand, dragging him over the threshold of my condo.

The first guy I ever let into my heart.

The first guy I ever let into my home.

And if I'm truly as lucky as he claims...he'll be the last.

Epilogue

Penny

Four Months Later

I inhale the salty air and settle back into the chair. The front porch is quaint, and we are still unpacking everything, but it's quickly becoming ours.

"You want this hung here?" Jesse asks, lifting Nan's copper windchimes to the hook suspended from the porch ceiling. A ceiling I had Jesse paint haint blue.

"That's perfect, thank you."

The windchimes sound the moment Jesse lets go, wiping sweat from his brow.

"It's only May, and I'm roasting." He pulls off his shirt, showcasing a masterpiece of inked art, telling the story of his life. Me included.

"You won't find me complaining," I mumble, running my eyes over the muscled valleys of his body.

Jesse cockily smirks and leans down to kiss me. "Your sister called, said she'll be over for dinner later," he says when he pulls back.

"Of course, she will," I reply with a chuckle.

I told Fia we'd come to her, because my niece, Daisy, is only four weeks old, but she said there's no way she's missing out on seeing our new house.

Our.

After Jesse showed up at my condo that chilly January morning, everything changed. It took barely ten minutes before we knew we couldn't keep living without each other. Ten years apart had been long enough, and we weren't willing to lose another day.

It wasn't easy, though. There were months of tender arguments and quiet compromises—him wanting to move to the city, me refusing to let him give up the business he was building. In the end, we chose something neither of us had expected but both of us needed: neutral ground.

We found a beach cottage, tucked behind large fronds and a white picket fence, four blocks from the ocean. It was close enough to Fia that I promised to keep the tradition of Tuesday night dinners.

It's small, but it's ours. It's everything we need.

There's a little yard where Tank bakes in the sun and chases his ball. Then there's the screened-in front porch where I plan to spend all my mornings editing photos, coffee in hand, ocean breeze against my skin.

I had to admit to Audrey—she was right.

My business didn't suffer from the move; if anything, it flourished. Less travel, more time here. I'm letting myself breathe for the first time in a long while, and it feels really good. Really right.

I've also become one of those obsessive aunts. Daisy is only four weeks old, but my phone is full of pictures of her perfect round face, and I can't imagine missing any part of her growing up. Fia's surprisingly chill and doing a great job. Of course, I'm only a phone call away at all times. Which I've reminded her daily.

In the evenings, when Jesse gets home from work, we walk Tank to the beach—it's easily become my favorite ritual. There's something healing about the rhythm of waves and the way Jesse smiles at me, like I'm still the best part of his day. I'll never tire of that.

But if you asked me about the *absolute* best part, it's what happens at night, when I slip into bed and this handsome, gentle, fiercely loyal man climbs in next to me.

And like the teenagers we once were, we stay up late into the night, talking, laughing, and dreaming, holding each other close like there's no tomorrow.

"Close your eyes and tell me where you'd go right now," he says, the white duvet settling over my chest.

It's our old, familiar game, and it still gives me butterflies, even after all this time.

I roll onto my side, eyes closed, hand reaching for him in our moonlit bedroom. His fingers find mine, and he lifts my hand to his lips, pressing a kiss against my knuckles. I melt deeper into the safety of the soft bedding and wiggle closer to him, until our noses are almost touching.

It's just us.

"You remembered our game?" I whisper, a smile tugging at my lips.

His green eyes meet mine, and he nods.

"When we were eighteen," I begin, bringing my hand down to rest over the steady, slow rhythm of his heart, "I couldn't imagine anything better than leaving everything behind."

I pause, letting the moment wrap around us. Because I never want to forget it.

"But the truth is, I can't imagine any adventure better than this…better than a life with you."

Acknowledgements

I wanted to keep this short and simple, but there are so many people to thank. First, to all my incredible beta readers who helped me shape this story and reassured me that Jesse was, indeed, THE MAN—I love you all. Of course, to my "Spice Girls" group chat (you know who you are), thank you for entertaining my rambling voice memos and hyping me up every step of the way—I couldn't have survived this crazy ride without you. And to my street team, who literally shouted this book out, a million hugs to you.

And to all my readers, thank you. I hope you loved Penny and Jesse as much as I did.

P.S. If you liked this book, the best thing you can do is leave me a review or share it with a friend.

xx,
Katherine

Also by

The Hometown Series
Unravel Me
Lucky Penny
Fia's Story (TBA)

Standalones
Time to Bloom
The Way You See Me
Strayed